Sarah Whitman, Clara Louise Burnham

Miss Archer Archer

A novel

Sarah Whitman, Clara Louise Burnham

Miss Archer Archer
A novel

ISBN/EAN: 9783337000417

Printed in Europe, USA, Canada, Australia, Japan

Cover: Foto ©Andreas Hilbeck / pixelio.de

More available books at **www.hansebooks.com**

MISS ARCHER ARCHER

A Novel

BY

CLARA LOUISE BURNHAM

BOSTON AND NEW YORK
HOUGHTON, MIFFLIN AND COMPANY
The Riverside Press, Cambridge
1897

The Riverside Press, Cambridge, Mass., U. S. A.
Electrotyped and Printed by H. O. Houghton and Company.

CONTENTS.

MISS ARCHER ARCHER.

CHAPTER I.

HOMEWARD BOUND.

MISS DEXTER had arrived at that stage of sea-sick misery where one fears the ship will *not* go down. She lay supine in her berth, and watched the garments hanging on the opposite wall sway out toward her, as if they had suddenly become sentient, and, tired of inaction, were coming over to discover the cause of her doing so long without them. Especially did the big buttons on her ulster glare at her like curious eyes, nearer — nearer, with the strain and quiver of the ship, which this time heeled over with such persistence that it seemed an impossibility that it could ever right itself.

But Nathalie Dexter had no hope of this. The motion had recurred too often. She knew the ship would right itself, and she turned her head away from the glare of the fiendish button-eyes and the smothering effect of the advancing dress brigade.

"Oh!" A little scream from the door of her cabin broke in upon her sick oppression. The ship, in struggling for her perpendicular, had evidently robbed Mrs. Archer of hers.

Mrs. Archer was Nathalie's chaperon, — a woman with the steadiest of heads and the most cheerful non-comprehension of *mal de mer ;* and the recumbent sufferer gained a remote gleam of satisfaction as she realized that Mrs. Archer had just come into involuntary and sudden contact with the jamb of the door.

"Does n't she roll, though!" exclaimed the visitor. "I believe my shoulder is black and blue."

Nathalie's vague pleasure deepened, even though she perceived feebly that the retiring ulster would be back in a minute.

"How are you feeling, this evening?" pursued the strong voice.

"Thanks," murmured Miss Dexter.

Mrs. Archer saw her lips move, but heard nothing.

"Well, one day less," she remarked with a laugh. "You *do* look forlorn! Ah!" with another little cry. "This won't do for me. I think I 'll go and lash myself to something. Goodnight;" and Nathalie was alone.

She closed her eyes. Tears had stolen from them many a time since she started on this voyage; but they did not come now. She thought of the woman who had just left her. She had fallen to Mrs. Archer's charge unexpectedly, and at the last minute almost, before sailing for home, and that lady had taken her duties very lightly. She had not even engaged a seat for Miss Dexter at table when they started, and Nathalie had the mortification of being obliged to retire from the dining-room after entering and finding it full, and afterward to make her own arrangements with the steward.

Mrs. Archer was a Philadelphian by birth and breeding, and although she had married a Virginia gentleman whose pride of blood she adopted after his death, her worship of the Quaker City and of its old families never weakened. She had now been making a short sojourn in Europe in charge of a Scion of one of these, and her absorption in her sacred trust made it quite impossible that she should take more than a nominal interest in Nathalie Dexter, a girl recommended to her care by a mutual friend, and who, while presentable and sufficiently well behaved, had failed to be born in Philadelphia, and if she had been born there, would probably have been reared on the wrong side of Market Street.

Miss Dexter, being an independent New Englander, and discovering in a day how the land lay, determined not to annoy Mrs. Archer and her select charge ; and had she been as well as on the smooth, happy trip over, with her mother, a year before, she would probably have been sufficiently amused by the humorous aspects of the situation to have retained undampened spirits.

Seasickness, however, obliterating as it does all earthly interests, swamps first of all the sense of humor; and that daily momentary apparition at the door, of her perfunctory chaperon, whose attentions had never exceeded this, seemed to Nathalie insult added to the injury of her lonely, miserable day.

The following morning, the ulster clinging meekly to the wall, the girl came to the daring decision to put it on and to attempt to get on deck.

Finally dismissing the kind but over-busy stewardess, she crawled up the stairway, down which gleamed the blessed light of day.

A tall man standing idly above her, his hands crossed behind him, and gazing into nothingness, heard her stumble, and turning, became instantly alert.

There was a singing in her ears that made her unmindful of what he said. She knew that he was big and strong, and seemed friendly inclined, and that in some way he got her into her steamer chair and tucked a rug about her; and that the hurrying wind dashed life into her face and kept her from fainting as she lay back, too limp to do more than breathe.

Mrs. Archer materialized from somewhere.

"There, now, that is quite the most sensible thing you could do," she remarked brusquely. "You know I told you so, days ago. If people would only use a little more will power. 'Come

on deck,'—that is what I always say to them,—
'come on deck!'"

While she spoke, the lady cast a sharp side
glance at the tall, smooth-shaven stranger in the
big overcoat. He acknowledged it by lifting his
cap; then, after a moment's hesitation and a look
at Miss Dexter's white, immobile face, he moved
away.

Nathalie did not speak. It was a physical impossibility to do so. So Mrs. Archer, after a few
more words concerning the unwisdom of yielding
to inertia, returned to the congenial circle she had
temporarily deserted.

" I had to go and speak to my Yankee," she explained. "She has no more stamina to-day than a
wet rag; and the kindest thing is to let her alone."

Nathalie, in her half-alive state, had little idea
of the passage of time; but at one point in her
morning the deck-steward appeared at her side
with some refreshment.

She lifted her eyes to him weakly and shook her
head; whereupon the Tall Man loomed beside her.

"You had better take something," he said; and
she obeyed, ashamed to have him see her hands
tremble.

At intervals again through the day she ate at
his bidding, and when finally she went below, it
was his arm that she clung to, limply, until the door
of her cabin was reached.

"I thank you," she said, looking up into his

calm eyes.   She hadnever before known what it
was to be stirred to hr depths with gratitude.

That night she slpt; and the next morning,
when she climbed uphe stairway, he was waiting.
A touch of the comicappealed to her through her
feebleness when, aftr he had hastened to assist
her to her chair andprovide for her comfort, Mrs.
Archer suddenly appared as before, and with un-
easy glances and pltitudes waited until she had
seen him off to a saf distance, and then, her duty
done, returned to he chosen companions.

The Tall Man, aving already comprehended
the situation, again ssumed charge of the invalid's
diet.   Nathalie's had was still unsteady, and her
weakness made heranswers to him monosyllabic,
as he stood besid her with his slightly bowed
shoulders, and hads crossed behind him in his
usual attitude; buit was not quite such a dead
weight that afternon that he at last assisted down
the staircase.

"I wonder if o the following day it will 'all
happen as before,'is the fairy tales say?" thought
Nathalie that nigh, as she fell asleep.

But it did not. The Tall Man met her, and
when she was seatd Mrs. Archer scurried forward
to drive him off; ut after he had gone, the chaperon did not immdiately follow his example.   Instead, she lowerec her voice and let her offended
glance fall upon Nathalie.

"I wish, Mis Dexter," she said, "that you

would cease to allow marked attentions from that stranger. It is very disagreeable to me for you to become the talk of the ship."

Nathalie had been fed into strength sufficient to feel her indignation rise; but she thought of her mother and tried to control herself.

"I should think it was obvious," she said faintly, "that a limp, white thing like me, with her cap awry, is simply an object of charity."

"Pshaw! Your hair is curly!" answered the other; and the unexpected retort cheered Miss Dexter.

"He is a young man, and very good-looking," went on Mrs. Archer austerely.

Generations of New England directness looked up through the girl's gray eyes into the ones above her. "He evidently has a heart in his bosom," she said distinctly.

"Oh, indeed! And you, perhaps"— The speaker paused, and the unspoken sneer brought color into Nathalie's face.

"Stop right there, Mrs. Archer!" she exclaimed hastily. "I have n't given you very much trouble since we started, I think. I am entirely able to look after my own affairs."

Mrs. Archer bit her lip and fingered her chatelaine, but after a little hesitation she retreated, for Miss Dexter was looking out to sea and appeared to consider the interview ended.

The Tall Man was glad to see expression in the

eyes that had been so vague, and he said as much the next time he drew near.

She smiled up at him. "You have converted me to being glad that my bones are not turning to coral," she replied.

"Were you so low?" he asked; and then he drew a seat near her.

"Yes. I have been very ill, and very homesick."

"Ah! You are not an American, then?"

"Yes, I am; but — at the last moment my mother decided that her duty was to stay in Italy with a sick friend, and " — the girl made a praiseworthy effort to smile again — "what is America without a mother?"

"Your courage will return with your digestion," answered her companion, conscious of the quiver of her lips, and settling himself more definitely in his chair with a view to conversation.

Nathalie, disciplining herself with such mental expletives as "Cry baby! Goose! Imbecile!" wiped her eyes stealthily.

"America is a very good place," he went on, gazing out to sea. "I am very glad to be going back to it. I suppose you have been in Philadelphia?"

Miss Dexter's face at once symbolized an April day.

"Oh, dear!" she said. "Are you from Philadelphia, too?"

The Tall Man looked around at her. "Yes. Why not?"

"No reason at all why not. Every reason why you should be. You will be shocked, of course, to hear that I never have been there; but I shall make the pilgrimage some day. Has the city really golden streets?"

Her companion looked puzzled before he smiled. "Some one has been boring you about our town. Well, I like it too; but we can talk about something else, — where you live, for instance."

Nathalie met his questioning glance, already grown grave again. Yes; he was really very good-looking, in the best sense of the word; and he was scarcely over thirty. She hoped Mrs. Archer was watching them.

"Oh! *I* really *do* live in the Hub of the Universe," she answered.

He reflected her smile. "And yet you are intolerant of egotistical Philadelphians? The complacence of Bostonians has almost passed into a proverb."

"Yes, I know it. My father was a Connecticut man, and he always liked to make a little fun of his adopted city."

The Tall Man noted the softened glance and the use of the past tense, and discerned that neither was there a father in that motherless America to which the girl was returning alone, or worse than alone.

"I have been in your city many a time," he said.

"Perhaps you may have heard of my father, Dr. Dexter?" she said tentatively. "He was quite well-known."

No, her companion had not heard of Dr. Dexter.

"He died two years ago," she went on. Then she swallowed with difficulty. "I being the only child, mother and I"— Here her speech stopped, and after a second she smiled with tremulous brightness at her companion through the tears that this time she frankly wiped away.

"I don't know what makes me so ridiculously weepy this morning," she said. "I cry if one speaks sharply to me; and then if one looks kindly at me, I cry. It seems to be a monotonous way of taking things, does n't it?"

"You need something to eat," said the Tall Man, looking around for the steward.

"Indeed I don't. *Indeed* — not yet."

"I think you do. I do, any way. Excuse me, and I will see about it."

He withdrew, and Miss Dexter leaned back in her chair and took deep, quiet breaths until she had regained the poise of which her tilt with Mrs. Archer had robbed her.

By the time her benefactor returned, she was able to join him in the lunch that was served them.

"You are very, very kind to me," she said. "I think by another day I shall not need to be a burden to any one. My father was careful about teaching me what to do in emergencies, but he never told me any panacea for seasickness! "

" That is something I 'm afraid you won't find," responded the Tall Man, as he ate his sandwich.

" No. We are always hearing that common-sense goes a good way ; but this does appear to be a case where it does n't help. It seems strange, sometimes, to see how astonishingly little common-sense a person may have. I once had such a pain-ful experience. I was out in the country, and a tiny insect flew into my ear. He fluttered in deeper and deeper, in spite of my efforts to get him out, and at last he began to amuse himself beating my ear-drum, — that is, I suppose so. At any rate, whatever he did hurt me terribly, and made my brain seem all to be buzzing. The nearest doctor lived ten miles away, and I had to drive to his house, enduring this misery all the time. When I reached him finally, he put some instrument into my ear, and the insect fluttered more madly than before. I will spare you the harrowing details ; but I was in agony before he succeeded in getting out even a piece of the crea-ture, and when I came back to Boston and told father about it, he made me sit right down while he gave me a lecture on emergencies. What do you suppose I could have done for my own relief, and that country doctor ought *of course* to have known enough to do ? "

"I don't know," responded the Tall Man; "I'm not a country doctor."

"Well, can't you think? It is so simple. I felt silly when father told me."

"Go on, and make me feel silly; for really, I can't think what should be done."

"No, because it is so easy. I should have dropped a little oil into my ear and clogged the creature's wings. Then he could n't have fluttered, and could have been removed at leisure."

"Capital! Can't you go on with my education?"

Mrs. Archer observed this interview from afar with indignation; and the next day she approached Nathalie, triumph in her reproving mien.

"Perhaps you will listen to me now," she said. "The lady who has the cabin next to *that man* has had her diamonds stolen, and many people on the ship believe that he has taken them!"

Miss Dexter was standing this time, and she returned her chaperon's gaze without excitement.

"Impossible!" she answered, smiling. "He is from Philadelphia."

Mrs. Archer flushed. "There are rogues in Philadelphia."

"Really? Well, I don't believe he has stolen any diamonds; and I certainly shall not alter my treatment of him, — if that is what you mean."

"Oh! Very well! I wash my hands of the responsibility;" and Mrs. Archer flounced angrily away.

The Tall Man's conscience appeared to be either clear or callous as he approached Nathalie later and asked her to walk. She soon found herself talking to him as to an old friend. She told him how she had been studying the piano for the past year, and how she meant to work all summer, and of her hopes that the great Brandon of Boston would let her into the elect circle of his pupils the following winter; and he told her in return how he considered it of paramount importance that a girl should have a special line of work and develop it to the utmost, thereby securing at once her usefulness and independence. She thought his manner rather amusingly judicial for a man of his years, but she did not say so; and they were very friendly indeed as they passed Mrs. Archer and her coterie, unconscious of the withering glances which glided harmlessly off them.

At last came the final day of the passage. The Tall Man asked Nathalie if he might meet her and take her in to the last festive dinner. She assented; and the diamond accusation having come to naught, Mrs. Archer only bridled when she was informed of the fact.

"I shall do my duty by you, Miss Dexter, for Mrs. Annersley's sake," she announced. "She requested me as a favor to take care of you, and I insist that you remember that I am chaperoning *you* as well as my sweet bud here," and she imprinted a chaste kiss on the round forehead of the Scion.

They were waiting in the salon for the summons. All three had discarded the salted garments of the sea and donned trim walking dress. Suddenly there entered from the further door the Tall Man. He paused, before approaching, to speak to a friend.

Sweater, ulster, outing-cap had disappeared, and he was buttoned to his smooth chin in clerical black.

Mrs. Archer clutched Nathalie's arm and gasped: " Why, he 's a priest! "

"So I see," returned Nathalie, equally astonished.

"From Philadelphia, you said," pursued the other, in awestruck tones. "Some of the best people there are Roman Catholics! "

"He told me yesterday he was a professor of philosophy in some institution," said Nathalie. "Here is his card."

Mrs. Archer snatched it eagerly. "Lewis Andreas! An Andreas of Philadelphia!" The blood retreated to her heart. Her thoughts were in such a whirl that she momentarily forgot her sweet bud. Here she had been entertaining an angel unawares — No, that was the mischief of it! She might have been entertaining him, — and she had failed to do so!

Truly, there are bitter moments in life.

The object of her fascinated gaze turned, and catching sight of Nathalie, smiled toward her, and saying a last word to his friend, began to move in her direction.

Mrs. Archer's grasp tightened on Nathalie's arm. " Shall I ".— she ejaculated in a whisper. " Would you call him ' Father ' ? "

Miss Dexter freed herself. " No, I don't think ·I would," she returned dryly.

CHAPTER II.

THE EGG-ROLLING.

APRIL came in tearfully that season in Washington; nor can the most devoted lovers of the festive city deny that he who anticipates balmy breezes there during the early spring will be disappointed. It is an eager and a nipping air that rushes about the Monument and sweeps down the broad avenue from Capitol to White House. Nowhere does one cling more fondly to furs in March under a deceptive smiling sky.

But Easter Monday there came one of the relenting days when the tree-buds stretch rejoicingly and the sparrows chatter. It had rained during the morning, and every child in Washington, without regard to sex or color, had been flattening his and her little nose against the window-panes and casting imploring glances at the sky. It was their day, — the day of the annual egg-rolling in the " White Lot " behind the President's home.

Countless little baskets stood ready with their gayly-colored eggs, and it was not only the sky that rained tears as the precious morning, slipped by.

> " ' Between the hours of eleven and two
> Is the time to see what the weather will do,' "

muttered Priscilla Toothaker, as after lunch she
stood at her window and looked out.

"It's pretty near two now, and I guess it's
goin' to clear off."

The speaker was not one of the children, nor
did she have any; but she felt for the little things,
and she welcomed the rifts in the sky. "Now, if
it comes off real clear, an hour's good shinin' ought
to dry up the grass enough so 's they can go," she
thought. "I don't know but I'll go myself."

Sure enough, out came the sun with clear, ardent
rays, and before the hour was ended the streets
began to swarm with little folk from mansion and
hovel. White and black, in embroidery or calico
patches, they flocked from all directions toward
the White House, — as if the President had the
Pied Piper himself for a guest.

Miss Toothaker determined to follow after. She
was a busy woman, for she kept a boarding-house,
or at least, she took charge of its table. A man
who, he said himself, knew his "p's and q's,"
knew Miss Priscilla, and knew she had "faculty."
He had lured her two winters in succession from
her New England home to take charge of this
house for him, because his wife was an invalid,
and Miss Toothaker had performed the task to
everybody's satisfaction.

"I'm willin' to work; I like to," she said; "but
I won't take responsibility. It scares me."

Miss Toothaker was a person not often troubled

with doubts. Given a proposition, she knew very quickly what she wanted to do, and her decision made, she did it with her might.

She decided this afternoon that she was going to take a half-holiday and forget what there would be for dinner. She was her own mistress. Mr. and Mrs. Barclay, nominal heads of the house, never interfered with her. They knew better.

"I 'm goin' out, Junius," she said to her black factotum, a youthful person in a high shirt-collar.

"Yas 'm," he replied, with a gracious air all his own. "I reckon it don't seem to be so cold as it feels to-day."

"H'm," said Miss Priscilla, who did not always trouble herself to respond to the amiable but involved remarks of her aid.

"I s'pose you 'll be back in the co'se of quarter to six?" pursued Junius.

"Yes, I guess so; but keep your wits about you now. It won't do for us both to be off the same time."

"Oh, yas 'm. I won't disremember nothin'. Goin' to the egg-rollin', Miss Pris? I thought a while ago the chillen was April-fooled this time, sure."

Miss Toothaker was pulling down window-shades, tying her bonnet-strings, and taking last looks about the dining-room; so Junius proceeded: —

"Y' ought to seen a man git April-fooled oncet to a rest'rant whar I worked. He took his meals

thar reg'lar, and they put up a job on him. He
was always eatin' apple-pie; so they brung him one
filled with cotton wool. It was hot, an' it looked
so greasy an' nice he shet down on it, an' — well,
after that he did n't order no more apple-pie."
The speaker grinned appreciatively. "He said
the crust was short enough, but the wool was too
light for him."

"H'm. Now, don't forget to fix this side-table
for Miss Archer to-night. Don't try to squeeze
her in as you did this morning. It is n't comfortable. Goodness! I ought to take her out with
me, this afternoon! Mrs. Barclay is n't able to.
Go see if Miss Archer is home."

"She ain't, Miss Pris. Done went out fo' lunch,
and ain't come back. Said she wanted to go up
in the doom o' the Capitol."

"Well, I guess she 'll get along. With a tongue
in her head and money in her pocket, she won't
get lost. Plucky girl," added Miss Toothaker to
herself.

"She 's got kind of a queer tongue in her haid,"
hazarded Junius, moving a castor nervously. Miss
Priscilla did not encourage comments on the
boarders.

"What do you mean?" she asked curtly.

"She kind o' talks like — kind o' like she
could n't talk real — real plain or somethin'," stut-
tered Junius. "I like to hear her, though, fust-
rate, I do. It sut'n'y makes me want to laugh."

Miss Toothaker sniffed. " I 'm goin' now. I depend on you, remember. See that everything goes right."

A series of smiling "yas 'ms " followed her out the door.

She took a deep breath as she stepped forth into the sweet air so full of " green things growing."

"It feels like summer," she soliloquized, saunter-ing along past the Arlington and toward the centre of attraction. Priscilla seldom sauntered. She was usually going somewhere in a hurry, and it was often to market; but this was a deliberately taken outing, and she meant to enjoy it. There was not a frill about her severe and simple garb; yet the jauntily shabby carriage-drivers, basking in sudden sunshine against the curb of Lafayette Park, discerned her holiday spirit with their usual uncanny penetration, and starting toward her, their ebony faces wreathed in ingratiating smiles, became voluble : —

" Drive this evenin', lady? Take y' all round the city, cheap."

She shook her head at them. " Yes, I 'm out for an airin'," she addressed them mentally, " but when I spend my money to go off in a brooch, 'foot and alone, I guess you 'll know it."

Then the park allured her. The shrieks of the sparrows were mellowed in the budding trees. She stepped within, and strolling along the path until she reached the spot where Andrew Jackson in

bronze reins his rearing, mettlesome charger, she
sat down on an iron seat.

" I 'll go across to the White House in a minute,"
she thought. " Here 's a real quiet place to look
over my letter."

She drew from her pocket an envelope with a
foreign postmark, and took out the thin sheets
within. These she unfolded and read carefully
from beginning to end, not without an occasional
puzzled frown, and an uncomplimentary allusion
to the quality of the paper and ink.

Then she let hands and letter fall into her black-
silken lap, and her light eyes, with all their little
wrinkles, kindly and anxious, stared before her.

At that moment there came striding down the
same street by which she had come, a masculine
figure. When he passed the carriage-drivers, they
stopped their chuckling and chaffing, started up and
stared at him wistfully, some of them lifting a hand,
but they did not venture to address him. It was
not because his appearance was that of a " swell,"
although they recognized that; but because there
was such an unmistakable air about him of being
able to ask for what he wanted, and of getting it,
too. His was an imposing figure, tall above the
common, flat of back and broad of shoulder, and
he had a way of holding in his chin as he walked
which gave him a military erectness of bearing.
Added to this, the firm, heavy curves of his smooth-
shaven lips and chin, his large nose, and well-set

eyes gave him an appearance of power which, com-
bined with naturally graceful movements, made
him noticeable and noticed wherever he moved.
He was as accustomed to being stared at as the
hero-actor of the matinée girl's fancy, and certainly
thought less about it than must the man with whom
such popularity gauges success.

He had been one of Miss Toothaker's family off
and on during her two Washington winters, and
had, moreover, been once upon a time nursed by
that efficient woman through a severe illness.
Therefore when he, also attracted by the aspect of
the park, turned aside and, entering it, caught sight
of her, wrapped in her brown study and staring
at the equestrian statue, he halted his long steps
beside her.

"If here is n't the fairest of her sex," he remarked, lifting his hat.

Miss Toothaker raised vague eyes to him and
then looked back. "They do say his tail balances
him," she said musingly.

The young man hesitated, then dropped upon
the rustic seat beside her. "Miss Pris, there is
usually so little subtlety in your remarks that I
feel warranted in asking you to explain yourself,"
he said.

"Do you believe it?"

"I don't know. I should have to be introduced
to the tail."

Miss Toothaker was accustomed to paying as

little attention to the remarks of this young man
as she gave to those of the colored boy she had left
at home. If Junius's effusions savored more of
heart than head, so did those of this personage
more of head than heart. She did not understand
him half the time, and for the most part she did
not complicate existence by endeavoring to do so.

"They do say he ain't fastened to the pedestal
at all, — just balances perfectly, mane and tail."

"Oh! you are referring to yon quadruped?"

"Yes. Land!" Miss Priscilla suddenly started
and gasped.

"What's the matter?"

She laughed a little shamefacedly. "Did you
see that sparrer go into the horse's nostril?
Stopped my breath right up. I wish't he'd come
out."

"Why, Miss Pris, you're imaginative. Who'd
have thought it?" and her companion faced around
toward her and leaned his elbow on the back of
the seat.

"Comes from havin' a vacation, I guess. I'm
off on a spree this afternoon."

"Indeed?" The young man smiled. "Where's
your cardinal pigment?"

Miss Toothaker met the twinkling light in his
eyes. "Hey?"

"What are you going to do to celebrate?"

"I'm goin' to see the children roll eggs after I
get tired of Andrew Jackson; but I thought I'd
sun myself first."

"Quite right, lady. Warm, is n't it?" The speaker lifted his hat from his scrupulously parted hair, and suppressed a yawn. Resettling his hat and regarding his companion fixedly, he continued: "It is a pity to cloud the sun for you by referring to a bereavement at such a time, but I meant to speak of it the first chance I had."

"Goodness, Mr. Andreas, what's happened?" asked the kind woman, quick to perceive the mournful change which crept over her companion's face.

"I've lost a mouse by death, up in my room, — in the closet, I think."

"For pity's sake! Do you mean you smell it?"

"Dear lady!" Mr. Andreas laid his gloved hand on hers and drew his brows together in fastidious deprecation. "You put it so baldly! But I thought if you would set Junius on the — the scent, — since you will have it so, — it might be best for you and best for me."

"I'll see to it."

"And one more thing. If I must be squeezed, I should prefer it to be accomplished by youth and beauty; but when it comes to mealtimes, I prefer the use of my arms to any amount of sweet womanly propinquity; therefore if you could make it convenient to withdraw that" —

"Miss Archer — I know."

"Yes, the lovely Archer. Her elbows may not

be Cupid's darts, but she aims them with the certainty of the little god."

"Elbows! I guess she had enough to complain of between two such creatures as you and Mrs. Rathbun, poor girl!"

"O Miss Toothaker!" emotionally. "It makes me thrill to have you class me with Mrs. Rathbun. Tell me honestly, as man to man, does n't that amiable woman wear reform clothing?"

"It 's none o' your business what she wears. She 's goin' to learn the bicycle to reduce her flesh."

"She is! Does the bicycle know it?"

Miss Toothaker laughed a little.

"What bicycle, Miss Pris?"

"I don't know. A good strong one, I hope."

Andreas shook his head. "That settles it. I shall leave Washington. I hope I am an ordinarily brave man; but I owe it to my family not to stay in the same town where Mrs. Rathbun rides a wheel."

"It was merely Junius's mistake about Miss Archer," said Miss Toothaker, reverting, as usual, to practical matters. "I 've fixed it to have her seat changed to-night. She 's only goin' to be here two or three days, anyway. You know she 's the Barclays' guest. They do it to help her along, I guess. She lives down in Virginia, and does some kind o' dinner cards or favors, or triflin' paintin' o' some kind for stores here; so she came up to see

about her orders. This is the first minute I've
had to help her any to sight-see or have a good
time, and when I was ready to come out this afternoon she 'd gone. Kind of a pretty girl."

"Pretty is as pretty does," returned Andreas,
with gentle reproach. "I did n't get a fair look
at her. I informed her that it was a cool morning,
and she showed no surprise. Then she asked me
for the salt, and she did n't seem to have that mas-
tery of the letter S which one looks for from a girl
who does up her hair."

"She 's got a little impediment, and that Southern talk 's queer anyway; but it 's cunnin', too.
The way she always says 'Ah' for 'I' sticks in
my mind. I 'm always possessed to say it over
after her. 'Yes Ah will — Ah can — Ah do,' she
says. Then, anyway, you need n't criticise! You
pronounce *hard* and *regard* and such words 's if
they were spelled *hord* and *regord*, yourself."

"Miss — Toothaker! This personality — and
from you? What a world of surprises!"

"I should think it was a world of surprises.
Here 's this letter just came to me this mornin'."
The speaker lifted the sheets in her lap. "It 's
from the best woman that ever breathed, but she
puts me out. She expected to come home this
spring, and now she 's got to stay over in Italy,
and wants me to fill in her place here this summer.
A relative of hers has lent her his cottage at the
seashore, and she wants me to go there — it 's up

in Maine — and open the house and take charge
of her daughter. I have n't seen Nathalie since
she was a little girl and Dr. Dexter used to bring
her to his old home once in a while."

"See what you pay for having ' faculty ' ! That
is what Mr. Barclay says you have, — ' faculty.' "

" I can't even make out the name o' the place.
See if you can." Miss Toothaker indicated a
word on one of the pages.

Her companion examined it a moment, then
started back dramatically, staring at the paper.

" Is it ? It can't be ! It is ! Miss Pris," tenderly, " there is something more than chance in
this. We are not constantly thrown together in
this way for nothing."

" For mercy's sake speak out ! " said Miss Toothaker.

" There 's no mistake about it. Fate intends
that you shall make me a huckleberry-pie."

" Does it, indeed ? Well, perhaps *I* don't."

" That place is Pulpit Point; and Pulpit Point
— be brave, Miss Pris — is where my people have
their summer cottage."

Miss Toothaker sniffed and took back her letter.
" So you think I won't get rid of you ? "

The young man shook his head. " Not unless
Nathalie is awfully disagreeable," he returned.
" Why don't you want to go ? " he added.

" Oh, I don't know. I s'pose Nathalie ain't a
child any longer. I s'pose there would n't be so

very much responsibility. I " — She recalled her
wandering thoughts suddenly and rose. " I 'm
goin' to see the egg-rollin'," she said.

Andreas strolled along beside her, and they
looked over toward the teeming lawn of the White
House.

" See ! They 're not using the White Lot," he
remarked. " Too wet, perhaps. How many families in the land would submit their grounds to be
invaded by such an army of small vandals? A
good deal is expected of our Executive, don't you
think? Thankless job being President of these
United States, anyway. For my own part, I 've
determined to refuse the nomination."

CHAPTER III.

THE next morning, the weather not having re-
considered its pleasant truce, and Russell Andreas
having some insurance business which called him
to Alexandria, he suddenly decided to proceed
thither by boat.

He settled himself in a quiet corner of the deck
with his newspaper, and becoming absorbed in its
contents, noted nothing of the passing and repass-
ing near him until the bell, ringing for the start,
caused him to look up and discover that a good
many people beside himself had taken advantage
of the sunny morning for a river trip.

He let his glance stray mechanically over his
neighbors, and it was quite a matter of course that
many of them were looking at himself. Only one
face did he recognize, and that only after a minute's waiting to make sure that he was not mistaken. He had not before seen her with a hat on,
and she was not one of those now honoring him
with an inspection. He obtained only a three-
quarters view of her face as she looked absorbedly
toward the river-bank.

There could be no doubt, as time went on, what

she was watching for, for when the boat passed
near Washington Barracks, she started up from
her chair and gazed eagerly at the unsatisfactory
view of quarters and parade ground, the dash of
bright color where a sentinel guarded his post, and
the stars and stripes floating over all.

Now the girl's lips parted, and her color deepened in the spring wind, while the soft touch of her
brown hair caressed her temples.   She looked very
young and innocent in her tall girlhood ; her large
blue eyes were exceptionally childlike in expression, Andreas thought, — for by this time he had
moved to where he could see her eyes, although he
was careful not to appear to observe them.   He
was a wary young man, and, owing to his physical
peculiarities, more accustomed to avoiding snares
than to setting them.

"Yes, it is Miss Archer," he decided, "and she
is evidently enamored of brass buttons."

When the Barracks were passed, the girl sank
back in her chair, but still looked about her with
interest.

Andreas recalled what Miss Priscilla had said of
her.   The statements did not indicate a lively existence.   There was a certain pathos in the fact of
her lonely outing, and the way she was making the
most of her little holiday.   Too bad she had to go
about in this solitary fashion ; and all the time he
was indulging in these magnanimous and compas-
sionate thoughts, Andreas was holding himself in

readiness to flee if the girl-tourist showed symptoms of recognizing him. He had known too often what it was to be seized upon, definitely, irremediably, and he had developed marvelous elusive ingenuity.

How fresh and sweet she looked! Southern girls were a nice lot. Though slender, she was not thin. He had been hypercritical to complain of her elbows. It was a moral certainty that they were rounded.

Standing thus in idle meditation, he suddenly realized that he had relaxed his guard unwarrantably. The brown head turned, and the blue eyes under the wide brow ran with childlike indifference along the faces of her neighbors. Andreas's time had come. His hand stole mechanically toward the hat which he would raise in turning, and then put his faith in his long legs. She was a Southern girl; she would not attempt to detain him.

But the hand did not reach his hat. Miss Archer saw him, — there could not be a doubt of that; but there was none of that recognition, — not a gleam of that radiant recognition which he was most apt to read in the faces of his woman friends. The blue eyes met his without changing expression, and moved steadily onward.

His hand dropped, and the long strides were not called into requisition. Her complexion had shell-like tints, and she liked brass buttons!

"Too shy to bow, poor thing," he thought.

"After all, it won't be so far to Alexandria, and it's lonely for her, unsophisticated little girl."

Whereupon, the magnanimous impulse being given its way, in a moment more the serene blue eyes were looking up into a pair of brown ones, as Russell Andreas stood beside the girl, with uncovered head.

"Good-morning, Miss Archer. You don't recognize me."

She did not change her position at his advent. "Yes, I do, perfectly," she said with calm deliberation. "Yo're the gentleman who showed temper yesterday because we were so crowded at table."

"I!" Andreas laughed in his discomfiture. "I! Showed temper? Miss Archer!"

"Yes, you cert'nly did. A sort of Jove-like, repressed wrath, you know. It was right amusing. I hit yo' arm once or twice on purpose; but then it was awfully impolite, and I had no business to do it."

"And you were well punished for it, too," retorted Andreas, who, bewildered by her drawl and her lisp and her demureness, could not decide what this innocent impudence might betoken, and was only conscious of being suddenly glad that Alexandria was no nearer. "You were put at the side-table last evening like a naughty child."

"Oh, the side-table is a great improvement. Junius treats me like a queen. Won't you either step aside or sit down, please? Yo're so big, and I've never been up the Potomac before."

Andreas, in whose experience this was the first girl who had preferred scenery to him, took the alternative in an exhilarating condition of astonishment. She went on talking, imperturbably.

"I live on a creek at home, but this river is something different. I was so glad it was pleasant to-day, for I must go home to-morrow, and I've never been to Mount Vernon in all ma life."

"Oh! you're going to Mount Vernon?" said Andreas.

"Yes, of co'se. Are n't you?"

Andreas hesitated a perceptible instant, during which the interests of the insurance business trembled in the balance. She turned her innocent face fully toward him and regarded him attentively. "You look like such a nice man," she said musingly.

"I am," admitted Andreas, with prompt ingenuousness.

"Oh, dear, no." She smiled for the first time, faintly, showing the edges of small white teeth; and it was at that moment that Russell decided definitely not to get off at Alexandria. "Yo 're not nearly so nice as he is, that is, I don't believe you are. *He* is a priest."

Andreas raised his eyebrows. "Same name as mine, perhaps?"

"I did n't catch yo' name. I 've called you ma Lord Touch-me-not."

The young man flushed. " Russell Andreas, at your service," he said, lifting his hat.

She gave a soft cry. " Not *Russell* Andreas ! " she exclaimed, and the owner of the name congratulated himself that it boasted so richly of the letter S.

Then she laughed, — the most mischievous, bubbling little laugh that ever fell from a girl's lips.

" I think that 's too funny," she said.

He shrugged his shoulders. " You will have to let me into the joke," he answered.

" Why, Ro — somebody was talking to me about you only last week."

" Favorably, I hope."

" And to think you are yo' brother's brother ! "

" Why, it has always seemed very natural to me. You know him, do you ? "

" I met him at Fort Monroe. Are you a Roman Catholic, too ? "

" No. I tell Lewis he is so high and narrow, I have to be low and broad to balance him. Who is it who has been talking to you about me ? "

The serene blue eyes were again busy with the scenery. " Would you rather know who he is, or what he said ? "

" Oh, it is a man ? I am not afraid to hear what any man says of me ; and I 'm curious — as curious as you please."

" But he said a lot of things. It came up because I was coming to Washington, and he said

you were very likely here, as yo' insurance business often called you this way. Some of the
things he said probably would n't be good for you
to hear, but I 'll tell you one, if you really want
me to."

" Of course I do."

The childlike gravity had all returned to Miss
Archer's face. " He said that wherever yo' insurance did n't take you, yo' assurance did."

Russell's short laugh had a conscious ring. It
occurred to him that he was proving the truth of
this assertion at the present moment.

" After that I demand your friend's address, in
order that I may call him out," he said.

" Then I reckon I won't give it to you, for he
is n't at all well."

By the time Mount Vernon was reached, these
two had made some strides in their acquaintance,
and Andreas had not once regretted Alexandria.
As they climbed the tree-laden hill toward Washington's tomb, Andreas spoke.

" I have given you my full name, and you have
not returned the compliment."

" Is n't Archer enough for you ? "

" It is a good name."

" I fear you don't half realize what a good name
it is."

Andreas looked at her questioningly, but the
innocent directness of her gaze was absorbing their
surroundings. They were approaching the iron

grating behind which reposes the eagle-crowned sarcophagus of the Father of his Country.

"I have never been here before, either," said Andreas. "So this is where the truthful gentleman lies at last."

His companion shook her head. "You should n't say funny things about Washington." Her roving glance embraced the fine estate. "Let us go on. It is more beautiful here than I supposed."

They wandered around by the old tomb and to the pavilion, where they sat looking down the steep bank with its fine trees, to the stately, broad river.

The girl looked up toward the pillared mansion. "I should like to live here with a steam yacht," she said.

Andreas smiled at her. "Would you? I should prefer to live here with a lady, — a very nice lady, you understand. Pretty, and amiable, and all that, you know."

Birds were calling each other from height to height in the ecstasy of the sunshine. The scattered tourists did not interfere with the effect of breadth and seclusion about them.

"Oh, that 's very natural if yo 're in love," she answered. "I 'm in love with steam yachts. I went out in one once at Old Point Comfort."

"Out — out," repeated Andreas, pursing up his mouth. "If I could pronounce ' out ' the way you do, I would n't work any more."

She flushed a little. "You say enough queer

things," she retorted. "Yo 're from Philadelphia, I reckon."

"I don't see what you mean; but then, if you
know my brother, you guess that easily. When
did you meet him? He has been abroad most of
the winter, and has just come home."

"Last fall. It happened I met him twice, for
he was visiting a friend of mine. That 's the way
I learned that there were some nice people in Philadelphia."

"Indeed? You don't trouble yourself to flatter
my city."

"I don't need to. We have a Philadelphian in
our house."

"Look here, don't rub it in! See how polite I
was to you in advance. I went to college in your
State."

"The University of Virginia. Yes, I know you
did."

He stared. "You do!"

She suddenly regarded him with eager interest.
"Were you an Eli?"

"Yes."

"Oh!" in poignant regret. "I wish I 'd known
you at that time instead of now; but then," —
with a shrug, — "I dare say ma hair was in plaits
then. I don't suppose you would have looked at
me."

Andreas smiled. "Then you are not entirely
given over to the military."

"The military?" she repeated with interest.
"How did you know I was fond of the military?"

"I watched you as we were passing Washington
Barracks."

"You did?" No one seeing her wide eyes
could have doubted that this news surprised the
young woman, — although in fact she had been
perfectly aware of his espionage as long as it
lasted. "That was very rude of you. However,
seeing you have discovered it, I don't mind telling
you that I do love an army officer."

"Better than steam yachts?" inquired Andreas
dryly.

"Oh, yes. *An* army officer, you understand,"
explained the girl. "I prefer steam yachts infi-
nitely to some army officers of ma acquaintance."

"Well," said Andreas, somewhat stiffly, "considering you have so much mysterious information
about me, it is perhaps only fair that you should
tell me these interesting details concerning yourself. Shall we go on up to the house?"

"Yes." She slid from her perch on the rail,
and advanced beside him. "You turn rusty sometimes, ma Lord Touch-me-not, don't you?" she
added after a silence. She met her companion's
sudden sharp glance with eyes that sparkled out of
their usual demureness.

"You have made a pun without being aware of
it, Miss Archer."

"You don't suppose I would make one *being*

aware of it, do you? There, that piazza, I know, is the very best of all," she added. "Let us save it until the last."

She was so fresh and simple, she spoke with such a relish. Andreas wondered if that officer might not be her brother. He would believe so for the present.

They strolled around the house to the garden, and wandered into the box-edged paths.

"This box! Think what it has witnessed!" said Andreas, impressed by the gnarled and tough wood of the pungent-smelling border. "The satin knee-breeches, gold snuff-boxes, brocaded skirts, and court-plaster, — think of them, right here."

"Yes," returned his companion. "Supposing those old fogies had seen a few bicycle girls racing around these grounds: I suppose it would have shocked them so their wigs would have stood right up."

"Miss Archer! I'm afraid there is a hollow where your bump of reverence ought to be. And you reproved me for being funny about Washington! Steam yachts and bicycles at Mount Vernon! You grieve me."

"Oh, but Washington is different. What a splendid place this would be to entertain in! I'd like to give a German here."

"Hush! You disturb my day-dream. Don't speak of anything more lively than the minuet! Think of Washington himself dignifiedly patrol-

ling that majestic piazza and straining his eyes,
scanning the river for a sail, — possibly bringing
him vital news. Oh, the good old times!"

"Nonsense!" remarked the girl airily. "The
good new times have spoiled us for them."

"Miss Archer." Andreas faced her squarely.
They had reached the end of a garden path, and
the girl, by his sudden motion, was placed with her
back to a greenhouse, as he looked directly down
into her face. "I am being obliged to revise all
my first impressions of you. I had no idea that
there were any new women among the soft-spoken,
charming maidens of the South. I now begin to
suspect that you are the very latest thing in new
women."

She returned his gaze with smiling defiance.
"Why do you think so, Mr. Rusty Andreas?"
She drawled the name teasingly.

"What!" He laughed and frowned. "You
even know my nickname?" He paused and
shook his head slowly. "This has gone on long
enough. You may be a new woman of the most
novel description, and be tolerably independent of
men, — all except army officers, of course, — but
there still remains a slight balance of physical
strength in our favor, and I am going to get quite
a little information before you come out of that
corner."

"Oh, you mustn't take that tone. I don't like
people who coerce me. Ask me prettily as we go

up to the house. We have n't been in yet, and there are spinets and armchairs and vases and lots of things to assist yo' day-dream."

" I don't care for detached relics. Do you?"

" Love them. Let me go."

She darted lightly to one side, but he caught her with one arm, and gently but irresistibly set her back.

She breathed fast. " I don't want to take part in a vulgar romp," she said.

" I would n't," he answered. Their gaze, half-laughing, wholly challenging, met, and they were mute.

" I reckon you won't lose the boat?" she asked at last.

" I hope not."

" Do you mean you would?"

" If you insisted, of course I should have to. I ought not to, for I ought to stop off at Alexandria sure, going back. Perhaps you will go with me. I will take you through the Braddock house, show you the black mahogany staircase where Sally Fairfax came tripping down to dance the minuet with Washington, — show you the room where the deed was done, — show you the deep stone chambers under the house where the horses were kept, — show" —

" Never mind! As if I should ever go anywhere with you again, when you treat me so!"

" I protest. I say you have treated *me* so, ever

since we started. Now then: What's your first
name?   Fair exchange, remember.   Rusty Andreas!   Well!"

She flushed.   " Do you remember the Mother
Goose riddle beginning, ' Elizabeth, Betsy, Bessie,
and Beth ? '   That's ma first name."

" Oh, well.   I'll think that over and take my
choice later.   Your middle name, please."

" Archer."

" No — your middle name."

" Archer."

" Very well," indifferently, " if you don't care to
see the detached relics " —

" Mr. Andreas — I 'm a Virginian, and in
George Washington's home at that."

" Then what is your *last* name ? "

" Dear me!   Yo 're an awfully stupid man,
are n't you ? "

He gazed at her firmly.   " I can stay here as
long as you can.   My insurance takes me to Alexandria, to be sure ; but my assurance keeps me
here.   I 'm coming to *that* traducer presently, — or
to-night, or to-morrow morning, — whenever we get
to him."

" I wish he were here now," remarked the girl
coolly.   " He would have you out of that path in
a twinkling."

The decided curves of her captor's mouth widened over his even teeth.   She read his expression.

"Oh, yes, he could do it, too, although he is n't quite so big as you are; — or he could if he were well. He is n't at all well."

" Then as he is n't here and is n't well," said Andreas gently, " don't you want to save time by telling me your full name? "

" I see I shall have to, yo 're so slow witted. I 'm sorry I can't do it in words of one syllable. Now listen." She spoke slowly. " Ma name is Elizabeth Archer Archer."

At her companion's look of surprise, she smiled. " You remember the story of the old woman who was entertaining her minister, and sweetened his coffee by filling his cup half full of molasses? When he protested, she hushed him, saying it would n't be any too good fo' him if it were *all* molasses. Well, I 've always been convinced that ma father did n't think it would have been any too good for me if ma name had been *all* Archer."

" Elizabeth Archer Archer," mused Andreas, putting his hand to his temple. " Where have I heard that ? "

His companion laughed low, enjoying his perplexity. " You don't expect to compel me to tell you that, I suppose ? "

" No," he answered absently, still chasing the elusive memory.

" Then I 'll surprise you by ma generosity. Might it have been at the University ? "

A light broke over her companion's face. " My

chum, Gerard. Best all-around fellow in the class.
Why, I do believe it was he. You were the little
girl whose picture stood in our room. He went to
West Point afterward. Why," more light irradiating the questioning eyes, "it's he — confound
him ! — it's Roger Gerard who has been making
epigrams about me. It is he who is your army
officer."

"Indeed it is; and wait till he hears how you
wasted my time at Mount Vernon, blocking the
way so rudely, and keeping me penned up in the
end of a blind alley ! He'll do something more
than make epigrams."

"Was he — I forget —   Is he any relation to
you?"

"No," returned Miss Archer loftily. "But
that doesn't make any difference, does it?"

"N-no," replied Andreas.

CHAPTER IV.

SOMEBODY has likened a New England conscience to "a case of moral hives." That of Priscilla Toothaker possessed the average local irritability, and was not prone to allow inaction in its owner.

Mrs. Dexter's letter had prepared her to receive another from Nathalie; and in due time this arrived.

It was a very pretty note which found Miss Priscilla in Twombley, Connecticut, whither she repaired on the first day of June, her Washington duties ended. She left that city a mass of bloom and foliage, which made Twombley look bleak by contrast. Moreover, Miss Priscilla's family having one by one died or married, she no longer lived in her old home in Twombley, but boarded, when she was there, with a family who were sufficiently kind to her, but to whom her comings or goings mattered little.

Miss Toothaker's conscience did not hesitate to remind her that she was foot-loose, and that there was no good and sufficient reason, beyond her own disinclination, why she should not oblige Mrs. Dexter at this time.

"Neither," Miss Priscilla replied defiantly to this suggestion, was she "at all beholden to the Dexters." She had earned a right to a good vacation, and no one could criticise her if she chose to take it.

Miss Dexter had offered in that pretty note to come in person to Twombley and talk things over with Miss Toothaker, if that lady would like her to do so.

"Like her to," repeated Priscilla suspiciously. "I don't know as I like anything about it. I don't know why they should pitch on *me*."

"Every reason," remarked Conscience inexorably. "They know how you are situated, and there are very few — perhaps no one else — whom they could call upon."

"Well, I won't be driven into it, so there!" said Miss Priscilla, quite to herself, and affecting not to have heard this remark of Conscience at all. "It'll just be changin' the place and keepin' the pain to go up there into Maine and cook and keep house again all summer, and I'm kind o' surprised that Mrs. Dexter should ask it of me. Perhaps it would be better for me to see the girl and talk it out. I wonder what she's like? If she's stuck up, that'll settle it."

So she told Nathalie she might come, and by dint of constant strengthening of her own position by arguments, and unremitting repression of Conscience that untiringly popped up like a Jack-in-the-box, she was able to assume a non-committal and discouraging demeanor when one day she went to the parlor to receive her young guest.

In spite of her knowledge that the child she remembered must have passed twenty, it gave her a sensation of surprise to be met by the graceful and elegant young woman who rose at her entrance into the dim and shaded room, and came to meet her with cordial outstretched hand.

"Here I am, Miss Toothaker," said the girl brightly.

Priscilla cautiously received the hand, her own elbow trussed to her side. "I thought your hair was red," she said, inspecting her.

The girl laughed frankly. "It did start out to be, and it has n't entirely relented, you see. You don't know how strange it seems to be in Twombley again," she added, as they sat down together on the haircloth sofa. "The dépôt has grown small, and so have the rocks; but the maples and beeches, — after all, one must come to Connecticut for trees. You have only just returned, yourself."

"Yes. It does seem good to get home and settle down again," returned Miss Toothaker, with subtle intent; and Conscience recoiled, for, in truth, there was an emptiness and a homelessness about Twombley for Miss Priscilla of late years.

"I suppose it does. I'm afraid you are n't at all pleased with our proposition for the summer."

"Well, you see just how it is. I work pretty

steady all winter, and summers I have the feeling belong to me."

"Of course you do. Mother only thought that as there would only be two of us " —

" What two? " suspiciously.

" Why, you and me."

"Oh!"

— "and since Pulpit Point is a quiet, pleasant resort, that you might not object to going there, if you had no other plan. She had to think quick, you know, for she decided so suddenly to let me come without her." Nathalie bit her lip, and her listener saw her eyes fill. " You don't know what it has been to me to come back to Boston alone. We've never been separated before since papa died. Twombley reminds me so of papa. O Miss Toothaker, forgive me!"

And, to Priscilla's vast astonishment, the next moment her arms were embracing her guest's fine, smooth jacket, and the jaunty quills of the hat she had been admiring were crushed against her shoulder.

Conscience viewed the situation, saw its chance for an hour off, turned over, and went to sleep.

"Do cry if you want to, Nathalie. Do, child." Miss Toothaker winked vigorously herself as she patted her. "You know nobody liked your pa any better'n I did."

In a few minutes the girl sat up, wiped her eyes, and straightened her hat.

"There would be one thing about Pulpit Point you might not like," she said, ignoring the little shower, and trying to smile. "Do you dislike hearing people practice on the piano?"

"I don't know as I do."

"Because I want to work this summer. Work with a capital W, you know. It will be good for me in every way; and I am pleased with the thought of going where I don't know any one. I can accomplish so much more. If it does n't suit your plans to go, though" — She paused.

"Well, what would you do then?"

"I should stay in Boston, try to find an unexacting boarding-place, keep the windows open, and practice."   ·

"Oh, I guess it would be better for you at the seashore."

"Of course it *would*." Miss Dexter smiled questioningly; and as it had been settled in Priscilla's mind that she was going to accede to her proposal, from the moment Nathalie accomplished the unconscious *coup* of weeping in her arms, the matter was soon settled between them.

It was the last day of June when they opened the cottage.

Pulpit Point is a bit of granite-bound land jutting into the water, the Pulpit itself being a huge rock of striking form situated at the furthermost point, rising above the surrounding ledges, and looking out to sea as if to suggest a congregation of mermen, maids, and fishes.

The cottage placed at Nathalie's disposal was breezily situated, only twenty rods from the Point, and surrounded down to the rocks themselves by hummocks of green grass; most uneven ground, which, if one walked over it by night, was full of pitfalls into which a foot, dipping unexpectedly, brought the jaws of the pedestrian together with a snap.

"Cap'n Levi's pastur'," it had been for many a year; but cows and oxen are being turned out of their happy hunting-grounds along the Maine coast with almost the same persistence as met the Indians before them. What Cap'n Levi called "bobbed wi-ar fence" curtailed the privileges of the livestock at Pulpit Point, and although Cap'n Levi gave it as his opinion that "the man who invented bobbed wi-ar ought to had a roll on't drawed through him," he yielded to custom and used it, now that specimens of tired humanity from the cities wanted his "pastur' lots" to rest in, untrampled by oxen.

Indeed, these odd human beings wanted so many things that Cap'n Levi did not find it convenient to go to sea any more, but stayed at home to supply them from a little general store; and they wanted them so quickly that the oxen could n't move fast enough, so Cap'n Levi had to buy a horse, of which he stood in considerable awe.

Nathalie and Miss Toothaker had not been long at the Point before discovering that Cap'n Levi was the guide, philosopher, and friend to whom they must turn in every emergency.

" Though molasses in winter ain't a patch on him for slowness," commented Priscilla.

" We must just remember that we have all summer," said Miss Dexter, when the captain went to Portland for the second time and forgot a necessity she had sent for.

" Yes, it 'll be a real comfort to go back in the fall and know we put those ceilin'-hooks up in the closet before we left," returned Miss Toothaker; but she laughed. Priscilla had laughed more in the week since they came here than she had done before in six months. The little cottage was pretty, the kitchen convenient, and as she sat down at table alone with Nathalie in a room where every window framed a marine view, and contrasted the situation with the fifteen hungry mouths she had had to feed in the dark dining-room on Fifteenth Street, she breathed many a sigh of inward content.

Nor was she grudging in letting Nathalie understand her satisfaction. " As convenient a house as I 'd care to have," she remarked; " but you 'll be lucky if I don't forget to work, lookin' out the windows."

" Oh, I fancy the pangs of hunger will assail us at about the same time," replied Miss Dexter.

Miss Toothaker's comments on the furnishings of the cottage afforded the girl much amusement.

Especially did Miss Priscilla take umbrage at the
Hawaiian tapas which decorated the living-room.
In vain Nathalie explained to her the interesting
handiwork of the natives, their only material being
pulp made from wood, and the coloring matter
from roots and berries.

"I could get calico for six cents that would be
more genteel," averred Miss Priscilla. "Those
sprawlin' patterns that look as if they was painted
in red clay and laid on with a stick! The idea!
But then, I did n't mean to hurt your feelin's.
It 's your cousin owns the cottage, and her taste
ain't any o' my business, and 't ain't the thing to
look a gift-horse in the mouth, either. I tell you,
Nathalie, this air alone is meat and drink, and a
very little clothing, as my mother used to say."

"It is fine; and now, Miss Priscilla, we 're strangers here, and if we can do so without rudeness, I
want to remain so. Callers are such thieves of
time in summer. Let us look the other way all we
can."

Miss Toothaker sniffed, and eyed her companion
thoughtfully. "There 's a young man I 'm most
afraid will appear to me before the summer 's
over," she said.

"O Miss Priscilla! If you are going to have
followers!"

"He 's a feller boards with me in Washington.
Says his folks come here summers. He 's a well-
meanin' young man, I think. He ain't real sensi-

ble in his talk always, but I 'm kind o' used to him."

"Now, Miss Priscilla, I can read partiality in your eye."

"No, I don't know as you can."

"Snub him, snub him if he comes," said Nathalie firmly. "Tell him to wait till you get back to Washington."

Miss Toothaker smiled. "It makes me laugh, 'cause that 's just what he said. He said, says he, 'I 'll come and see you, if Nathalie ain't very disagreeable,' says he."

Miss Dexter's bright eyes grew brighter in her surprise. "How charming!" she ejaculated.

"Oh, he 's always sayin' those gassy things. I 'd told him about your mother's letter, that 's all. Mr. Andreas did n't know a thing about you, of course."

"Andreas!" with a quick sigh. "The dearest man in the world is named Andreas."

"Nathalie Dexter! Why, I never thought of such a thing till this minute! Are you engaged?"

The girl shook her head mournfully. "Alas! no. He is a priest."

"Russell Andreas, this man I was talking about, has got a brother, a priest."

"Why, it must be the same! Is n't that an odd coincidence? How *very* odd! Well, it will be hard, then, for Nathalie to be very disagreeable to him; but I shall be firm!"

And now all was ready for the most important member of the family, namely, the piano.

Nathalie was obliged to have recourse to Cap'n Levi several times on this subject, and one morning she found him coming around the side of his store.

"Jest killed a skunk out he-ar in my hen-house," he announced conversationally.

"Are there skunks at Pulpit Point?" with horror.

"Plenty of 'em, plenty of 'em," was the cheerful response. "Guess ef the wind wa'n't east, you 'd find out right now there was *one*, anyway," and Cap'n Levi exhibited a solitary tooth in a wide chuckle at the girl's look of consternation. "Wood-pussies, the cawtage folks calls 'em. They do kind o' favor cats, you know. Kin I do anything fer ye?"

"Yes. You know I was talking to you about my piano. Well, the people in Portland say they will deliver it for me at this dock, but that I shall have to get it up to the house myself; and that means that *you* will have to bring it."

"Does, hey? Dunno as I ever hauled a pianner."

"Oh, Vixen will do it beautifully," said Nathalie persuasively.

Cap'n Levi scratched his head. "When 's she due?"

"It will come down to-morrow by the afternoon boat."

" Wall, I hope it don't rain and make the goin' bad," observed the captain. " Vixen ud balk, like 's not."

He evidently felt a weight of responsibility at the prospect, but the next afternoon's boat-time found him at the dock with his wagon, watching the incoming steamer with a boding countenance.

So great was his absorption in looking for the piano that he did not notice a familiar figure which left the boat with the other passengers, and after exchanging salutations with several lounging Pulpit Pointers, approached the open-mouthed captain.

" Wake up, Cap'n Levi. Are n't you going to speak to me ? " cried the newcomer.

" Hello, that you, Russell ? " absently allowing his hard hand to be gripped.

" What 's the matter, cap'n ? You look as if you 'd lost ten dollars and found a quarter."

" Seen anythin' of a pianner ? Thar — thar 't is now. They 're a-puttin' her off ! "

" What 's this ? You been investing in a piano ? Made your fortune ? "

" It 's Miss Dexter's pianner, an' she expects me to haul it fer her."

" Oh, there is too much style coming to the Pulpit. Dexter is a new name."

All the same, Andreas was wondering why it had a vaguely familiar sound.

" She 's darned *set*, — that 's all I know," muttered the harassed captain. " One o' the sort 'll never let ye rest, if she wants anythin'. She looks jest as pleasant 's a curly, bright-eyed lamb; but, b' gosh, if she ain't worse 'n Miss Toothaker, come right down to it."

Russell Andreas smiled in enlightenment.

" I 'll help you, Cap'n Levi," he said generously. " Don't be excited."

The captain accepted this offer eagerly; but he *was* excited and, moreover, he retained command of the expedition. As several hands hoisted the upright piano upon the wagon, Vixen laid her ears back inquiringly. She was tied and double-tied, after the captain's usual cautious fashion, for he lived in a state of constant apprehension as to possible outbreaks of his steed.

" Stiddy, stiddy ! " he cried, as the piano settled into place. " Ketch this rope and make her fast across thar, so 's the thing won't slip out the stern o' the wagon. Now we 're ready," to Russell. " Cast off, will ye ? "

"Ay, ay, sir," returned Andreas, and untied the mare. Then he jumped up beside the ex-mariner, and Vixen started.

Nathalie was watching the approach eagerly from the open window, whither came stentorian " Gees " and " Haws " as Cap'n Levi guided his mare up the stony road.

" Oh, Miss Toothaker," she called to Priscilla, who was busy in the kitchen, " they 've sent a man from Portland with the piano, after all."

" That 's clever," came the reply.

" It is a relief to me. I was so afraid these poor fishermen would break their backs trying to handle it."

So saying, Miss Dexter came out upon the piazza and waited, until with many a jolt, the wagon with its precious burden drew up to the house, and stopped.

The sunshine picked out the red lights in her chestnut hair, and the satisfaction of the moment made her bright youth radiant to look upon as she stood there. She beamed upon Andreas with an approving smile.

" Good-afternoon. I 'm very glad you could come," she said. " They are not accustomed to moving pianos down here."

Andreas smiled appreciatively after his first surprise, and accepted the rôle thrust upon him.

" Think we can h'ist her alone ? " asked the captain doubtfully.

" Easy as lying. This is n't like the dock, you know."

Nathalie watched eagerly as, with many a grunt and " Stiddy, thar," from Cap'n Levi, the piano was moved inside. She directed where it should be placed, giving Russell many a quick command in the transit, and smiled with satisfaction when she saw the coveted instrument safely at her disposal at last.

" Now, it was n't so very bad, Cap'n Levi, was it ? " she asked coaxingly.

" Wall, I hope ye 'll get an orgin next time. Want to go along o' me, Russell ? " turning to his able assistant.

" No, thanks."

A movement of Vixen's head, visible through the open window, attracted the notice of her anxious owner. " Hi, thar ! Hi, thar ! " he cried, and, hastening out, mounted into his wagon and drove away.

Andreas regarded Nathalie soberly. " What a man for such a position ! " she thought. " Did they want me to pay you to-day ? " she asked.

" By no means," he returned, with a gesture which was the most polite disclaimer ; but he made no movement to go.

" Then — I should like to ask you to sit down and rest," said Nathalie civilly ; " but you have not much more than time to catch the boat on its return from Mericoneag."

" Thank you. I am not going back to Portland to-day."

Miss Dexter returned his gaze, bewildered. He smiled into her eyes, and she retreated and colored. There was some awful blunder here. He was too — oh, too many things to be a piano-mover. Beside, he looked so much like somebody. Who was it ? She groped wildly for the fleeting memory.

" I have — made a mistake," she stammered.

" You have given me a pleasure, Miss Dexter."

That little bow; the tone; the turn of the head. Ah! she had it now. " Mr. Russell Andreas! " she ejaculated.

" There is evidently no resisting fame," he remarked, surprised.

" You see, your brother " — she exclaimed eagerly.

" Indeed? Why, I 'm so glad I am Lewis's brother. I find it such a recommendation."

" You look so like him."

" Miss Dexter," plaintively. " That grows monotonous. Could n't you find it in your heart to detect some resemblance in Lewis to me? "

Miss Toothaker suddenly appeared in the doorway, rubbing her forehead with her wrist. " Oh, '*t is* you. I thought 't was your voice."

" Miss Pris! The only woman I ever loved! "

" Look out! I 'm all flour. I can't shake hands. Glad to see you, though. You 've got acquainted with Miss Dexter, I see."

" Mr. Andreas moved my piano with Cap'n Levi. I am under the greatest obligation to him." Nathalie spoke with fervor.

After Russell had taken his departure, saying he had not yet reported to his own household, she sat down with hot cheeks and, laughing heartily, told Priscilla her experience.

" I shan't stop blushing for a month! I ordered

him about so.　You should have heard me!" she finished.

Miss Toothaker's low laugh rumbled forth as an echo.　"Well, I s'pose he's come to the seashore for *change*," she remarked.

CHAPTER V.

IT was a glorious morning. The clear green waves were rollicking about the Pulpit. Out on the ledges snowy garlands of foam sent up a fine, smoke-like spray, and the gull's wing was whiter as it rose from the crested wave.

It was one of the mornings when the breathing apparatus seems too limited. One opens one's arms to the sunlit air, and lifts a thankful face toward the downy fluffs of cloud along the blue.

Miss Priscilla had lagged in her determination to shake rugs. She had left them hanging over the piazza rail, and gone to see how her grass was coming on. She was helping Nature to clothe a bare patch of ground, which had lacked either time or courage to procure a new garment since those ruthless times of digging when the cottage was built.

Smiling at the tiny clover leaves which scrutiny revealed in the brown earth, she rose at last, humming a tune, and went back to her rugs. She had shaken one, and was turning to get another, when the figure of an approaching man caught her attention. He was a stranger to her, and he was about

to pass near the piazza. Instantly her precious
baby clover occurred to her. She waved to him
warningly. " Keep off the grass ! " she called suddenly.

. The startled stranger leaped aside, directly upon
the long brown patch.

Instantly Miss Toothaker's voice rang out in a
transport of feeling: " That *is* the grass ! "

The stranger leaped back again, and laughed.
So did Miss Priscilla. It was such a jubilant
morning, and the treasured spot was so bare.
" Excuse me; but it 's just beginnin'," she explained, " and I do want to get it covered."

" Why don't you put a little fence around it? "
suggested the young man, lifting his cap, as he
paused to contemplate the forbidden ground. " It
lies too temptingly in the path to the shore."

" That would be a good idea," replied Miss
Toothaker.

" There 's no time like the present. If you have
some twine, why should n't we do it now ? I 'll be
glad to atone for the blow my heels have dealt
your hopes."

Miss Priscilla looked at him in some surprise at
the offer of assistance. He was well built, with
broad shoulders, strong-looking hands, and goodly
length of limb; but his face was pale, and his
mustache not so heavy as to conceal that his lips,
too, told mutely the need of precisely this invigorating air. His eyes were remarkable, and as he

made his proposition, they held Miss Toothaker in momentary admiration of the light in their radiant brown depths.

"I'm sure you're very good," she said rather awkwardly. Then she added, her lips twitching: "You've got a good deal of energy for a Southerner."

The young man lifted his eyebrows in quiet amusement. "How do you know I'm a Southerner?"

"I haven't lived in Washington two winters without learnin' to know a Southerner when I hear him."

"Oh, when you hear him," said the other, smiling. "Well, may I help you?"

The manner of the question enchanted Miss Priscilla. There was no impatience in it; but a quiet courtesy, and just a suggestion of deference.

"Yes, if you really want to; and thank you, too," she answered promptly, and disappeared.

Miss Dexter was busily sending scales rippling out the window to the waiting stranger. Miss Toothaker stooped in passing, and spoke: —

"There's a *gentleman* come to Pulpit Point."

"Indeed?"

"Yes, I've got another follower;" and Miss Priscilla hastened on. Returning a minute later, she spoke again, while Nathalie's deft fingers raced on.

"You and I are kind o' high-toned in the help

we employ.   If you know what's good for yourself, you'd better peek after a while.   He's got eyes like the Hindoos at the World's Fair."

These mysterious words moved Miss Dexter, when she had finished her scales, and before she proceeded to the next step in her morning's work, to go cautiously to the window and reconnoitre.

What she beheld was her housekeeper and a strange man erecting a protection of sticks and twine around a bare spot of earth.   As Nathalie was not unaware of Miss Toothaker's hopes and her clover nursery, she saw at once what was going on, and gazed amusedly for a time at the pair, without being able to catch more than a glimpse of the man's face ; then she returned to her work, much to the satisfaction of Miss Toothaker's helper, for he had a passion for music, and was sufficiently intelligent in it to deduce the existence of better things from the avalanche of thirds and sixths, whose ceaseless flow from the windows proclaimed an accomplished pianist.

"Now, then, I can have some hope," said Miss Priscilla, looking fondly at her incipient grass, when their task was done.   "And you, sir, you can remember this evenin' that verse : —

> 'Count that day lost whose low, descendin' sun
> Views from thy hand no worthy action done.'

Seein' the way I hollered at you, I consider your action uncommonly worthy."

The young man, his cap set back on the thick hair that waved loosely above his forehead, regarded his completed handiwork, and then looked off toward the dancing waves, tumultuous this morning, apparently, from mere excess of frolicsome joy.

"It is a pleasure just to live on a day like this, is n't it?" he said in his deliberate, reposeful manner. "I must continue my explorations, and," lifting his cap, "I hope I shall not do any more damage."

Miss Toothaker looked after him as he walked on, fascinated. "Yes, a gentleman has come to Pulpit Point," she mused. "I hope Mr. Andreas will get back in time to entertain him."

For Russell's stay had been short on his first trip to Maine, though upon his departure he had cheered Miss Priscilla by the assurance of his speedy return.

The stranger moved on down to the shore, and ascending into the Pulpit, vaulted up on one of its massive sides, and sat there viewing the kaleidoscopic changes before him, until the incoming tide had sprayed him well. Then turning his steps inland again, he began to hear faintly the tones of Nathalie's piano. His rather mournful eyes brightened at the sound, and he moved faster, leaping from cradle-knoll to cradle-knoll, until he had drawn near the cottage. A large solitary boulder invited him to eavesdrop.

Throwing himself down on the further side of

the rock, he gave himself up to enjoyment. He did not know the Præludium that Nathalie was playing; indeed, he knew very little music by name save the music of his band. Neither would he have excused this fact by the *bétise* of declaring that he "knew what he liked," — astonishing platitude, which falls complacently from the lips of many a person who might be expected to pause and consider that instead of being peculiar, this fact is really one of those things which goes without saying.

What he did comprehend was that a plaintive melody with strange and alluring intervals and rhythm was coming to him from an invisible source, enriched by a rippling accompaniment, and that the same flowed on under an assured touch, now strong and fiery, now modulated to a delicate whisper, and that it gained a wonderful enchantment from the limitless view of sea and rock and scudding cloud all about him.

Day-dreams, sweet, vague, visited him, lying there in the soft grass, his senses enthralled. He lost all count of the passage of time while the music went on, varying movements succeeding one another in delicious succession as the player, unconscious of a listener, exhausted her repertoire.

At last, after a triumphal climax of chords, the tones ceased.

"Miss Priscilla," called a voice distinctly. "*Is* n't dinner almost ready? I'm starved."

The lotos-eater under the lichens started guiltily, and seized his watch. " Mine hostess! mine hostess! What shall I say?" he ejaculated, horrified.

Miss Toothaker saw a form skim by her kitchen window.

" I do believe there goes my gentleman on the dead run. He 'd better look out. He 's been sick, or I miss my guess."

She was watering the precious clover when he went by the next day, and she returned his salutation with a friendly nod.

" You don't want to be too smart," she said. " I saw you runnin' yesterday. You must remember you 've been sick."

" I 'm bound to remember that, for if I had n't been ill I should n't be here," he returned. " I can't regret it, you see."

" Yes ; I don't know as ever I was in a more sightly place. Well, get strong as fast as you can. We 've got all the air there is up here."

" Looks paler 'n ever," she muttered when he had passed on. " Sober-lookin' feller, too. I 'd go out o' my way, though, to see him smile, any day. Wonder if he ain't lonely. Wonder if he 's boardin' at that little one-horse hotel. I 'd like to cook him a meal o' victuals myself. Ain't he as straight as a die ! "

All of which goes to prove what good capital it is for a young man to possess a pair of long, Oriental-looking eyes, and a serious, interesting cast of countenance.

Miss Toothaker did not forget him when she went into the house. On the contrary, she addressed Nathalie, busy at the piano, with a lack of candor so new as to sit awkwardly upon her.

"Now, I'm goin' to make a fuss about this, Nathalie. You sat here the whole livin' mornin' yesterday, and to-day's so perfect, it's a regular weather-breeder. There'll be plenty o' storms when you can sit and thump those keys. Do you get up now and go down to the rocks — for half an hour, anyhow. I know your mother'd say so."

"Yes, I do know she'd say so," muttered Miss Priscilla, when Nathalie had protested, then laughed, then obeyed. "How do I know she'll meet him? And what if she does? I don't s'pose he'd speak to her, lonely as he is; but he'll see there is somebody here beside a hatchet-faced old woman, and then maybe it'll come around." And Miss Priscilla smiled dreamily out of one side of her mouth as her imagination leaped forward and began to draw the ménu which she would serve to the straight, pale young man who had built her fence, when the conventions permitted of his being invited to dinner.

Nathalie, hatless, happy, went singing down to the rocks. Miss Toothaker was right. Pianos we can always have, but only one month in the year is it July on the Maine coast.

Lightly she ran up into the Pulpit, and standing on tiptoe to lean her elbows on its edge, looked down into a clear pool, left below by the tide. Starfish, anemones, hermit crabs, urchins, swam, palpitated, crept, before her. Millions of barnacles crusted the rocks.

The breakers rushed past the Point in orderly, stately procession, and the neighboring island lifted its clump of evergreens like a crown.

> "Why thus longing, thus forever sighing
> For the far-off, unattained, and dim

(that 's Paderewski),

> While the beautiful, all 'round thee lying,
> Offers up its low, perpetual hymn ? "

she quoted aloud, in her splendid solitude.

Her voice brought from behind a neighboring ledge the man Miss Priscilla had shamelessly sent her down to see.

For an instant their eyes met. Nathalie, her uncovered curly head glorified in sunshine, addressing the universe from the Pulpit, was a preoccupying sight. Miss Toothaker's protégé had not taken the precaution to wear rubber-soled shoes; and that was the way it happened.

In endeavoring not to stare at Miss Dexter, and, moreover, trying to get out of her way, he leaped to a rock which chanced to be covered with treacherous, slimy weed, and fell in a way to strike his knee against the massive ledge he had just quitted.

He uttered a suppressed exclamation, and then lay still. Nathalie came flying down to him.

"Are you hurt?"

"Pardon me; but — I believe — my knee-cap's off. Yes, it is."

"Don't touch it again. Don't move it," she said imperatively. "I think I can — I'll try. Put your arms around these rocks and hold yourself firmly. Can you hold?" Unhesitatingly she stepped to his feet, and seizing the heel belonging to the injured leg, she pulled with all the strength of her young, piano-trained arms; then, when the strain was at the utmost, she gave a quick, sharp jerk.

Her victim bit his white lips. Her heart beat suffocatingly. She felt of his knee. "It seems to have gone back. Oh, are you going to faint?"

"Faint! No."

"The tide is just turning, but it won't reach you. I'll send some men down at once, and get the doctor. What cottage?"

"Andreas."

She fled up the hill and by the house. Miss Toothaker saw her pass. "Seems to be somethin' in this air that makes folks terribly frisky," she remarked. "Wonder where Nathalie's bound, goin' like the wind. Wonder," Miss Priscilla's shoulders twitched up, and she murmured it half guiltily, — "wonder if she saw him."

Cap'n Levi, his chair tilted back against the sunny side of his store, was entertaining some other leisurely Pulpit Pointers with an account of the manner in which the day before he had disci-

plined the small son of one of the cottagers who was
making himself dangerously at home in one of the
fishing-boats moored near by.

" I was out in my dory, and I see him monkeyin'
around thar, tryin' to drown himself, and I says
to him, says I : ' Come out o' that bo't,' says I.
' Whose bo't is this?' says he; jest like that. I
saw it wa'n't no time for cawnversation, so I took
him by the collar, and the breast of his breeches,
and hove him ashore. Who's this runnin'?
Why, it's Miss Dexter."

For Nathalie's flying feet had brought her upon
the nonchalant conclave, — a sudden, breathless
apparition. .

" Where does the doctor live?" she demanded.

" Who's sick?" drawled Cap'n Levi; but one
of the younger men pointed out the way.

" Two of you go right down to the rocks by
the Pulpit," she went on, catching her breath.
" There's a man there hurt so he can't walk. Take
him to the Andreas cottage. You'll let me take
Vixen, Cap'n Levi? Unfasten her, please." She
turned to the fellow who had given her information, and he started to the spot where, as usual,
the horse-of-all-work stood ready harnessed.

" You can't never drive her in this world! "
said Cap'n Levi, startled at last out of his apathy,
and hurrying forward as he protested.

" I think I can do it quicker than you," replied
the girl.

"She'll run away and kill ye, like's not," shouted Cap'n Levi after her, as the mare started at a good pace, "and you'll pay fer her, let me tell ye. B' gosh! if she ain't the settest piece that ever come to the Pulpit," he added in an aggrieved tone, watching his wagon go jouncing over obstacles, as Vixen rattled along under the excited urging of her new driver.

"We'd better hustle after the feller," remarked one of the bystanders, grinning. "She looks as if she'd make the fur fly, if folks kep' her waitin'."

Had Cap'n Levi been her messenger, Nathalie would assuredly have blamed him for the doctor's tardy arrival; for, with her best efforts, it was nearly two hours after the accident that he was brought to the door of the Andreas cottage, and Miss Dexter, dropping him, drove slowly back to Cap'n Levi's store.

To her relief the place was deserted, as was often the case. She tied the horse, then patted her, and laid her cheek against the smooth neck.

Meanwhile the country doctor was congratulating his patient while he examined him. "Mighty good thing for you, young man, that you weren't alone when this happened to you. That knee-cap's been off, and now it's on again. Miss Dexter wasn't sure whether she'd done right or wrong; but I can tell you now that if that cap had been off all the time that plucky girl has been chasing 'round after me, you'd have been lame for *life*."

The patient shook his head. "A bad thing in my profession."

"A bad thing in any profession, I take it. Says her father was a physician, and he told her how," said the doctor, whose thoughts had harked back to Nathalie. She had made a deep impression on him, with her uncovered head, her bright eyes, and her reckless driving in the old wagon. "Well, we'll fix you up in a little plaster, and you'll go around here a few weeks on crutches, and after that you'll be as good as new, Mr." —

"Gerard." An added mutter of impatience set the doctor off again.

"Yes, 't-ain't pleasant; but think what it might have been. You'll let Miss Dexter know that you're all right as soon as convenient, I hope. She's all worked up about it, you understand," were the last words the doctor said in leaving.

His motive was most benevolent. He had no doubt that there was a romance here, and the agitation which the girl had betrayed concerning her own part in the affair had been so highly becoming that he pitied his patient for not having seen her while she related the experience.

His astonishment would have been great could he have known that the two young people were strangers, and that he had informed Gerard of the name of his friend in need.

"Dexter." Roger fitted the name to the figure he had seen as a sudden bright vision in the gray

Pulpit. All her subsequent, quick-witted action seemed like things seen and felt and heard in a painful dream.

A keen appreciation of the absurdity of his own position afflicted him. "I hope her sense of humor is latent," he thought. "Rusty will never let me hear the last of this. I'll never chafe at conventions again. The young lady ought by every precedent to have sprained her ankle and let me carry her lightly and gracefully to the house. I wonder if I could have done it?"

He was in bed, and he bared his arm and examined his muscles. "Hang typhoid fever," he observed. "And now comes this handicap — I mean knee-cap. What next?"

As for Nathalie, she went laggingly home from the store.

"Well, I thought you was lost," observed Miss Toothaker when she came in. "Why, you are pale as a ghost! What in the world possessed you to run so hard? What — why "—

For Nathalie had sat down in the nearest chair, and now, bowing her face in her hands, began to sob.

"Nathalie Dexter, what *has* happened?" implored Miss Priscilla, stooping beside her.

"I'm — I'm — enjoying it," declared the girl thickly.

Miss Toothaker's conscience alertly suggested that in some mysterious way she was probably to blame for this; and indeed, when her companion had become calm and told her story, Priscilla had a heightened color.

"You see, it was my shouting out so suddenly, thinking I was all alone, that made him turn quickly and slip on that weed," explained Nathalie forlornly.

"H'm," returned Miss Priscilla. "I won't say anything against your practicin' mornin's, after this. I find usually it's first rate policy to keep in mind that firm that made so much money mindin' its own business!"

CHAPTER VI.

AN IMPROMPTU PICNIC.

MY DEAR MISS DEXTER, — The doctor told me yesterday that but for your prompt action, the injury to my knee would have resulted in chronic lameness. The surgeon who came from Portland to see me this morning confirms his words. Your presence of mind, your kindness in going in person to bring the doctor for an utter stranger, — these are favors for which thanks seem tame; but I ask you to believe, Miss Dexter, that your noble action will be held forever in grateful memory.

Sincerely yours,
ROGER GERARD.

This was the note Nathalie received on the following morning. She read it to Miss Toothaker, who listened approvingly, her chin resting on her hand.

"He's got a sense of what's becomin', I tell you," she commented triumphantly. "Didn't I say he was a gentleman?"

Nathalie looked beyond her. "He hates me for it," she said with conviction.

"You must be crazy," returned Miss Priscilla with vast contempt.

"Yes, he does. He hates to feel that he, a man, was put in a humiliating position. Mr. Andreas will tell his friends."

Miss Dexter had seen considerable of Russell before he took his forced departure from the Pulpit, and she thought she knew him.

"Hate you! The idea! That letter don't sound much like it."

Neither did the box of roses which reached Nathalie the next day seem to evidence an uncharitable heart. She lifted the card which lay on top of the tissue paper.

"Lieutenant Roger Gerard, —— Artillery, U. S. A.," she read aloud. "Miss Toothaker," excitedly, "he is an officer!"

"And a gentleman," added Priscilla, with sonorous devoutness. "Oh, he hates you, he hates you bad," she added, lifting out the glowing roses, which Nathalie had forgotten for the fascinating bit of pasteboard.

"This is nothing. I dare say he will keep *on* sending me flowers. If a box should come every day, it wouldn't surprise me in the least. He loathes his obligation. He *writhes* under it. He will try to work it off. You watch," announced Nathalie oracularly.

"The cat's foot in the bandbox!" returned Miss Priscilla contemptuously.

It was a few days afterward that she was going out the front door with a rug, when she was surprised by an apparition at the far end of the piazza. It was Mr. Gerard seated there in a chair, his crutches leaning against the rail near him.

She exclaimed, and he laid a finger on his lips, and then pointed toward the invisible piano where Nathalie was playing a Bach fugue.

Miss Toothaker understood. He enjoyed the music, and he did not wish to have the player disturbed. So she stood silently beaming a welcome upon him for a moment, and inwardly bemoaning the pallor of his countenance; then, after shaking her rug, she turned back into the house and went about her business in the kitchen.

Nathalie played on for nearly an hour; then Miss Toothaker could stand it no longer. As the pianist came to the end of a piece, she put her head in at the living-room door.

" Do go out on the piazza for a breath," she said. " The air 's like wine."

Nathalie, humming what she had last played, obeyed mechanically. Outside the door she was met by the unexpected sight of Roger. He arose.

" Don't — don't rise, Mr. Gerard," she begged, hurrying toward him.

" Thank you, but I am becoming quite proficient in standing on one leg like a stork."

They shook hands.

" Why did n't you let me know you were here? "

" I was so well entertained. I only prayed you would not stop."

"Oh, do you care for it? I am so glad, for then perhaps I can make up — I mean I can — yes " — she caught her breath, " I believe I can't— Is n't it a beautiful morning ? "

The vivacious face had grown so flushed that Roger was mystified by her embarrassment.

"Never mind the chair. Let me wait on my- self," she went on, and then blushed deeper. " I know it must be so annoying for you not to be able to do everything, — so trying for a man to be laid up this way. I know how they dislike to be waited on. I — I " — she stammered, and then, as Roger said to himself, she ran down.

Her whole manner was so hesitating, so doubtful, so different from the prompt decision she had shown in their former memorable meeting, he was puzzled by it for a second, and then the explana- tion came over him in a flash.

" She is sorry for me because I was ridiculous, — nearly fainted, and all the rest of it. Of course. She plays that way. It was mighty hard on her, the whole thing." After which mental aside he proceeded to reply.

" Yes, this accident was rather unfortunate for a convalescent. I was ill all the spring, — the first time in my life, too. If the fortunes of peace are going to treat me so badly, I shall have to pray to try the fortunes of war. Mrs. Andreas sent kind messages to you. She says her son explained her invalidism to you, and that she does not visit at all."

It was a fortnight after this meeting that Mr. Russell Andreas arrived again at his summer home. His friend had deemed it best to write him an outlined account of the misfortune which had befallen him, thinking that if by the time Russell reached home it had become an old story, he might escape some chaffing.

Gerard went to meet him on his crutches the morning of his arrival, and the two friends exchanged the heartiest of greetings after their years of separation, inspecting one another with affectionate scrutiny.

" It's a confounded shame," declared Andreas. " Here you were seedy from the fever, anyway. It seems like kicking a fellow when he's down, does n't it ? You 've a fine red nose on you, though. How soon are you going to throw away these wooden legs ? "

" In a week more, I think."

" Say," Andreas chuckled, " is n't the military intellect up to a more romantic way of scraping acquaintance with a pretty girl than that? I 'm surprised at you ! "

Gerard smiled philosophically.

" Miss Dexter, too," went on Andreas. " Nice, well-bred girl she seemed to be, what I saw of her. I had n't an idea she 'd pull your leg " —

" See here, Rusty. Leave her out of it."

" Why, where would the story be then ? " laughed Andreas.

"Forgotten, I hope. At any rate, I want to know if you are intending to speak to Miss Dexter about it?"

Andreas well remembered this extra soft and slow speech of his college chum, and what it meant.

"I refuse to fight a crippled man," he declared, highly entertained.

"You have some imagination, Andreas."

"Thanks, old man."

"Please apply it right here, in regard to Miss Dexter's standpoint in this matter. I won't have her chaffed."

"Sure you won't?"

"Sure I won't stay to see it, anyway. Listen, Rusty: it was awfully white in you to insist on my coming up here, when we had n't met in so long. I did n't know how much I needed it till I breathed this air; but we 'll call it off right now unless you give me your promise not to refer to the part Miss Dexter played in my accident, — at any rate, not to mention it to her in any manner whatever. If you can't see why, that's no matter. If you should speak to her of it, I should have to punch your head, and as I could n't very well punch my host's head, I would take the boat instead. I 'm not fooling."

"Oh, I know you 're not fooling when you leave out all your *r*'s, my flower of Southern chivalry," returned Andreas, flinging an arm around his friend's shoulders. "All right; mum's the word, — until you are able to punch my head, anyway. First catch your hare, you know; and for the present the hare is a little swifter than the tortoise."

"No," returned the lieutenant stiffly. "Your promise for all time, or I leave on the morning boat."

"Take your playthings and all?" Russell patted the crutches. His friend stopped, and faced him with a steady look of the heart-stirring brown eyes. "Oh, Roger, you old idiot!" he went on, "of course I'll promise. What's the matter with you? Swing along lively now. There's my mother at the window."

So it happened that Nathalie gave Mr. Andreas great credit for delicacy at their first subsequent meeting. Beyond certain twitchings of his deep-cornered mouth when he referred to his friend's mishap, he did not err even against the spirit of his promise.

One morning some time afterward, Russell came to the open door of the Dexter cottage. No one was in the living-room.

"Oh, Miss Pris," he called, his voice penetrating to the furthermost niche of the little house.

"Hello, Mr. Andreas. Kitchen."

Following the sententious suggestion of the muffled tones, he presented himself at the door of the culinary department, to find Miss Toothaker deep in the mysteries of making cake.

" I have called " —

" I heard you."

" Miss Pris," with grave reproach, "are you being funny?"

" Funny! Well, I guess if you make me lose count o' these cups o' flour, you'll think I ain't very funny. Was that two or three, — did you notice?"

" That was two, — yes, I'm positive; " and Mr. Andreas picked up a particularly plump raisin.

" Here! don't you eat one o' the stoned ones, or I'll set you down here and make you do another cupful."

" Plum cake is good for picnics," observed the visitor musingly.

" Yes, that must have been three cups o' flour," said Miss Toothaker. " I can tell by the looks. Now what do you want? Speak quick, for I don't like to talk when I'm beatin' eggs."

" Give me those eggs, woman. If I couldn't beat eggs with one hand and talk with the other, I'd go out of the insurance business."

Miss Toothaker tied an apron around his neck on the instant.

" Go right at it," she retorted; and the famous maker of salad dressing accepted the plate and its slippery burden with conscious power.

" What I was saying when you interrupted me so rudely," he said, as he began to ply his fork, " was that I called to know why Miss Dexter was neglecting her music. The house was silent as the grave as I approached."

" Why, I don't know, I 'm sure. She must have just stepped upstairs."

" What rent do you charge Gerard for that boulder out yonder?" Andreas jerked his head toward the side of the house.

" He does seem to take comfort out of it, don't he? Sometimes I creep out just to see if he 's there, and he usually is. I believe he 'd lay there the whole day, if Nathalie 'd play that long. I often think how surprised she 'd be to know how much o' the time she has an audience."

" Think she does n't know it, eh?"

" I know she don't. Mr. Gerard asked me not to mention it. He thought she might feel freer, you know."

" Roger is a very considerate fellow, — ever noticed it?" Russell's eyes laughed at Miss Toothaker above the checked apron.

" Well, I guess he is," she returned seriously. " He 's the most perfect gentleman *I* ever saw."

" Miss Pris, Miss Pris! And I sitting here beating eggs for you so pleasantly with a bib on!"

" You do it first-rate, too."

" I wonder if you can guess what this cake is for?" remarked Mr. Andreas ingratiatingly.

" It 's for tea. Want to come?"

" Oh, I am coming. This cake is for a picnic tea over at Gull Island this afternoon at five. Such a select picnic, too. Nobody but you and Miss Dexter, Roger and myself."

"Russell Andreas, I would n't go in your sailboat if you begged me on your bended knees, and you know it."

"Yes, that's why I 've borrowed the Bensons' little vapor launch."

"No, I 'm afraid o' big water anyway."

"Miss Pris, pause. This is the first day Roger has walked with a cane. It must be celebrated. Miss Dexter must be chaperoned. There is no way out of it. You and I must go to take care of the young people, and with the aid of my mother's tea-basket we 'll do it. That launch goes along like a settled old steamer. You 'll like it."

It was one of the occasions when Miss Toothaker's ever-ready conscience took a hand in the argument. For a trifling cowardice she ought not to cheat Nathalie out of a good time. So she gave herself up to the dangers of the deep in the pretty boat with its flying flags. The wind was steady, and the waves blue as the sky.

"You see," said Andreas, as at last they steamed away from the landing, "with only four of us, if Roger wants to keep up the bluff of interesting invalid, he can lie down on these cushions and rest his game knee."

"Yes, indeed! Lie down, Mr. Gerard," said Nathalie joyously. "Mr. Andreas is going to let me steer ; are n't you, Mr. Andreas? "

"Nathalie Dexter, sit still. Don't you think o' steerin' this boat," said Miss Toothaker solemnly. She was balanced on the very edge of the seat, preparing to meet her Maker.

"But I have the chart here, see?" explained Nathalie. Her ruddy brown hair was tied up in a white silk handkerchief, away from the ruthless wind, but a short burnished lock escaped here and there. "There is n't a bit of danger. Mr. Andreas is obliged to stay by the engine, and," turning wheedlingly to the lieutenant, who was lying stretched out under the awning, the picture of luxurious contentment, "Mr. Gerard does n't feel any too well, do you?"

"Jes' po'ly, thank Gawd," responded Roger, smiling.

Miss Toothaker cast a glance at Russell as the arbiter of her destiny. Nathalie laid a covetous hand on the smooth little wheel, and spread her chart out before her.

The boat steamed on merrily, the water splashing to right and left, and the vitalizing sunshine lent such a gay security to the scene that even Miss Priscilla relaxed as time went on.

"If you had only brought the piano, Miss Dexter," said Roger lazily.

"Why did n't you remind me?" returned the girl.

"Well, to tell the truth, I should think you'd both be sick of it," remarked Miss Toothaker

"Why? Are *you*, poor Miss Priscilla?" asked Nathalie, without turning.

"Oh, I ain't obliged to listen to it."

"I'm sure Mr. Gerard has n't bored himself by coming very often."

The lieutenant lifted his heavy lashes, and exchanged a smile with Miss Priscilla.

"What are you doing with the rudder, Miss Nathalie?" called Andreas. "Our wake looks like a snake in pain."

"Oh, do, pray, Nathalie" — besought Miss Toothaker, becoming grave with great suddenness.

"I'm avoiding ledges on the chart," explained Miss Dexter with dignity. "Such ingratitude!"

Roger left his couch, and approaching, leaned over the chart beside her, humming a Pastorale she had taught him.

"This chart is rather good fun," he remarked, after a minute.

"Take hold there, Roger," called Andreas. "We'll be chasing our tail in a minute."

Nathalie sent him a withering glance, but she relinquished the wheel, and Miss Toothaker breathed a sigh of partial relief.

Nathalie took her seat with dignity. "I don't suppose it is at all good for Mr. Gerard to stand up there and steer. He might be jolted and strain his knee," she said, addressing space.

"Oh, Roger is almost ready for anything now," remarked Andreas cheerfully. "He will be dancing next. By the way, Miss Dexter, when you see Gerard dance, you will be glad you " —

The lieutenant cast a swift glance over his shoulder.

" Ahem ! " continued Russell with a sudden cough, — " glad that you know him. Yes, Roger, that's Gull Island to the right there. Nice little cove it has, and a nice cup of tea Miss Toothaker will make us. Many a one she has made me. Ah, Miss Pris, are you going to take me under your wing again next winter ? "

" I doubt it." Miss Toothaker spoke curtly, not from any ill temper, but because she was afraid if she allowed her attention to wander from her surroundings, the boat might go down.

" What ! You would allow me to run the risk of mumps and chicken-pox all alone in the big city ? What do you mean ? Explain."

" When we get on land, I will."

And she did. After they were seated in a clump of evergreens, fragrant with many a fir balsam, the sliced cake before them, and cups of hot tea in hand, Miss Priscilla spoke : —

" I 'm gettin' superstitious about receivin' letters," she announced impressively. " I almost never in my life got a letter with nothin' in it, as most folks do."

" It 's a shame, Miss Pris," said Andreas. " I 'll write to you as soon as I leave the Pulpit."

" When I get a letter it always means : ' Here,

come now; change all your plans and do somethin'
you never expected to.'"

"Oh, Miss Toothaker," protested Nathalie plaintively, "you are so personal!"

"Now I've heard from Mr. Barclay to-day. It's
the time o' year I always do hear from him. You
noticed, Nathalie, when you handed me that letter
this mornin' I was n't surprised."

"No; you remarked with the utmost noncha-
lance that it was from Mr. Barclay, and have left
me to burn with curiosity ever since as to who Mr.
Barclay may be, and what he is saying to you."

"H'm. Mr. Andreas knows who he is;" and
Miss Priscilla took a long drink of tea.

"He has a very agreeable wife, Miss Dexter,"
announced Andreas gravely.

"Yes, with one foot in the grave," added Priscilla, emerging from her teacup.

"Well, don't exult openly," said Andreas, in a
gentle aside. "It is n't good form."

"It's his house I've kept for two seasons in
Washington; and I expected he would go on
leasin' it and I should go on keepin' it indefinitely.
We've given each other pretty good satisfaction,
and I was all ready to say 'Yes' before I read his
letter this mornin'. As long as the subject has
come up, I'll tell you what he said; for anyway, I may get drowned goin' back to the Pulpit, and then I should want one o' you to answer
him."

"Never!" said Andreas dramatically. "I'm not going on living without you, Miss Pris. We will go down to the sharks together!"

"Do hush up!" ejaculated Miss Toothaker.

"It is absolutely safe," said Gerard, his eyes comforting her more than his quiet words. "The proprietors of that sort of launch, I understand, offer a thousand dollars to any one who will blow it up."

"Generous offer," put in Andreas. "So tempting to the winner."

"Land! Will it blow up?" exclaimed Miss Priscilla. "I never thought of its doin' anything but tip over."

"There! You see, Roger, how unwise it is for you to put in your oar."

"No, Miss Toothaker," laughed Nathalie. "It can't do anything on a day like this but creep-a-mouse-y-creep-a-mouse-y right home as soon as we're ready; but do tell us what Mr. Barclay wants you to do."

Miss Priscilla turned to Andreas. "Do you remember that Southern girl that came up to Washington at Easter, — Miss Archer?"

"Of course I do. But look out, Miss Pris. You are on dangerous ground. Miss Archer is a very particular friend of Gerard's, and he's a regular fire-eater; run you through as soon as look at you."

Miss Dexter regarded the young officer with

interest. He was leaning on his elbow, making dabs with his teaspoon at the slice of lemon in his cup.

"It is owing to her that I am in this clover now," he said. "It was Miss Archer who recalled me to Rusty's mind with sufficient vividness to gain me this invitation."

"I want to know! Well, 't ain't likely I should be goin' to say anything against her. She's a real nice girl. It seems her mother has been writin' to Mr. Barclay" —

"Her stepmother," suggested Gerard.

"Is it? Her stepmother, then. She wants Mr. Barclay to take their house for the winter instead of the Washington one; and Mr. Barclay thinks the climate might be better for his wife, and it might be just as good a business scheme. So there 't is; and he wants me."

Roger Gerard was listening with fixed attention.

"For a boarding-house?" he asked. "The Archer place?"

"Why, yes. I s'pose so."

He nodded. "It was bound to come to that," he murmured. "Poor Betty!"

"Well, now, ain't it queer that they are your friends! I see you don't like the idea. Any reason that *I* ought not to like it? It would be real friendly in you, Mr. Gerard, to tell me all you can. I ain't a bit enterprisin'. I don't like new things, or new places, or new people; and my first

impulse is to say ' No.' Perhaps you 'll bear me
out in it. He says it 's Old Point Comfort, or it 's
practically that. It 's close by, and his wife would
have the benefit o' the sea air."

" Yes." Gerard bowed gravely. " The house
is on a creek, — salt water. Miss Archer's grand-
father built it long before the war. I have spent
much of my life there, for her father was my
guardian. Of course, I 'm fond of the place ; but
it was bound to come. The present Mrs. Archer
is not a woman of much sentiment, and they are
not too well off."

Something in the lieutenant's manner and tone
as he referred to the present Mrs. Archer roused
Nathalie's suspicions.

" Can you describe Mrs. Archer ? " she asked.
" Perhaps I know her."

" Oh, I don't know that I can describe her.
She is rather hurried and nervous in her manner,
not domestic at all in her tastes " —

Miss Dexter did not care for this. " Does she
wear her hair straight back ? "

" Yes."

" And wink her eyes fast and squint them up ? "
" Yes."

" And does she come from Philadelphia ? "
" Yes."

" It 's the same ! " ejaculated Nathalie triumphantly. " Well, what a strange world this is !
Three of us know the muffin man ! She was my

chaperon coming across this spring. Miss Toothaker, do they want you to keep house for *her ?* "

" Not exactly; why ? "

" Oh, I won't say anything; only I fancy after
you 've been there a month, a vapor launch
would n't have any horrors for you. I 'm not sure
you won't put to sea in a tub."

" Forewarned is forearmed," returned Miss Priscilla. " What a good thing the subject came up !
No, ma'am ! This Mrs. Archer, whatever she is,
or whoever she is, won't have anything to do with
me, or I with her. I make my arrangements with
the Barclays, and I mind my business, and give
everybody else the privilege o' mindin' theirs."

CHAPTER VII.

EDGEWATER.

By the time Lieutenant Gerard's leave expired, he was a credit to the invigorating properties of Pulpit Point.

Nathalie congratulated him on his altered appearance as they stood on her piazza at the close of his farewell call.

" I go away, Miss Dexter, carrying an abiding sense of obligation to you," he said in his earnest, slow, Southern speech.

" Can't you forgive and forget?" she returned. " A sense of obligation is so unpleasant."

" Do you think so?"

" Yes, I know so," she answered, an irresistible impulse driving her to meet his gentle courtesy with brusque frankness. " I have never apologized to you for startling you and making you slip that dreadful day. I do now."

He gazed at her in astonishment. " Were you to blame for my clumsiness, and did n't you make the *amende honorable* on the instant?"

" Did that make it right?" she insisted, her cheeks tingling under his reposeful gaze. " You have suffered pain, been set back in your convalescence, gone about on crutches, — all on account of me. You might write an essay on ' Woman in the Pulpit.' " She finished with an embarrassed laugh.

" But, Miss Dexter, you forget that had I not been a cripple, I should have been led off into all sorts of expeditions away from your piano."

" You have not asked me to play a half-dozen times. I did think you were going to care for it." She allowed her disappointment to be apparent. " I counted on it."

His eyes shone with quiet amusement. " Do you see that boulder over there ? " He pointed to it. " On the further side of that rock the grass is almost giving up the ghost. Miss Toothaker may have to sow some more clover."

He noted the surprise and pleasure that slowly altered the girl's expression.

" It would convict me of being the idlest fellow in the universe to own how many hours you have enchanted for me. One does not hear music at its best except undisturbed, in such surroundings as this. That is what I meant by carrying away the sense of obligation. The pleasantest day-dreams of my life have been enjoyed over there by that rock. I will go back now and drill my men, and march daily to the music of the band ; but the past will go with me. I shall recall a melody and taste this crisp air, see the breakers fling themselves against the Pulpit and watch the white sails pass. Nor," he lowered his voice, " shall I forget that it

is owing to you that I can march. Don't belittle
what you did for me."

"You don't mind it, then?" she asked, almost
imploringly, and her hand was in his.

"Take care of these clever hands," he said,
smiling. "Who knows but I may come under
their magic again some day?"

When he was gone, Nathalie went slowly into
the house and sat down at the piano; but she
did not touch the keys. When Miss Toothaker
returned later from some errand, she found her so.

The girl started up from her reverie. "Mr.
Gerard has been here to say good-by. He was
sorry to miss you."

"Pshaw! Well, I'll see him off at the boat."

"He said he should see you in a short time,
anyway, at the Archers'."

"Yes, indeed. That surely is one advantage
that 'll come with my Virginia experiment: I shall
see Mr. Gerard occasionally."

"I think he is probably engaged to that Miss
Archer, by the way Mr. Andreas spoke." Miss
Dexter had already extracted from her housekeeper
all the particulars she could give of the Southern
girl.

"I wonder, now, if he is?" said Miss Priscilla,
at once pleased with the idea.

"Of course he is," thought Nathalie, sinking
back into her reverie, "and I have been orchestra
for the sentimental and dramatic scenes of his day-

dreams." She tried to think back. What had she played most? What had she played best? How strange that he had been listening all the time. Well, he was going now, and forever, so far as she was concerned. She should never, in all probability, spend another summer at the Pulpit; though, for that matter, neither was it very likely that he would. He was gone, and it mattered nothing. He was engaged to a Southern girl who lisped, — how could he admire a girl who lisped! — and she, Nathalie, had her object in life, her career just the same, whoever came or went. The Reverend Lewis Andreas had been right. Nothing was so important, nothing such a protection to a girl, as to have a career.

So she went on with her work, and when, lingeringly and reluctantly, she and Miss Toothaker at last closed the cottage and bade farewell to the Pulpit, she went back to Boston, and there began her study with the famous teacher.

Her mother remained away until the last of March, and Nathalie, boarding with some friends who were sufficiently in sympathy with her to endure her practicing, threw an amount of energy into her work which, by the time of her mother's home-coming, made her gowns rather loose and her eyes hollow.

"It is time I came," said Mrs. Dexter to herself, at the moment when Nathalie at last closed the door upon all other welcoming friends, and they

sat in her room, blessedly alone, feasting upon one
another with their eyes.

Mrs. Dexter's were blue, and her hair white.
The lines about her mouth showed that her life had
not been all calm; yet the serenity of her smile
was a charm that one waited for, and even with her
white hair she looked young, — young enough to be
the sympathetic companion of her daughter, and
this she was.

" You write good letters, Nathalie, and yet there
are some things for me to learn. You have been
working harder than I knew. Harder than last
winter ? "

" No, but it is different over there, where one
only works and recreates. Here there are people
one knows, — kind, dreadful people, who invite one;
and being pulled different ways is wearing; but I
am well, — perfectly well."

" Your summer was a success ? "

" Oh, entirely so."

" And good Miss Toothaker, I suppose, is in
Washington? I must write to her."

" No, she keeps a boarding-house in Virginia this
winter. Did n't I tell you? She wrote me once
soon after she arrived there, but that is all I 've
heard. All I deserve, too, for I don't write to her.
There is an odd coincidence connected with her
new home."

Nathalie had unselfishly concealed from her mother the details of her homeward trip a year ago,

and now she told her the story, laughing gayly over circumstances which had seemed so dire during their occurrence. " Miss Toothaker wrote me that Mrs. Archer was away visiting in Philadelphia when she arrived, so I 've never heard how she gets on with her, if she is there," she finished.

" My dear, brave daughter! " said Mrs. Dexter, holding the girl's hand and regarding her affectionately. " I have hungered for you, Nathalie. What a reward this is, for us to be together again." After a minute she added unexpectedly : " Instead of my corresponding with Miss Toothaker, let us go to see her."

" Oh, how can I?" returned Nathalie, with quick protest.

" Try to manage it by the second week in April. Don't you think you could ? "

"Yes, I could," answered the girl slowly. " You want me to stop studying?" Mrs. Dexter nodded, with a brightening of the eyes and a smiling tightening of the lips.

" Oh, mother! It would mean all summer."

" I know it would; and I think that would be best."

" What makes you think so ? "

" I see that you are tired."

" We have never been to Virginia," said Nathalie thoughtfully, and she thought of the girl who lisped. " I have a queer feeling about going," she added quickly. " I would rather not go."

"You are tired enough for all your feelings to
be queer. German, harmony, Mr. Brandon, and
some society! It has told upon you."

"Why should we go to *that* place?" asked
Nathalie.

"Because I want to see Miss Toothaker and
thank her. Where is she?"

"It is near Old Point Comfort."

"And you are reluctant about going!" Mrs.
Dexter laughed. "My dear, you are in a worse
way than I thought. A girl who makes difficulties
about going to Old Point Comfort is in need of
heroic measures."

"The house is called Edgewater, Miss Toothaker says," remarked Nathalie. "It is on a creek."
She remembered the clump of firs on Gull Island,
where she had first heard about it. She recalled
how Mr. Andreas rallied his friend. She saw
Roger Gerard and his interest in the lemon in his
cup.

"I think we must see it," said Mrs. Dexter.

She wrote Miss Toothaker to make arrangements
for a room, and received a reply which came as
near to enthusiasm in its expression of satisfaction
at the prospect of seeing them as Miss Priscilla
could come. This she read to Nathalie, in the
expectation of inspiring her with anticipation; but
the girl received it with quiet assent.

"If you were not thin, Nathalie, I would change
my mind," remarked Mrs. Dexter. "I would leave

you here and take some other girl, who wanted to go."

"Oh — you are good to me, mother! I would like Mr. Brandon to go with us, — that is all."

"But he does n't wish you to go on with your lessons. He says it will be gain to you to rest. I should suppose that would make your mind so easy that you would be charmed at the prospect."

"I ought to be," answered Nathalie slowly, and with such speculative eyes that her mother laughed infectiously.

"You are dazed with study," she said. "We will leave cobblestones, and east winds, and shut-up rooms, and the din of traffic, and live out of doors awhile. It will make a new girl of you."

It was in the last twilight of an April evening that they reached the little Virginia station near which were the grounds of Edgewater. As soon as they alighted from the train, they perceived Miss Toothaker speeding across a green field in the direction of the depot, followed by a colored boy.

"I expected to be right on hand to the minute," she cried, when she had hurried within earshot. "But, land! you can't calc'late a thing down here about *time*. You can't get your help to have one idea of it. There ain't a day passes that I don't wish I had a whippin'-post in the yard."

"Worse than Cap'n Levi?" asked Nathalie;

but the name was cut short by the hard, pecking
kiss that Miss Priscilla bestowed on her.

" Junius, take these bags to the house, and then
get the trunks over. Mrs. Dexter, how 've you
been? You look well. Welcome to Old Vir-
ginny. What's the matter with you, Nathalie?
You look like the heroine of an old-fashioned
novel. Where 's those cheeks you had at Pulpit
Point ? "

" We hope they 're down here," said Mrs. Dexter. " We thought it worth while to look, anyway. This girl has worked too hard, you see; that
is all."

" And how have you liked Edgewater? " asked
Nathalie.

Miss Toothaker's lips twitched. " Very well,"
she replied non-committally. " I fetched my same
colored boy with me I had in Washington, and he
knows my ways, and the Barclays are well pleased
from a business standpoint. It 's all right, and
it 's a pretty place. Tea 's ready; we have it late
here. I must go right in. Junius will show you
your room, and you come soon as you can."

It was too dusk, being a cloudy evening, to get
more than a general idea of spacious grounds
before they hurried into the square brick house.
Emerging a few minutes later from their room,
they met Junius, who with an airy bow conducted
them through a latticed walk and into the well-
lighted dining-room beyond.

Here was a long, well-filled table, and as they took the two vacant places, Miss Toothaker named them to their immediate neighbors.

A lady across the table put up her lorgnette and surveyed Nathalie.

" I cannot be mistaken," she said, and her voice sent thrills of unpleasant association over the girl. " Surely it is Miss Dexter. Why, Miss Dexter, this is a most unexpected pleasure."

" Good-evening, Mrs. Archer," responded Nathalie composedly. " My mother, Mrs. Archer."

" Happy to meet you, Mrs. Dexter. Your daughter and I had a very pleasant trip together a year ago. · Oh, Miss Dexter, have you ever seen any, more of that delightful Father Andreas ? "

" I never have."

" By a strange coincidence, I found when I reached home that my daughter had met him. Betty? Where is Betty? Oh, yes! I remember; she is taking tea at Hampton to-night. Was n't it strange that she should have met him? We have never seen him again, but his brother has been here once. My dear, if you could see his brother, you would lose your heart. You really would. Never have I seen a young man who carries in his person the sign and seal of fine antecedents more markedly than Russell Andreas. You know the strange part of it was that my daughter met him, too, at a time when he was residing with our good Miss Toothaker at the capital; so when business brought him this way he naturally looked in upon us. I really hope you will meet him some time."

Good Miss Toothaker caught Nathalie's eye with an expression which made her smile.

The lowered tone in which Mrs. Archer delivered her address across the table was distinctly patronizing.

"I have met him," returned the girl.

Mrs. Archer lifted her lorgnette in surprise.

"Miss Toothaker is an old friend of ours," said Mrs. Dexter gently. "She took care of my daughter for me through the summer."

"Then you knew they were coming," remarked Mrs. Archer to Priscilla in a changed voice. "You did not speak of it. However, of course you did not know that Miss Dexter and I were acquainted."

After this Mrs. Archer applied herself to her crab salad, her thoughts running something after this fashion: "I knew she was nobody" (*she* being Nathalie). "Friends of Miss Toothaker! My instinct never deceives me. Mr. Andreas claims Miss Toothaker for a friend also; but a lonely young man, so, is different. There are friendships *de convenances*, and I've no doubt she was very useful to him when he boarded with her. Fortunate that Betty was out to-night. I shall have a talk with her."

"Hope springs eternal in the human breast," and Mrs. Archer never despaired of making an effect upon her stepdaughter by the words of wisdom she was always willing to bestow upon her. Probably Betty's attitude contributed to this misplaced confidence. She had a quiet, receptive manner, as gentle and non-resistant as that of an amiable little child; and she wore it that evening in her mother's bedroom, when called there upon her return from the Institute.

"Some new people have come to-night," began Mrs. Archer. "Betty," fretfully, "I wish you would turn the bows on that hat, if you can't do any more; they really are too faded."

The girl took off her headgear and examined it attentively.

"They are not the sort I care to have you mix with."

"I don't care to mix with faded beaux, maself."

"Be serious! I am. These people are friends of Miss Toothaker. That is enough. Of course, Miss Toothaker is a very good person. The daughter will probably try to claim an acquaintance with you. She is the girl I told you I chaperoned across the water last spring, and who behaved so boldly with Father Andreas."

A trace of eagerness came into Miss Archer's passive manner. "What is the name?"

" Dexter. Nathalie Dexter."

" Roger's friend."

" Why, no ! He does n't know her."

" Yes ; she is the girl who played the piano at Pulpit Point. Have n't you heard him talk about it ? "

" No, I have not."

" I have. He and Miss Toothaker often speak about the good times they all had together last summer. Mr. Andreas spoke of it, too, when he was here."

" Well, last summer was last summer," returned Mrs. Archer decidedly. " Young men go anywhere and do anything that amuses them ; but with a young lady it is different. They are not the sort of people who would ever have come under the roof of Edgewater in its palmy days."

" Nor now, then, had it not been for you," returned Betty.

Despite the cool, dispassionate tone in which the words were said, Mrs. Archer colored deeply. " Then I hope you are sufficiently obliged to me," she retorted. " We had come to where we could not even scrape along any longer ; whereas now you do not even need to paint unless you like. A few years like this, and I could invite you to Philadelphia for a season. You would find out then whether I could be a useful friend. In fact, any time when you will put sentimentality aside, as *I* can, and give your consent to sell the place, we can live and travel as we like."

"You have said that before."

"And I shall say it again, very likely!" Mrs. Archer winked fast, after her habit when excited, and kept on muttering to herself after Betty had left her.

CHAPTER VIII

VACATION.

"EDGEWATER stands on a creek." Nathalie remembered Mr. Gerard's description of the Virginian homestead as she stood on the gallery in front of her room the day after their arrival.

The " creek " was to her eyes a large salt-water bay, flowing like a river this morning under the soft wind, the high tide bringing its waves to the very fence that edged the grounds. Across its broad, rippled spaces came sweetly a bugle call from the fort.

Fortress Monroe. There it lay in warm sunshine, its distant verdant parapet guarding the post. "Lieutenant Roger Gerard, —— Artillery, U. S. A." Nathalie believed she had his card somewhere yet.

Again came the mellowed notes of the bugle. She wondered if it were calling him, — wondered with a blissful lack of interest. Such contentment, such leisure were in this place of heavenly rest. In her tired condition the girl could think of nothing desirable to add to the present blessed moment.

The wide, smooth lawns of Edgewater rested

her eyes. At her left a dozen peach and pear
trees in full bloom feasted her soul with their ethe-
real, snowy, rosy blossoms. Down the gentle
slope toward the water, spreading shade trees
upreared their massive trunks and stretched
symmetrical boughs, delicately clothed in spring
foliage. Rustic seats surrounded these. Tall
magnolias and sturdy rosebushes stood all about,
full of promise; but Nathalie scarcely noticed
them. Her eyes rested affectionately on the vio-
lets and buttercups striving for space in the grass.
She inhaled the breath of the old box hedge which
everywhere bordered the walks. She felt herself
as truly in paradise as did the butterflies rollicking
and frolicking on every hand, or the birds that
lighted near her and regarded her with trustful
eyes.

She forgot to regret Mr. Brandon and the circu-
lating musical library. Those catbirds were better than the Symphony concerts. Even the bell
of the trolley car which raced across the bridge
dividing the creek from Hampton Roads was a
remote suggestion of the city's noise, which but
heightened her content in this utter contrast.

She had not known until now how tired she was;
and a grateful acknowledgment of her mother's
wisdom stole over her. She appreciated being left
alone at the present moment, to drink in the novel
loveliness. This was indeed rest. It was new
life.

At this point in her meditations she became conscious that there was another person beside herself on the gallery. Involuntarily she turned her eyes to see who it was, pausing over there beside a pillar.

Instinctively she felt at once that it was the girl who lisped. Nathalie had been aware of her, fluttering in some remote corner of her consciousness, every moment since her arrival, but as yet she had been a will-o'-the-wisp. This young person, with the smooth brown hair and observant eyes, must be she.

Now that the moment had come, Miss Dexter shrank anew from meeting her. Ah, the girl was approaching. Why was not Edgewater a desert isle!

"Isn't this Miss Dexter?" asked the clear, pleasant Southern voice.

Nathalie had learned enough of this stranger from Miss Toothaker at the Pulpit to be certain that she was of a different order from her stepmother. Nevertheless, she now admitted her own identity in a cool manner.

Betty's expression of indecision vanished, and she smiled with pleasure as she took in the details of her companion's face.

"You don't know who I am," she said, "but I know who you are. We have several mutual friends."

She was like the landscape, — piquant, and sunny,

and winning. An added charm surrounded her to Nathalie as the latter realized that this home of beauty was the girl's natural environment, her native element. What wonder that her face was fair and her voice reposeful! Instantly her suitability to the peculiar characteristics and tastes of Lieutenant Gerard of the —— Artillery suggested itself with force.

"Miss Toothaker and Mr. Gerard have spoken to me of you," went on Miss Archer, "and we had a call from Mr. Andreas during the winter, and he talked of you, too. I'm Betty Archer. Perhaps you've heard ma name."

"Yes, I have, Miss Archer." Nathalie felt her manner to be stiff compared to the other's geniality, and hated herself for it, especially because she found she took a certain enjoyment in her own coldness, and had no intention of thawing. "Your home here is ideal."

"I'm so glad the sun shines fo' you this morning. It has been unpleasant fo' nearly a week; but you see Nature was only preparing fo' yo' reception — getting her bouquets ready. You deserve it, you know, fo' the grand time you made Roger have at Pulpit Point. We feel just as grateful — Mrs. Archer and I — as if you'd done it fo' us."

"I did nothing, — absolutely nothing." Nathalie raised her eyebrows.

"Oh, he does n't think so."

Miss Dexter was silent for a time.

" Is he quite well again ? " she asked at last, with chilling politeness.

" Entirely so, thank you."

" Not lame at all ? "

" Lame ? " asked Betty, with courteous surprise. " Why should he be lame ? "

Miss Dexter crimsoned with conflicting sensations, in which impatience at her own stupidity was dashed with a strange gratification that Mr. Gerard had not told their adventure to this sweet girl. Then, as quickly, she rebuffed the pleasant emotion with a reminder that it was not strange he had refrained from mentioning a circumstance of which he was ashamed.

She turned her flushed face aside to smooth back a breeze-blown lock. " Oh, he had a slight sprain at Pulpit Point. It passed right off, probably," she said carelessly.

" It must have. It would n't do to have Roger lame," added Betty, with a little laugh. " I should lose a lot of dancing."

" You go to the Hygeia, I presume," remarked Nathalie perfunctorily.

" Yes, occasionally."

Betty pursued her valiant attempt to be companionable for some time longer, and ended by asking Miss Dexter to accompany her that afternoon to parade, — an invitation which Nathalie refused with a decision faultlessly polite.

As a consequence of this interview, when Roger Gerard found Betty under her accustomed live-oak fifteen minutes before parade, she reproached him.

He lifted his cap as he drew near.

"Didn't Miss Dexter arrive?" he asked with concern.

"Yes."

"You promised to bring her over."

"Yes, in ma innocence. I'd no idea what a contract I'd undertaken."

"Why that tone, Betty? I was sure you would like each other."

"We do — to a degree. I like her hair, and she likes ma home. She is good enough to say it is ideal."

Gerard smiled. "And she prefers to stay in it, does she?"

"Apparently. Why didn't you tell me how impossible she is?"

"Impossible? What an idea! I found her not only possible, but probable. Even actual."

"She's that kind, then," mused Miss Archer aloud.

"What do you mean?"

"Some girls are that way," explained Betty. "The masculine element acts on them like chamois leather on silver."

"She is very unaffected," averred Gerard.

"I found her so," rejoined Miss Archer.

When Mrs. Dexter finally joined her daughter

on that same morning, Nathalie had strayed out into the pavilion built half a dozen rods from the shore in the water, directly in front of the house.

As the girl perceived her mother advancing along the narrow pier, she waved her hand to her.

"I should like this day to be a week long," declared Nathalie, as she rose to meet her. "I am renewing my youth."

"Really?" Mrs. Dexter smiled. "I think, too, that we are very much obliged to Miss Tooth-aker."

They entered the pavilion, and Mrs. Dexter refusing the hammock, Nathalie took possession of it, while her mother seated herself by the railing.

"Obliged to Miss Toothaker?" repeated the girl. "I should say the thanks were due your guardian angel. I suppose he is around just the same as ever."

"I hope so, I 'm sure," returned Mrs. Dexter. Nathalie had been used to say that her mother's reliance on this unseen guide was as practical as the confidence she gave her grocer and butcher.

"One thing is certain. We had no idea of the loveliness we were coming to." Mrs. Dexter's glance swept about her surroundings. "This is not much like the waste of boards and sand about the hotels across there at the Point. I have just been talking with the daughter of the house."

"You mean the stepdaughter."

" Is she ? She certainly does n't resemble Mrs. Archer in any particular. I 'm afraid I may be prejudiced against that lady a little. At all events, the daughter is very attractive."

" Is n't she ? "

" Her talk is bewitching, and her face makes you want to hug her. Don't you think so ? "

" She is charming," declared Nathalie, with all the enthusiasm she could throw into her manner.

" It is good fortune for you to find such a girl here. A congenial companion for you to go about with " —

" Don't mention such a thing," interrupted Nathalie quickly. " I have n't seen you for a year. Don't fancy you are going to put me off on any girl. I don't want to see anybody but you ; not anybody at all."

The unnecessary warmth with which this declaration was made was another proof to Mrs. Dexter of her child's fatigued condition.

" You set me up, my dear," she returned gently. After a minute she went on : " Miss Archer has just been telling me about a Mr. Gerard whom she says you know well."

" Yes ? " Nathalie's hands were crossed underneath her head, and her eyes lazily regarding the masts of the shipping in Hampton Roads.

" He was at Pulpit Point, I understand. I don't remember his name."

" Did n't I write of him ? It is n't remarkable.

I did n't see very much of people. I was so busy."

" That suited him, it seems. Miss Archer says he was never weary of hearing you play."

" Well, I don't mean to tire people with it."

" I am just waiting for the right time for another feast."

" Then you 've brought me to the wrong place. I feel that I shan't want to do that kind of playing here."

" You thoroughly enjoyed Pulpit Point, did n't you ? There was a Mr. Andreas you wrote me about, — the brother of your kind friend of the steamer."

" Yes. Did n't you hear Mrs. Archer talking about him last night ? He is one of the elect, in her estimation. It was a blow to her to learn that I knew him."

" Poor lady ! "

" Now, mother, don't begin using that tone about Mrs. Archer ! Next thing you will be telling me I 've got to love her."

" Don't worry, my dear. There are only two things we must love."

" Well, so long as Mrs. Archer is n't one of them " —

" You remember — Goodness and Truth."

" Very well ; then my chaperon is out of it."

" On the contrary, they are at the soul of her, or she would n't be alive. Perhaps there is a good deal of excavating to be done in her case; or perhaps the rubbish can be burned away by love. Aversion, repugnance, never accomplished anything worthy. Don't try those instruments."

A friend of Mrs. Dexter's had once said to Nathalie : " My dear, your mother lives more nearly transparent to heaven than any one I ever knew." The words had remained in the girl's mind, and she remembered them now as she met her mother's tranquil, clear gaze. A provoking recollection of her own recent interview with Betty Archer flashed across her. She stirred in the hammock.

" It is my vacation, and I wish you would let me be as bad as I want to be," she returned plaintively.

Mrs. Dexter laughed. " Here is Miss Toothaker," she announced, as Miss Priscilla approached on the narrow walk.

" I thought I recognized Nathalie's striped waist," called the newcomer, " and I made up my mind I 'd snatch a minute to ask you how you was ' likin',' as Cap'n Levi used to say. Remember that, Nathalie ? "

" Yes, I remember. What a different sea air this is, Miss Priscilla ! — as soft as velvet and cool as satin."

" Yes." Miss Toothaker came into the pavilion and dropped on the wooden seat. " This and Pulpit Point are both sea air, and a banana and a cucumber are a good deal the same shape; but there's just as much difference between the two airs as there is between the fruit and the vege-table.

"Cap'n Levi would call this 'hahnsome wea-ther,'" remarked Nathalie.

"Ain't it pleasant!" Miss Priscilla looked about approvingly. "Miss Betty says she's made herself known to both of you; says she asked you to go to parade, Nathalie, but you did n't favor it. Now, Mr. Gerard would be real glad to see you again."

"Give me time; give me time." Nathalie spoke lazily. "I can't do everything at once. Just now I feel that I should like to be doomed to remain inside these grounds for a month."

"I guess you're a tired girl; that's what I guess. Mr. Andreas is comin' to stay with me awhile. He's got insurance business to do in Hampton, and Newport News, and Norfolk, and it'll be real convenient for him. We'll have a Pulpit Point reunion, as it were, with your ma and Miss Betty thrown in."

"What an attractive creature your Miss Betty is," remarked Mrs. Dexter.

"Yes, I like that girl. 'T ain't every one as young as she is that would know how to carry sail as well with Mrs. Archer." Miss Toothaker low-ered her voice, as though wind and waves might carry it inland. "That girl's got pluck and tact with the best of 'em; and then she's got Mr. Gerard close by."

Nathalie smiled. "Had Miss Toothaker been your correspondent, mother, you would not have remained ignorant of Mr. Gerard."

"You know we thought they might be engaged," put in Priscilla. "Queer if they ain't, but I can't be sure. Well"— Miss Toothaker sighed and arose. "There's Junius comin' after me already. Come in in a few minutes. It's almost dinner-time."

"MR. GERARD wished to be remembered to you, Miss Dexter," said Betty the following morning. "He regrets that his duties will not permit him to call to-day, but he is watching for the first opportunity."

The Archers and Dexters were still lingering at the breakfast-table after the other boarders had dispersed.

"From what I understand," remarked Mrs. Archer, "Miss Dexter is here for rest, and will not care to have people calling upon her."

As Nathalie made no reply to this, Mrs. Dexter spoke pleasantly: —

"Oh, I am glad to say my daughter is not ill. I am sure she will be pleased to see your nephew again."

"Roger is not my nephew. It would be a little difficult to say what he is to me," — Mrs. Archer laughed consciously, — "except that he is very, very dear. He is my husband's ward. Naturally he and Betty have always stood almost together in my affections."

Betty just glanced at the speaker with the innocent eyes which had learned to keep their owner's secrets.

Her memory was unfolding a panorama of scenes in which she and Roger were always conspirators, engaged in escaping or foiling the unsympathetic wife of her adored father. Mrs. Archer was not the cruel stepmother of the fairy tales, but she was indifferent to children, and had never sought to gain the confidence of her husband's daughter. Betty had never been asked to call her " Mother," and had never done so ; but the sweet wholesomeness of the girl's temperament, and a strong and saving sense of humor, had enabled her to preserve an unruffled attitude toward Mrs. Archer, who complacently assumed all credit for their friendly relations.

That lady had heard of the interest which Nathalie's music had inspired in Gerard, and could not deny to herself the attractions of this Yankee girl. Being extremely forehanded, and given to preparing for war in time of peace, she succeeded now in catching Nathalie's eyes with a full gaze.

" Neither Mr. Archer nor I was ever able to think of Betty without immediately thinking of Roger, nor to think of Roger without thinking of Betty."

" Naturally," returned Mrs. Dexter, with her usual manner of kindly interest. " I suppose they grew up together like brother and sister."

And Betty, who had felt surprise at hearing Mrs. Archer's impressive declaration, smiled at her plate.

The next day was Sunday. Junius, who approved of Nathalie's graceful and dignified carriage, and the poise of her bronze-crowned head, stepped up to her as she was leaving the breakfast-room : —

"Goin' to be a baptize in the creek this mawnin', Miss Dexter, yas 'm," he said, his face beaming from between the points of his amazing shirt-collar, and his manner more airy than usual. "I thought you might like to be thar. I thought it might give you a little amusement. Up to Hampton Bridge, yas 'm."

Nathalie thanked him, and soon afterward, while she was writing a letter, seated in the peach-tree bower, she heard him singing at his dish-washing.

Such stentorian and sustained tones as Junius was capable of would be the envy and despair of the average student of singing, groping for the secret of breath-support!

> "Naro, my God, to Thee,
> Naro to Thee,"

he bawled, until Miss Dexter began to wonder laughingly what a chorus of such would sound like, and realizing the present impossibility of letter-writing, she determined to go to the "baptize."

Hastening into the house, she found her mother, and proposed the trip.

"Let us get Miss Archer," responded Mrs. Dexter at once.

" Let us *not* get Miss Archer," returned Nathalie gayly. " Let us get tired of each other first,
mother. I am fairly jeal — "

She had been going to declare herself jealous
of Betty, but for some reason she stopped herself.

"Oh, you may admit it," remarked Mrs. Dexter,
as she put on her bonnet. " You have seldom had
so good reason to be jealous of any one. She be-
witches me. How many girls would behave as well
as she does? Just think! This is the first year of
having the privacy of her home invaded by any one
who chooses to pay the price. The child is like
a dear little unostentatious hostess all the time."

Nathalie's cheeks flushed. " I have n't seen
very much of her," she said.

They left Edgewater and took the electric car
for Hampton, the kindly colored people with whom
it was filled squeezing up to make room for them.

Arrived at the appointed place, they found the
crowd already gathering. From all directions
streamed the concourse of men, women, and children. Some perched on the edge of the bridge,
but most of them stood patiently on the bank of
the creek, while a large gathering of various craft
assembled on the water near the scene of the pro-
spective baptism.

The sun beamed down ardently, and it was tire-
some to stand and wait. Not even the curious
variety in the congregation could prevent the minutes from dragging.

Nathalie found a vacant space on a log, which she insisted that her mother should occupy, but the color had left the girl's own face.

"Let me walk about a little. It will tire me less," said her mother. "Keep this seat for me a few minutes, please."

Mrs. Dexter made her way through the crowd back to the road, and scanned the surroundings for some point of vantage where she and Nathalie might both find a comfortable spot to pass the time of waiting, and yet be able to view the proceedings. It was a hopeless search. Every desirable spot except the private grounds of the pretty homes whose lawns ran back to the water's edge had been preëmpted. She stood, her parasol on her shoulder, looking about in a somewhat anxious way, when suddenly a voice accosted her.

"Can I help you, madam?" She turned her head and saw an officer in artillery uniform. He held his cap in his hand as he spoke.

"I'm afraid not," she answered, smiling. "My daughter and I found it fatiguing to stand down there on the bank. I was looking for a possible seat, but there is n't any. I will go back."

"No, no, wait, please. I have friends in this house," indicating the spacious brick residence on their left. "They would like for me to make use of their veranda, I know. If you will bring your daughter, I will meet you at their gate and see that you are comfortable."

" But are you sure " —

The officer met the doubt with the smile which had won Miss Toothaker's unyielding affections.

" You need not hesitate, madam. I will speak to my friends."

Mrs. Dexter hurried back to her daughter. Later, Nathalie laughed over the subdued excitement of her mother's manner.

" Come, dear. Come quick!" she said. " There is a gentleman who is going to take care of us."

" What 's this ? " asked the girl, as she rose.

" The most fortunate thing," explained Mrs. Dexter, as they forced their way through the crowd. " He just happened to come along, and saw that I was puzzled, and he knows the people in that house over there, and we are going up on the piazza."

" Oh, no ! " returned Nathalie, protesting even to the extent of stopping when they were nearly at the gate. " Truly, you won't be uncomfortable down where I was, and this is so queer " — The erect lieutenant emerged from the door of the house. " Such an intrusion ! " went on the girl. He ran down the steps. " I don't like it ! "

" Why ! " exclaimed the approaching officer; and Mrs. Dexter saw that the reassuring smile he had given her was nothing to the radiance which could illumine his face.

" Why ! " ejaculated Nathalie in the same breath, all her pallor fled. And then they were clasping hands, and his head was uncovered, and Mrs.

Dexter's lips were parted as she wondered what all this might mean.

For a moment Nathalie seemed tongue-tied. The truth is, she had prepared so many phrases to say to him when they should first meet, that now they all escaped her in a body.

"Well, have you taken care of them?" he asked, looking down at the hand he held.

It slipped from his.

"Mother, let me introduce Mr. Gerard."

"Oh, *this* is Mr. Gerard," said Mrs. Dexter graciously.

"My mother has heard the Archers speak of you so much," explained Nathalie hastily. "What a coincidence this is!"

"Isn't it? I went over to Edgewater, thinking you might like to go to church, and there Junius informed me where you had gone. There is no telling when or whether I might have found the needle in the haymow, had my good angel not prompted your mother to go on an investigating expedition."

"Oh, that wasn't your good angel," returned Nathalie gayly. "That was mother's. She has one which permits of no rival."

"Perhaps they're friends. Don't you think it quite likely, Mrs. Dexter? Now if you will come around this way. The nurse has put some chairs out on the veranda for you, and I shall add a third, if you will permit me."

They were soon ensconced. How dramatic the scene had grown to Nathalie's changed vision! The sea of dusky faces on the bank, the gently rocking boats at anchor in the waves, now formed a significant picture.

The minister finally appeared, and, staff in hand, his gowned form waded out into the flood, sinking deeper and deeper in the sparkling tide, until he had found the requisite spot, where he planted the staff.

Then began a procession of black-robed men and boys, who advanced to their immersion while the crowd on the shore raised a hymn of praise.

After this came the crowning touch of the picturesque ceremony. A larger procession of women, their dusky faces the darker for the costuming of white robes and turbans, filed to the bank. Two of the dripping men conducted between them the form of an emotional sister, whose immersion seemed to the onlooker suffocatingly long.

Upon emerging from the flood, some of the excitable creatures wrung their hands, shouting, "I'm redeemed!" Others broke into singing; others again swayed their bodies from right to left with groans of rapture, during the whole of their laborious transit to dry land.

The Dexters watched it all with the rapt interest of novelty. Mrs. Dexter held her breath each time a turbaned head disappeared beneath the flowing tide in the deliberate hands of the clergy-

man, whose sonorous intonations sounded across
the water.

Gerard, looking on with wonted eyes, received
the comments of his companions with gentle assent
or demur; but never once, Mrs. Dexter observed,
did he ridicule any feature of the scene. She liked
him for it. Indeed, it inspired her with a sort of
dismay to see how easy it was to like him for all
his obvious characteristics, — those not only for
which he was not responsible, but such superficial,
acquired ones as she could already observe.

Her mother-heart took alarm, and she began in
an uncertain way to put two and two together, and
to send her thoughts, or rather her imagination, on
scouting expeditions into that past summer, which
had evidently thrown these two into familiar relations. And she had insisted on coming to Edgewater in spite of Nathalie's reluctance!

"Would you like to do it, Mrs. Dexter?"
Gerard's eyes were interrogating her.

The crowds on the bank were dispersing. Her
far-away look drew a laugh from Nathalie.

"I don't think mother has caught her breath
comfortably yet, after all the sympathetic gasps she
has been giving."

"I beg your pardon?" asked Mrs. Dexter.

"I have been telling Mr. Gerard that I want to
go to a colored church, and he says he will take us
where he knows one of the teachers in the Sunday-
school. Would n't you like to go?"

"This woman used to be a plantation hand," explained Gerard as they neared the church, "but she is simply a genius as a teacher. She does occasional work at Edgewater, and Miss Archer is interested in her. She took me to visit this class of 'Mis' Jackson' once lately, and I don't know of anything more original to show you."

The regular service of the little church was very brief that morning, owing to the "baptize," as the sexton explained, and very soon the Sunday-school assembled.

Mrs. Jackson recognized the lieutenant with an expansive smile and a delighted bow, and cordially welcomed the ladies, whom he introduced to her as visitors to her class.

"I does have right smaht of a class mos' days, Mist' Gerard knows," she declared, blinking behind her spectacles, "but I don't guess I will this mawnin', 'long o' the baptize. Kind o' breaks 'em up, ye know."

Nathalie thought it well worth while to have come here, if it were only to meet Mrs. Jackson. The teacher was a heavy-lipped African, as nearly black as could be found. Her costume was a scarlet flannel gown with skin-tight sleeves, over a petticoat of mazarine blue, which was visible below it all around, and she wore a turban hat which rivaled the red-bird's wing.

In spite of Mrs. Jackson's fears, about a dozen little pickaninnies appeared after the general exercises of the school to receive her instruction.

She beamed upon them proudly. "This *wuz* the banner class up till two months ago," she remarked, turning to her guests, who were decorously seated at her right, "but then we done lost de banner, and it's puffic'ly rediklus, but we hain't ever ben able to git it back."

"What decides who shall have the banner?" asked Mrs. Dexter.

"It's jes' the number o' pennies the chillen kin bring," explained the teacher.

Mrs. Dexter's lips twitched over the materiality of this arrangement, and her gaze strayed along the row of strangely dressed little darkies, with their rolling glances and woolly heads. In jackets made of old bed-blankets, or frocks of faded calico, and odd head-gear, they sat there in a motley picturesque row, the short, tight braids standing out stiffly all over their heads, and their solemn, shifting stares fixed upon the lieutenant's red and gold, or the pretty costumes of the ladies.

But soon there was no idle time for worldly considerations of either army or civil life. Mrs. Jackson took up her Testament, and supplied each of the older children with one.

"Who kin tell me the Golden Tex' fo' to-day?" she inquired.

No one answered, but every pair of round eyes was instantly fixed upon her in an unblinking stare.

"All right! Then we've got to learn it now.

Come on! 'Bless'd are the merc'ful, fo' they shall 'btain mercy.' All together now, — come on! 'Bless'd are the merc'ful,' — ye ain't dumb, are ye? Say it with me, now. 'Bless'd are the merc'ful' " —

Mrs. Jackson had laid down her book and risen from her chair, and was hovering over the children with outstretched, waving hands, like an enormous tropical bird. Her pupils sat on the very edge of their seats, their braids electrically erect, and gazed up into the round spectacles that moved from one face to another as the teacher exhorted and coaxed and repeated by turns, frowning at a delinquent, and smiling with admiring pointing finger at some bold and successful spirit who, galvanized into speech, loudly proclaimed the text.

Whenever she perceived the flagging of the children's interest, with perfect tact she veered off suddenly upon Moses in the bulrushes, or one of the Commandments, until she recognized the proper moment to return to the main object of the lesson.

Finally, in the general excitement, it was discovered that the teacher herself had forgotten the precise wording of the text, but, turning for her Testament, she found that it was closed and the place lost.

After an instant's futile search, she stretched out her quick, heavy hand toward the largest girl. "Here, yo Rena. I ain't got time to fool. Gimme yo' Bible. Yo Gunnavere, take that gum out yo' mouth, an' don't yo put it back again. 'Bless'd are the merc'ful,' — now, then, come on! Yo goin' to sleep there? Wake up yo' brains an' go into it! — '*fo*' they shall 'btain mercy'!"

By this time Nathalie, too, was on the edge of her chair. There was no cessation of the camp-meeting whirl in which "Mis' Jackson" kept her flock until the bell sounded for closing, when, instantly hushing, she turned to her guests with the calm, expansive smile which seemed to indicate an absolute freshness and willingness to begin over again.

And that smile crept around the class when the three guests, constituting themselves pupils *pro tem.*, augmented the class fund to such an extent that, amid a satisfied display of ivories, Guinevere marched across the Sunday-school room, and brought back the silken banner to its old home with "Mis' Jackson."

CHAPTER X.

NATHALIE's behavior on the way home from church, and throughout the dinner that followed, was so much more like that of her old light-hearted self than Mrs. Dexter had seen since her home-coming, that the mother put aside her vague suspicions with relief.

Gerard stayed to dinner, and Mrs. Archer's sharp eyes glanced many times from him to Nathalie, and thence to Betty, as if exhorting the latter to observe the degree of friendship which existed between these two.

Nathalie's cheeks were pink, and she talked more than usual, striving from time to time to bring Betty into the conversation ; but it was Miss Archer's turn to be monosyllabic. Her direct glance and slight, amused smile were as spontaneously attentive as ever, but she permitted Nathalie to absorb the lieutenant.

After dinner Miss Dexter yielded to persuasion, and played the piano for half an hour.

"You don't know what those things bring back to me," said Roger, while Betty, with sparkling eyes, stood close to the piano in her enthusiasm.

Gerard went on to describe to the Archers his *dolce far niente* season beside the granite boulder ; and Mrs. Archer listened with set thin lips.

Nathalie excused herself at last to write letters. Her heart beat fast as she took her bright leave of the group, and a look of excited triumph was on her face when her mother followed her into their room.

" I could n't tell you before all those people how I enjoyed your music," said Mrs. Dexter fondly. " What good work you have done in the last year ! And what a rapt audience you had ! It was a satisfaction to watch Mr. Gerard and Miss Archer. Those two young people are perhaps as congenial in their tastes as Mrs. Archer wishes them to be. No wonder she likes the idea of having him for a son-in-law ! Are they really engaged ? "

" Don't ask me. I really know Mr. Gerard very little."

" Indeed ? I judged from your sprightly table-talk that you had seen considerable of each other."

" No." Nathalie smiled at herself oddly in the glass, where her bright eyes confronted her. " There was always a granite wall between us. You just heard him say so."

Meanwhile Betty was bidding Roger good-by at the gate.

" I envy you living in the house with that music," he said.

" You need n't. I probably shan't hear any

more till you come again. Yo' Miss Dexter is as different from mine as can possibly be imagined."

"She probably needs time to become acquainted," returned Gerard.

"No," laughed Betty quietly; "she needs the chamois leather, just as I thought. You need n't look martial. It 's a matter of temperament. You know there are men's women and women's women."

"I don't like for you to try to be cynical, Betty."

"Oh,. I 'm not cynical," she answered equably, "only I 've noticed so many things since I was bo'n."

"I 've taken you too often to the Hygeia."

"Yes, I 've learned some things there. Then you know it 's very educating to live with Mrs. Archer."

"Oh, Betty! Keep the circle drawn about your white self," rejoined Gerard warmly. "Keep those eyes as clear as they are now. Notice some things only to reject them, just as you always have. It seems you are n't infallibly keen-sighted. You are n't right about Miss Dexter, for instance."

Miss Archer made a mock courtesy. "We all know men are infallible where reading a girl is concerned."

"I like to see a woman stand up for her own sex," remarked Gerard.

"Does any one accuse me of not doing that?" A rare color showed in Miss Archer's cheeks. "I didn't know this was a personal matter with you, Roger. I supposed I could indulge in a little character-study with you, who are near to me as a brother, without harming any one."

"Hush, dear! hush!" he said, taking her hand. "There is no shadow to be allowed to creep in between us. You know you would not allow any one to say of me that I was a woman's man."

"You — you are a Virginian gentleman," said Betty proudly.

"And you are a Virginian gentlewoman," returned Roger with a laugh. "Now honors are easy, and I had better go. Let me prophesy, though, that before a fortnight is out, you will admit to me that Miss Dexter is a woman's woman, and of a rare sort."

Betty's lips drew together, and her eyes were solemn in their gaze. "She will never be mine if she comes between you and me, Roger. I wonder if you ever stop to realize, as I often do, that you are all I have in this wide, wide world!"

He returned her look with a steady, affectionate gaze. "Don't you know that I can't imagine life without you?" he answered.

"It is still so, is it?" she asked.

"It is still so, Betty. Why should not something come of it?"

"Something does come of it," she answered,

smiling at him with such sweetness in lips and eyes as seldom shone through the demureness of her expression. " All the content of my life comes of it."

" Yet you don't want to marry me, dear ? " he asked gently.

" I don't want any one else to," she said seriously.

He laughed a little. " Then perhaps you 're coming on. Good-by, I must go."

He lifted his cap and hurried away.

Miss Dexter's window overlooked the gate. She sat .beside it, her letter-paper before her ; but it was a virgin sheet.

The following week Nathalie and her mother devoted to sight-seeing. They visited Hampton Institute, set with all its wealth of happy work and usefulness in a very garden-spot of earth ; then they went to the Whittier School, where the singing of hundreds of little colored children took close hold on Nathalie's heart.

" How old are you, dear ? " she asked one mite.

" I 'm thix. I uthed to be five," answered the big-eyed cherub in the flapping misfit shoes, which sorely handicapped an effort at skipping in the kindergarten games.

There were so many infants who had not yet outlived being five, and even four, and whose wardrobes were grotesque, that the Dexters wished a realizing sense of this school could be conveyed to the North.

"The children seem to enjoy everything so much," observed Mrs. Dexter to a teacher in one of the sunny, spacious rooms.

"Yes," she replied; "it is great happiness to them. When our first building burned, the vicinity became crowded with mourning children and their parents. One woman told me the day after the fire that she had had no end of trouble with her little ones. She declared she had had to 'be up all night spankin' the chillen to keep 'em from cryin' '!"

The teacher went on to explain how, owing to the shiftlessness as well as poverty of the parents, the children were illy fed, even to an extent which led to many a fainting little one's falling down in the ranks during the school exercises.

"The peppermint bottle does poor service in the case of that sort of cramps," said the patient teacher, smiling.

After this talk, when all the children gathered in the pleasant hall to sing, their voices gained additional pathos to the hearers' ears.

The pupils stood in close lines, and sang from memory. One little fellow who stood directly in front of Nathalie especially interested her. Large patches of brown skin showed through his stockings, his ragged trousers were held on by a bit of twine, and his corduroy jacket literally hung in ribbons from his shoulders. His large head swayed to one side in a sad fashion, and he lisped hopelessly.

"Who fwallowed Jonah?" he sang with the others.

"Whale did fwallow Jonah whole!"

Nathalie swallowed, too, with the clear, soaring strains in her ears.

She behaved very well until the sweet cadence of another hymn began; but when the child before her, with downcast eyes, sang:—

> "Nobody knows de trouble I see,
> Nobody knows but Jesus,"

her wrought-up imagination overcame her self-control, and she precipitately left the room.

"Yo' mother says you found a sorrowful side to the Whittier School," remarked Betty Archer that afternoon, as she joined Miss Dexter on the rustic seat under one of the great trees.

"Oh, yes, I rather disgraced myself." Nathalie gave her skirts a welcoming push to make more room for the newcomer. "We waited, though, until I could find out where my little boy lived. His big sister finally informed me, although she was almost discouraged in the effort when she found I was so ignorant as not to know where 'Barnes's Bar' was. I could only discover that my little boy lived near this saloon, and mother and I set out upon a pious pilgrimage on foot to find it. The affectionate persistence with which we inquired for Barnes's Bar must make the Hampton loafers believe that at least two women in this place need the Keeley cure badly!"

"Did you find the house at last?"

"Oh, yes, and our visit quite relieved my mind. Another comfort is that I believe I can make my friends at home take an interest in the school."

"If you knew how cheap co'n is here, you would be out of all patience with such need as you speak of."

"Yes; but the children are n't to blame for the parents' shiftlessness; and they are not to blame for the saloons. How the streets bristle with them! In this lovely, lovely part of the world, too!"

"Yes; you see there are the soldiers from the fort to support the saloons, and then the Old Soldiers' Home, — though *they* have their own saloon, run by an officer of the institution. That regulates the drinking somewhat there, and a great deal of money is taken in, — enough to pay for all the old soldiers' amusements, such as the plays that are given there, and their temperance lectures, and" —

Nathalie's laugh interrupted the enumeration.

Betty smiled appreciatively. Each of the girls had intended to maintain a cautious and non-committal attitude toward the other, but Nathalie's genuine new interest had lifted her out of a personal rut, and her novel geniality at once disarmed the gracious Southern girl.

"I seem to do service as chamois leather maself to-day," thought Betty.

She renewed her invitation to attend parade, and Nathalie accepted it. Mrs. Archer, when she heard of the plan, decided to chaperon the girls, and Mrs. Dexter was glad to support her in this pleasant duty.

The easy refinement and innate kindness of Mrs. Dexter's manner had won Mrs. Archer's reluctant approval.

" Mrs. Dexter is a gentlewoman, whatever her daughter may be," she remarked oracularly to Betty. " She is n't like the usual bores who have infested Edgewater since the autumn. She is really very agreeable."

And having settled the status of her new acquaintance, Mrs. Archer proceeded to patronize her, and enlighten her dense ignorance concerning the characteristics and movements of some of Philadelphia's best families, with an affability which Mrs. Dexter received with courteous submission.

Nathalie sighed rebelliously this afternoon as the four skimmed in the electric car across the bridge to Old Point, to observe the animated chatter which Mrs. Archer continued to pour into her mother's ear.

They sought the pavilion in front of the Hygeia, and there Nathalie adroitly managed to slip into a seat between Mrs. Dexter and her lively bureau of information. The present was too exhilarating to make digging into the musty past endurable.

The White Squadron added majesty to the wide

sweep of Hampton Roads; the waves broke noisily against piers and foamed upon the sands. The bright, soft wind shook out the folds of flags. The uniforms of army and naval officers enlivened the long promenade before the hotel. The gay strains of a band on one of the battleships proclaimed that dainty feet were tripping about among its grim steel guns. All was life, motion, color.

Mrs. Archer viewed the glowing interest of Nathalie's face and heard her comments with disapproval. It was distressingly provincial to show so much pleasure; and she had been just about to tell Mrs Dexter about Mrs. Bartholomew Baumgarten's reckless second marriage.

"Three cheers for the red, white, and blue seems to be in the very air, does n't it?" said Nathalie. "There should be a few eagles screaming over the parapet of the fort yonder."

"Oh, we're nothing if not patriotic down here," returned Betty. "Even the very crabs would scorn to be disloyal. Have you noticed?"

She indicated the walk just outside the water-bound pavilion where they were. A little group of people were engaged there in catching crabs. The shellfish would attack the lump of meat at the end of a string, and then find themselves snapped out of the water upon the sunny boards, where they wildly waved their brilliant red, white, and blue arms in comical conformity to their environment.

"I want to take you up on the parapet before parade," said Betty, "so I think we had better go."

They sauntered on toward the hotel, and as they turned east on the board walk, Nathalie could hear fragments behind her of the resumed history of the Bartholomew Baumgartens.

Entering the fort, the quartette wandered on beside the cannon, which stand like horses in their arched stables along the outside of the quiet moat, each gun trained upon the waters of Chesapeake Bay. Mounting an inclined plane which led to the summit of the earthworks, the party walked along the rampart, high above the rolling expanse of water.

Out toward the open ocean, far as eye could reach, the ships were coming and going. The waves were breaking high on the deserted, crumbling fort, known as "The Rip Raps." The air was balmy. Nathalie stood still to view the marine picture, and the others stopped perforce.

"We might as well walk along," suggested Mrs. Archer curtly. She feared the girl was going to rob her again of her companion's attention.

"Yes, I think we might as well, too," observed a masculine voice.

"Mr. Andreas!" ejaculated Nathalie, wheeling about.

Gerard was accompanying his newly arrived friend, and there was a good deal of laughter and

hand-shaking, and Russell was presented to Mrs.
Dexter and beamed upon solicitously by Mrs.
Archer before he found himself moving along
beside Betty in the little procession.

"At last, Miss Archer Archer, we meet again.
Kindly admit that it seems long since I called on
you in the winter!"

"When you called on Miss Toothaker, you
mean."

"What a pity that blessed woman never
changed that excruciating name!" remarked Andreas. "Well, how goes art? All those fetching
little hearts and darts and cherubs and things that
you do? Miss Pris showed me some of your
pretty cards. Call that work, do you? Ah,"
sighing, "if you were only in the insurance business."

"It seems to be a nice, malleable sort of a business, — takes you No'th in summer and South in
winter in what looks to the uninitiated like a
mighty obliging way."

"Oh, well," turning out his hands in a gesture
of assent, "of course if you're not glad to see
me" —

"Well, what then?"

"Why," cheerfully, "I can drown myself.
There's plenty of water about."

"Don't drown yourself till you've seen Edgewater in the spring. Ask Miss Dexter."

"See Edgewater and die is her motto — eh?"

" Are n't you surprised to find the Dexters here? "

" Should have been stunned, only Gerard mercifully prepared me."

" Miss Dexter is a great friend of yo's, is n't she? "

" Well, I hope so. Of course, I 'm not in it with Gerard. I like music, upon my word I do : something you can feel the time to, you know; but I can't look soulful and entranced over a jumble of runs and jumps, the way he can, and she 's all wrapped up in that sort of thing. Besides," smiling with quick significance into his companion's eyes, "she has never rescued me, you know."

" What do you mean? "

" Did n't he tell you? Then, by the jolly jumping John Rogers, I must n't ! "

" But," imperiously, " you must, I assure you."

" My dear Miss Betty ! — say, you don't care if I call you my dear Miss Betty, do you? My mother said I might, — you don't know what you ask."

" Very well," frigidly. " I 'll ask Roger."

" Heavens ! I hate to get grass-stains on these ducks, but I 'll go down on my knees if you say so — plump ! Dear, good, kind Miss Archer Archer, don't give me away ! "

" But Roger never kept a secret from me befo'. It makes a lump come right up in my throat."

" Swallow it; swallow it. It was nothing, — the merest trifle. A little breach of the *convenances*,

—a mere nothing; but you know Roger. His sense of chivalry would force him to have me court-martialed, imprisoned. I don't believe you can look into my trustful eyes and have the heart to blight my young life. It is n't even insured. Shoemakers' children, you know, go barefoot."

" A breach of the *convenances* — chivalry? See here, Mr. Andreas, I really can't stand it."

" Do you know what I said to myself when I first saw you ? " impressively. " I said to myself : ' Now, there is a girl who must have had some ancestress other than Eve. She has no curiosity, — absolutely none.' "

" See here ! " called Gerard after the engrossed pair. " Are you going all the way around the fort ? Come down."

" Ah, that voice ! " shuddered Andreas dramatically. "I give you my unvarnished word as an insurance man that I 'm in a cold perspiration. Stand by me now, Miss Betty, and I 'll never forget. it."

" I 'm too proud to ask either of them," said the girl, as they turned and followed the others down the bank.

Russell took off his hat and mopped his brow. "In that case I 'm saved ! " he ejaculated.

CHAPTER XI.

RETREAT had sounded in the hush that precedes the resounding cannon, and the band was now giving forth the strains of the "Star-Spangled Banner." The ranks of artillery-men stood waiting for the. final drill, — long, brilliant lines of red-decked figures on the wide parade ground guarded by its live-oaks.

Mrs. Archer cast withering glances at certain women who had risen to their feet, obstructing her view.

" Deliver us from these ostentatious patriots who chatter all through parade when you want to listen to the officers, and then rise for the 'Star-Spangled Banner' and get in the way when you want to see the parade ground ! " she ejaculated.

" Yes, indeed ! " agreed Nathalie, who was viewing her first military pageant, and was naturally impressed thereby.

" Mrs. Archer never grows tired of parade," remarked Betty. " She sco'ns the side-glances one obtains from the quarters. Nothing satisfies her but a seat directly facing the clock on the barracks."

"Excellent taste," said Nathalie, giving Mrs. Archer her first approving look.

That lady seemed to consider herself accused of weakness, and bridled virtuously.

"I should assume an interest if I had it not, for Roger's sake."

The young officer soon appeared, and the party rose to make their adieux to him.

"Give my respects to Miss Pris," said Andreas, turning to Betty.

"Then she is n't expecting you this evening?"

"No, I believe there is n't room for me yet. I 'll stay with Gerard to-night, and run over to-morrow to see how the land lies. And remember, Miss Archer Archer, to remain a proud lady!"

"I think yo 're putting on a great deal of unnecessary anxiety. I think yo 're doing it on purpose to rouse ma curiosity."

Andreas made a gesture of dissent, and his expressive eyes spoke his comic yet real dismay.

"Indeed I 'm not, I assure you."

"It is so small to have secrets," said Miss Archer loftily.

"Still smaller to try to discover them, remember."

"Good-by, Roger." Betty intended the lieutenant to feel the coldness in her tone as she turned to him; and he did observe it.

He walked along beside her as the party moved toward the postern entrance to the Fort.

" The Dexters want to go to Newport News and to Norfolk," he said.

" Indeed ? "

. " Yes. Can't we take them together ? "

" The same day ? " asked Miss Archer.

Gerard smiled down at her. " What are you making difficulties for ? There are enough days, are n't there ? "

" Not for me. I have work to do. I 'm not an army officer with nothing to kill but time."

" Hello ! hello ! " murmured the lieutenant, in surprise more at her manner than her words. " What has happened, Betty, since we last met ? "

" Mr. Andreas has come."

" Well, he has n't made such a hit with you that you can't be civil to me any more, has he ? " Gerard smiled as he asked it.

Mortified color swept to Betty's cheeks at his jocose tone. " You would n't care if he had," she exclaimed. " You can laugh ! "

" What nonsense, dear ! Is n't it because we are sure of each other ? " and as they all just now entered the vault-like passageway beneath the parapet, the lieutenant utilized the darkness to press the hand that hung at her side.

. She withdrew it.

" What has come to you, Betty ? Tell me, child."

They emerged into the sunlight and crossed the moat in silence. Betty was a little pale, but she

looked at her companion now, calmly. " It seems
to me that this afternoon I 've waked up for the
first time in ma life. It has all been dreaming till
now."

" What roused you? "

" Mr. Andreas."

" Of course I don't understand you."

They had fallen behind the others. " Are n't
you going to tell me what portentous thing Rusty
said to you? "

" It does n't matter. Some few words he dropped
had a strange effect on me. They made me jealous. I believe I was never jealous befo', not even
when papa got married."

" What in the world should Rusty " —

" Never mind him. Really his part in it is
nothing. It is this strange feeling of mine that
I have to study and understand."

She looked at him with steady questioning, and
he felt as if some intangible veil was falling between them. He hastened to speak, lest in another
minute the words would not come.

" Do you mean — do you mean " — the gentle
chivalry of his manner was more marked than
ever. " Do you mean you felt jealous — concerning me ? "

It would have been so easy to ask the question
a week ago. Why now did it come with conscious
difficulty ?

" Yes, that is what I mean!" She looked up

at him wistfully. They had stopped on the quiet walk at a little distance from the spot where the others of the party were waiting for a car. "Do I," — her voice dropped still lower, in a sort of awe, — "do I — love you, Roger?"

"Did we ever doubt it, dear?"

"But *that* way — that frightening way? You asked me to marry you, Sunday. No — you suggested it."

"As I have done several times before."

"Yes; it used to seem the best plan to us. Don't you remember we determined not to be like the silly people in books and set ourselves against the match just because our fathers wished it? And we have drifted along, — drifted along."

A car whizzed by, and the waiting quartette looked over toward the absorbed pair with some impatience.

"Those foolish children!" said Mrs. Archer, consciously, loth to disturb what she believed was being a salutary object-lesson to this girl with her musical fascinations. "Shouldn't you think they had time enough to talk without detaining us like this? Betty!" calling; "Betty, how many cars do you want us to miss?"

The girl started. "I must talk to you again, Roger, and I must think."

"Don't worry," he answered soothingly. "Of course these matters don't stand still. Take your time. For one thing, you are sure of me."

She looked up into his beautiful eyes, and gave him a curious little smile.

"No," she answered unexpectedly. "I am not sure of you;" then she hurried forward to join the others, and Gerard followed perforce.

Andreas found an opportunity to seize Miss Archer's hand in farewell.

"Unfeeling girl! What have you been saying to him? What do you suppose my state of mind has been all this time?" he murmured, in the jingling of the approaching car. "I give you my word; I feel like an invertebrate animal. Nothing but heroic will-power keeps me from flopping down on all fours. What fate are you leaving me to!"

"You'll never get more than you deserve, I'm sure of that," returned Miss Archer lightly. Then she followed her friends into the open car, and fell into thought as they glided across the bridge in the transfiguring glory of sunset, soft reds and molten gold of sky irradiating the water, and bathing the still sails of ships in lovely Hampton Roads.

Gerard and his friend reëntered the fort in the dying glow, the former thoughtful, and the latter, to judge by his unsmiling countenance, equally so.

Andreas broke the silence. "Should you become engaged without announcing it to me, Roger?"

The lieutenant smiled. "I'll never marry without inviting you to the wedding, Rusty."

" Miss Archer is one of the most attractive girls I ever saw," said Andreas bluntly.

" You're a judge, old man. Thank you."

" What are you thanking me for?" retorted the other.

" Does it offend you?" asked Gerard, amused.

"Of course it does, unless you're engaged to her."

" That is something I can't inform you about."

" That's what hurts. When I was here in the winter, a dozen people on the post spoke to me of your engagement to Miss Archer. It seemed to me that I was as near to you as they, yet you never said a word to me about it."

" Nor to them, I assure you. It is a fact that I don't yet know myself whether Miss Archer will honor me."

"Oh!" Andreas's face expressed the most earnest interest. "You are on probation, then?"

The lieutenant kept a short silence.

"This is a good deal of a catechism," he suggested.

" Yes, it is," was the curt reply. " Beg pardon, old chap."

The conversation turning upon other matters, it was not until after the two men had parted for the night, and Gerard was thinking over Betty's unusual behavior and words, that the questions put by Andreas returned to his mind.

An entirely novel thought came with them, and

he suddenly threw himself into a chair to consider it. How much had Russell seen of Miss Archer in Washington? Then had come the few hours he had spent with her on a winter day at Edgewater. This afternoon they had met again. There were many cases on record of love at first sight. Was it possible that Andreas found himself so deeply impressed with the young girl that those questions had been put with a purpose deeper than curiosity or a friendly regard for his college chum?

Gerard interrogated his own sensations with sudden and lively interest. Provided the supposition had any ground, did he resent it? He had always supposed that some day he should marry Betty Archer. That he was fond of her went without saying. Now he searched himself for the symptoms of jealous alarm which the presence of such a rival as Russell Andreas ought to inspire.

Instead of the heat and excitement which the occasion demanded, he found himself dwelling with curiosity on the question of Russell's state of mind. That a man sought after as he had been should capitulate so suddenly to a simple Southern girl, who had never made the smallest pretense to fashion or position, as position is counted at the North, was strange, if true. How would Mrs. Archer like it? Gerard smiled as he considered the question. She had been more than favorable to himself, thanks to the fact that he possessed something beside his income from the government; but Andreas was a Philadelphian of the Philadelphians. Little doubt but that she would graciously transfer her favor to him.

"Well, how does that consideration affect me?" asked the lieutenant of himself, with some impatience of his own calmness.

He sighed after a vain attempt to detect some hastening of his pulses. "I suppose the truth is I'm too sure of Betty to be disturbed," he decided. "She said she was n't sure of me. What could she have meant by that?"

He rode over to Edgewater on his bicycle next day to find out. Leaving the dusty road, he entered the peaceful, green, blossoming grounds, only to meet Miss Dexter coming down the box-edged path, her hat on, and parasol in hand.

He met her brightly. "I am unlucky. You are going away."

"Yes, to the post-office; but Miss Archer is at home."

"So you do not consider that politeness requires you to turn around, then?"

"Not at all." Nathalie smiled. "Is n't this air delicious? I go about asking every one that until I suppose they think me imbecile; but does it ever storm here?"

"I hope it will pretty soon. The roads are dusty. I can't expect you will go with me on the wheel until the dust is laid?"

"I have n't mine here."

" I can get one for you."

" You are very kind ; but please don't feel the least responsibility of my entertainment. I came here to be lazy."

" Well, you find pretty good facilities. Too good, I fear."

" Why ? "

" I 'm afraid you may neglect your practicing."

" Oh ! "

" Still more afraid that you won't have regular times for it."

" Indeed ? "

" And let me know when they are."

" There are no rocks here."

" I know ; but perhaps some less solid ambush might serve by this time."

" No ambush would answer here. Good-by. I must go. I have been sent for the mail."

She made a hasty movement.

" Are you going to Old Point ? "

" Yes."

" Won't you let me run over for you on my wheel ? "

" Thank you. I want the walk."

" Then why may I not go with you " —

" Good-morning, Roger." It was Betty's voice which called from the gallery.

" Good-by," said Nathalie, speaking low, and moving quickly away.

" I just caught a glimpse of yo' red stripes

through the green," continued Miss Archer, as, lifting his cap, the lieutenant rolled his wheel up the path toward her and leaned it against a pillar. "Birds of bright plumage are convenient when it comes to locating them."

"But think what precarious lives they lead. They never know when they are safe ! "

"You are right saucy, sir, and you can go away. I don't want to see you."

"We differ, then, for I do want to see you. I came on purpose."

"Did you really ? Dear old Roger! But you have seen me now, and I 've had an order for some dinner favors, and I 'm obliged to begin them this morning."

"Bring your painting-table out here."

"And have the wind blow ma things all about ? No, thank you."

"Then I 'll come in and help you do them."

"Ah, Roger ! Is that you ? " Mrs. Archer came upon the scene. "Have you brought Mr. Andreas over ? "

"No ; Mr. Andreas is on his way to Norfolk by this time."

"I do think it very queer Miss Toothaker could n't arrange to receive him immediately," pursued Mrs. Archer impatiently. "This whole plebeian arrangement becomes frightfully annoying when it is our own friends who wish to gain admittance here."

" Well, Andreas is Miss Toothaker's friend,"
suggested Gerard.

"Nonsense! He regards her as he would a
good, faithful servant, of course. He is your
friend, and therefore Betty's and mine ; and I hope
he won't be discouraged because he has to be held
off in this way. I wish you would explain to him,
Roger, that Betty and I have actually no more to
do with the rooms here than if we were in Cali-
fornia at the present moment."

The lieutenant regarded the speaker thoughtfully. Her interest in his friend had gained a new
meaning in his eyes. His glance roved to Betty,
and a tenderness grew in his heart at the very
sight of her familiar face in the light of his new
thought. If the care of her happiness were to
pass out of his own keeping, how much of responsibility and solicitude he should feel !

" Rusty is very comfortable with me for the
present, thank you, Mrs. Archer. I think his
proud spirit can brook eating the bread of dependence till Miss Toothaker is ready for him."

Gerard followed Betty into the house to a little
room where, beside a window, stood the artist's
table. Drawing-board, sketches, pencils, paints,
brushes, bits of water-color paper, scraps of bolting-cloth, made a litter out of which she now proceeded to bring order, seating herself before the
table for the purpose.

" Don't you think Miss Dexter looks better than

when she first came?" asked the lieutenant, as he drew up a chair for himself, and began turning over the outlined sketches of æsthetic female figures.

"I reckon she does. Why? Did she look very different last summer?"

"Her face was rounder, yes, — and of course sunburned, you know."

"Do you admire sunburned girls?"

"We were all in the same boat up there in Maine, — shaded red and brown. Oh, it was fine! The music of waves, — nothing quiet and soothing like this, but inspiring and full of vitality and action. I would like to show you that place, Betty."

"But one should have the accompaniment of Miss Dexter's music, I reckon. I've been thinking about those day-dreams of yo's, Roger. What were they like?"

The lieutenant met her lifted blue eyes. "Can one tell day-dreams?"

"Yes."

"*Does* one, then? Dreams are great bores, — other people's dreams."

"Was I in them, Roger?" she asked slowly.

He smiled at her. "I believe I was fifteen years old when I had the pleasure of meeting you first, Miss Archer. I doubt if there has been a day since that time when I have not thought of you — Yes, possibly during my siege at West Point there might have been some seasons when math. and chim. and sundry other tortures drove you and all other joys out of my head."

" Yes, in winter that was all very well; but did n't any features of the summer ever drive me out of yo' head ? " -

Gerard laughed. " When you start in to be jealous, you cover the ground, don't you, Betty ? "

She dropped her hands on the drawing-board, and regarded him. " I told you yesterday that I must think, and I 've done so. I realize for the first time how much of yo' life has been lived without me. There were girls at the university. There were girls at West Point."

" You are not going to ask me to number those sands of the sea, are you ? " asked Gerard, lifting his eyebrows in mock dismay.

" Only those you were in love with."

He looked away a moment, then slowly back to her.

" Is this just a case of flippant give and take ? I suppose you are not in earnest."

" Are you trying to reproach me ? Are you going to say you did not flirt at West Point ? "

" Oh ! cadet officers all flirt. Even privates have been known to. It is part of the curriculum." Gerard's eyes smiled again. " And I was a captain, remember."

" You did it against your will, of course."

" I don't remember ever taking a very active part in the operation. It was n't necessary."

"Roger Gerard! That is the most unchivalrous thing I ever heard you say."

"Oh, no," protested the lieutenant quietly. "Custom, you know, — custom. That sort of thing is made very graceful and easy for a cadet. The regulations compel him to be comparatively passive, and to wait as a rule for aggression from the other side of the camp line. It usually comes, and then he slips easily along the path of least resistance."

Betty painted a minute in silence before she spoke.

"Roger, how many times have you been in love?"

He looked at her. She was gazing at him as if she must have his thoughts.

"Should I be likely to be in that condition without telling you?"

"How do I know?"

He looked down a moment, and then up at her again with a new, serious expression.

"I have a glimmering idea that to be in love is an extremely sacred thing," he said simply.

"But you do not know by experience?"

"I — scarcely" — He hesitated.

"Yet you have asked me to marry you." Betty spoke gravely. "How do you excuse yo'self?"

A bird-song floated in at the open window. The two sat absolutely still for half a minute, their faces averted. At last Gerard turned to her and spoke gently.

" Are not our lives the explanation? There is
no reason for you to feel bitterly toward me. If
you could examine into my life," — her very help-
lessness to do so smote upon him and made him
take her listless hand, — "you would find nothing
in it disloyal to you."

She regarded him with a strange little smile.
" Then if I 'm in love with you, ma fate is a sad
one, is n't it ? "

" No, no, Betty. Don't say it ! " he returned,
with quick pain. " Never was man more devoted
to woman than I will be to you, if you decide that
your happiness is to marry me. I swear that."

" And you will bury yo' regret, whatever
comes ? "

He looked directly into her eyes. " There will
be no — Hark ! " He interrupted himself suddenly, turned away, and rose noiselessly to his feet.
Through walls and closed doors came a delicious,
plaintive melody with a flowing accompaniment.
It was the first thing he had heard Nathalie play,
on his turf couch by the boulder at the Pulpit.

" Miss Dexter said she was going to Old Point,"
he murmured.

Betty looked up at him scrutinizingly, wistfully.
" People change their minds," she answered softly.

CHAPTER XII.

THE LIEUTENANT OFFENDS.

" Do you know that mother of yours is just the best woman in this world ? " asked Miss Toothaker of Nathalie, as she came out to where the latter was swinging in a hammock under the trees.

" Who would n't be good here ? " returned Miss Dexter. " I 'm good myself."

Miss Priscilla sat down on a rustic seat. She took her rests in odd moments and places, just alighting, as it were, occasionally, on her way from one duty to another.

" To watch the way she looks out to see if she can't help me, and does little things to make the other boarders enjoy themselves, and lets Mrs. Archer talk her to death, always havin' some work in those pretty hands o' hers, so 's nobody can really waste her time. It 's just a comfort to have her around ! I hope you realize, Nathalie Dexter, if you don't ever have another blessin' in life, that your mother, with her sweet face and the calm, happy light shinin' in her eyes, is blessin' enough for one girl."

" Do you know, Miss Toothaker, that is a very good thing to remember ? " said Nathalie, regard-

ing Priscilla and speaking slowly. " Miss Archer
has no such blessing as that."

" No, poor lamb."

" I probably appeared very idle to you when you
came out here under the trees," went on Nathalie,
looking up into the boughs, " but that was merely
an appearance."

" 'T was, eh ?   What you up to ? "

" I 've just discovered that I was meant to be
a poet.   I 've been turning into one ever since I
arrived here.   Now that the locust-trees have blos-
somed, and the roses are blooming, and the whole
atmosphere smells like sweet peas, I feel that the
time has come.   Wonderful things are seething in
my brain.   There is only a thin veil between me
and the most graceful poem of nature that ever
was written."

" Well, I wish you good luck.   That avenue o'
locusts out there in the road *is* sightly, ain't it?
The green is so fresh and delicate, and the clusters
o' bloom all over 'em makes 'em look as if they
were all trimmed up with festoons o' white lace.
Your ma likes those trees.   Says she had locusts
on her weddin' bonnet."

" Yes, she told me," said Nathalie softly.   " That
is part of the poem ; but, alas," — with a sigh, —
" though it would make a poet's fortune to look
into my brain, I fear I shall never be able to
straighten out the sweet tangle."

Miss Toothaker looked around approvingly on

the tall, thick rosebushes, rapidly covering with flowers in all stages of blossoming. "Folks down here say the roses are early this year. I guess your ma has loved 'em into bloom. I guess there ain't a day since she came that she hasn't gone around to every bush on the place, lookin' at the buds. I'd bloom in their place. There she is this minute, over yonder. Who's she got with her? Mr. Andreas? Yes. There ain't anybody else around quite so big as he is. Let's see what they're goin' to do. I'll bet she's goin' to show him the Pride of India tree. Yes, sir, that's just what she's doin'."

Priscilla watched with interested eyes as the pair crossed the lawn to the tree with its stiff and gorgeous purple clusters.

"Your ma's tickled to pieces with those flowers; says the calyx is just like wash-leather. See here, — they're goin' off! They don't see us. I've got to speak to Mr. Andreas. I know he wants me. Shall I call him?"

"No, no! He doesn't fit into my poem. He is too material."

Miss Priscilla started up and hurried after her friends, calling upon Russell Andreas, who turned. Excusing himself from his companion, he came to meet the housekeeper.

"Good-afternoon," she said. "I suppose you're after me."

"You know I have been for years, Miss Pris," he returned with sentiment.

" Go 'way, goose," she returned ; but she smiled, for she declared within herself that it was good for sore eyes to see him again.

" *That* 's unkind," he said reproachfully. " However, you have a rival at last."

" Who is it this time ? "

" Mrs. Dexter. Is n't she more than charming? I 've been talking with her for the last half hour, and I 've lost my heart entirely."

" Oh, cheer up ! There 's a string to that heart o' yours, sure."

" No, no ! " gravely. " This time it 's the real divine spark I feel. There is n't a doubt of it."

" The real ' divine spork,' eh ? " mimicked Miss Toothaker, laughing.

" That 's unkind again," remarked Russell.

" She says," he added, — " charming Mrs. Dexter says that she thinks the superfluous creature who has had my room here has at last consented to get off the earth."

" Sounds like Mrs. Dexter."

" That is a free translation of what she said, but is the spirit of it correct ? "

" Yes. You can come now whenever you want to. There was a woman over from one o' the hotels this mornin' wanted to come here so bad that when she found I had n't a room for her, she sat right down on the piazza and cried."

" Peri at the gates of Paradise, was n't it ? Well, that makes you realize, Miss Pris, what might have happened if you had met me with a negative answer. I tell you," impressively, " when I weep, I *weep*, and it is n't any laughing matter."

Miss Toothaker looked at the speaker kindly. " Well, I 'm glad we can take you. It does seem like good old times to have you 'round with your fool remarks."

Andreas lifted his eyebrows and smiled. " You do me too much honor," he said, bowing and bringing his hat to his heart.

Mrs. Archer gave the young Philadelphian the most cordial of welcomes, and in the days that followed showed such an embarrassing disposition to secure tête-à-têtes with him in order to discover and discuss mutual acquaintances, that he finally took refuge in a truly pitiable ignorance.

" The fact is, I 've been so much away, Mrs. Archer, I 'm afraid my mother's friends have forgotten me; and really, I suppose it 's a shame, but I 've pretty well forgotten them. You will have to make great allowances for me."

" An Andreas will never be forgotten in Philadelphia," she responded superbly. " When you return there, you will find open doors and open arms."

" You alarm me. I am naturally shy."

" We shall meet there some time," declared Mrs. Archer, in such an uplifted manner that Russell laughed frankly.

" You speak as if you believed that good Americans go to Philadelphia when they die. I've always understood that Paris was the goal."

"Excuse me," retorted his companion. "My idea of heaven is n't of a place where all the drivers try to run over you, and fine you if they succeed."

"Oh! he has such a manner!" she declared afterward to Betty. "There is such a *je ne sais quoi* about him! He is a kingly man."

Mrs. Archer fell into thought, regarding the figure of her daughter painting busily at her table.

"You are a very odd girl," she said at last impatiently. "Why don't you say something?"

"What, for instance?"

"Make some comment on Mr. Andreas. Tell me what you think of him."

"Why, you have covered the ground. I think with you there is a *je ne sais quoi* about him."

"And you admire him, of course?"

"I don't think I 'm a very admiring person."

"You never would confide in me," complained Mrs. Archer with heat.

"I 've nothing to confide, indeed I have n't," returned the girl mildly.

"Betty Archer, sometimes I think you are the deepest creature in existence, and then again I believe you are as transparent as a child of five! A blind man in a dark cellar could see that Mr. Andreas admires you."

"And Miss Dexter."

"I deny it. He does n't care a rap for all that

drumming that you and Roger roll up your eyes over."

"Well, what of it?" Betty gave a warmer tint to the blonde tresses of the quaintly gowned girl she was painting on an oblong bit of bolting-cloth.

"Well," rejoined Mrs. Archer with some sharpness, "I should think it would be a matter of some pleasurable excitement to be admired by a man like that. Most girls would like to talk about it. You're so queer; but," in a different tone, "I suppose the reason is Roger. Betty," impressively, "are you sure about Roger?"

The girl gave the faintest smile at her work. "Why do you ask that?"

Mrs. Archer seemed relieved by the gentle question, and settled back in her chair like one who sees a longed-for opportunity.

"I have been feeling it my duty for some time to ask you if you were sure that your childish fondness for Roger was the sort to make it suitable for you to marry him. I have been wondering if you would be led by a mistaken sense of honor in the matter; if you would feel that your father's wish was binding, and that you mustn't disappoint Roger, or something of that kind."

"I thought you wished me to marry him."

"I do, if it's the best thing; but I do feel that I ought to tell you"—Mrs. Archer stirred with some embarrassment—"that the Andreas family

as a family are people of more property and higher
position than Roger Gerard."

Betty slowly turned her head and gave her companion a long look before returning to her work.

"You are absurdly unsophisticated, my dear,"
responded Mrs. Archer to the unspoken reproach.
"I beg you not to encourage any false sentiment.
I only wish to tell you that you ought not to consider yourself bound to Roger by any childish ties
whatever. You have outgrown those now."

"Both of us have, then, I suppose."

"What do you mean?"

"I mean that of course he is no more bound
than I am."

Mrs. Archer bristled. "Roger is too much of a
gentleman, I hope, to take an initial step in this
matter."

"Yes, he is, bless him!" The girl spoke with a
fervor rarely displayed before her stepmother.
"One would almost think he had a claim to consideration," she added.

"If you are going to imply that I am lacking
in regard for Roger, you are extremely unjust; on
the contrary, I want him to have a wife who loves
him, not to marry a girl who is merely used to him."

And this sounded so extremely well that Mrs.
Archer said it over a second time with unction.

"He will." Betty said it softly as she put a
rosebud in her young woman's taper fingers. "His
wife will love him."

"Then you are sure about him," said Mrs. Archer with a touch of disappointment.

"I 'm sure about him," answered the girl.

"Sure about who?" asked Gerard himself, coming into the room.

"*Whom*, lieutenant?" suggested the artist, just glancing up. "About you, of co'se. Who else should we be talking about?"

"*Whom*, if you please, Miss Archer." Gerard bowed to the other lady, and sat down near the painting-table.

"Why don't you call me Miss Orcher-Orcher, as your friend Rusty does?"

"Because I think you are more sure to come when I call you 'Betty.' Don't you want to come out on your wheel? I think you stay in the house too much."

"Indeed she does, Roger. There is really no necessity for her working this spring."

"And because there is n't," said Betty, "of co'se the orders come pouring in."

"Why don't you reject them with superb disdain?"

"Because I 'm mercenary, I reckon."

"I 'll tell you why," put in Mrs. Archer, with impatience. "It is because she says that now she can use her money for charity. Those dinner-favors will probably all turn into baby clothes and grape juice."

"Oh, you make me feel so good," murmured

Betty; "just like a little angel with wings springing out. If both of you would *only* not object to minding yo' own affairs."

"That's it, Roger," remarked Mrs. Archer exasperated. "Betty appears to be such a gentle creature. I wish anybody joy who tries to influence her."

"What's this?" exclaimed Gerard suddenly, seizing the pencil sketch of a woman's head.

Betty glanced up to see what he had, then looked back at her work. "Well, what is it?"

"Miss Dexter. Did you do it?"

Mrs. Archer came to look curiously over his shoulder.

"Yes, I did it."

"Well, that is good," admiringly. "If you can catch likenesses like that, you will be doing something beside dinner-favors one of these days."

"Isn't it pretty? I've just had an order for cards with female heads for a men's dinner-party. That will come in very well."

"What! You are thinking of using this?"

"Copies of it, yes. It will do duty in several ways, — blondes and brunettes both."

"You would allow a likeness of Miss Dexter to go to a man's dinner-table?"

"Well, you need n't bite her head off," said Mrs. Archer. "Business is business. If it answers the purpose, why not use it? Who would be the wiser?"

"Would n't you like to be the guest to receive one?" inquired Betty, apparently unruffled.

"I could n't accept such a thing, — such a great thing." The speaker's agitation was evident. "What right have I? I am surprised at you for considering such a liberty as this. Even if Miss Dexter should consent in her desire to be of use to you, it should n't be allowed. To think that Tom, Dick, or Harry might have such a resemblance lying on his table for his friends to comment on — Why, Betty!" for utterly without warning the girl's false calm gave way, and burying her face in her hands, she became shaken from head to foot with violent sobs. Her drawing-board rested in her lap, her brush had dropped to the floor, while the festive rose-laden maid on the bolting-cloth doubled up ignominiously.

"*Betty!*" exclaimed Gerard again, desperately, starting to his feet and lifting away the débris of work.

"There! I hope you are satisfied, Roger Gerard," exclaimed Mrs. Archer. "I should like to know who Nathalie Dexter is, that you should scold Betty and hurt her feelings so on *her* account? As if there would be any likeness after Betty had worked it up into a fancy head, as she always does! Such a tempest in a teapot!"

"Hush!" exclaimed the weeping girl, convulsively waving a protesting hand toward her stepmother.

"Here, here's a handkerchief, dear," said Mrs. Archer, tucking one into Betty's hand, and looking daggers at the miserable lieutenant. Who knew but this unexpected difference might lead to vaguely better things? "My daughter, Mrs. Andreas." Like a faint, suggestive echo this pleasing phrase sounded upon her inner ear.

"You had better go right away, Roger," she said fussily; but Betty's hand suddenly flew out and seized Gerard blindly. He took courage then to seat himself close to her, and take the hand in his.

"I'm awfully ashamed of myself, dear," he said contritely.

"You — you — don't know what — I'm — crying about," she sobbed. "You — are n't to — blame!"

It was what she had always said. In every escapade of his boyhood she had always maintained, whether she proved it or not, that he was not to blame. He remembered this, and a strange tremor seized his heart. He had been deeply, unreasonably stirred just now, and bewilderment and remorse were at work upon him.

"You dear, forgiving girl! I was mad to talk to you so. How should you know what I meant, or why I felt such distaste " —

"Now, then, Roger, you are only exciting her!" Mrs. Archer's sharp voice aided Betty to regain control of herself.

In a minute more she tried to smile on him.
"Is n't this — ridiculous?" she said; then with a
sudden movement she leaned forward and picked
up the sketch of Nathalie and tore it in two.

Gerard started uncontrollably.

"There. Does that please you?" she asked.

Mrs. Archer saw the start. She had become
lynx-eyed.

"Perhaps he would rather have kept it safe for
you," she suggested sneeringly.

After Gerard, still quiet and penitent, had taken
himself away, Mrs. Archer gazed at the girl with
sharply thoughtful eyes.

"Well," she said at last, "I don't like the looks
of things at all. I don't see how you can say you
feel sure about Roger."

The speaker's voice showed her alarm. It did
not suit her at all to lose hold on Gerard until
she had seen how much that fascinating Mr. Andreas meant by his flattering ways.

She recalled how the lieutenant had one day
been chaffing Russell before the others on the slippery character of his affections. Roger had said
that whenever parents inquired into Rusty's intentions, it was that young man's habit to state that
they were "honorable but remote."

Mrs. Archer felt very doubtful of him. He
thought Betty was a pretty, simple creature, doubt-
less; but the more the stepmother reflected, the
less probable it seemed that his admiration was

more than skin-deep. Beside, he probably looked upon Betty as Gerard's intended; and now was Gerard going to be beguiled from his allegiance by a piano-playing nobody? The state of things was one which required watching.

CHAPTER XIII

UNDER THE WILLOWS.

"I AM glad you happened out, Miss Betty," said Mrs. Dexter. "I have just finished this little gown. Is that about the thing?"

Mrs. Dexter, sitting under a tree, her work-basket beside her, held up the gown by its two tiny sleeves.

"It is just the thing! How good you are to me!"

"I don't look at it that way. It seems odd to find a girl as young as you so interested in charitable work. It is only a pleasure to me to help you."

"There isn't anything odd about it if you understand," returned Betty, throwing herself down lightly on the grass. "I've lived here all ma life, and ma father never could deny help to the negroes. He always felt more or less responsibility of them. Of co'se, all his boyhood he saw them looked after, and I feel he'd like fo' me to do fo' them when they need it. They are such helpless, shiftless creatures."

"But when you visit Hampton, you feel that that will not always have to be said."

"Oh, I don't know," returned Betty, with gentle skepticism.

"My dear girl!"

Betty smiled. "Yo 're a No'therner. Of co'se, yo 're enthusiastic. The trouble is I 'm a Southerner and I know the negroes, and I know facts and the figures that never lie."

"It is too soon to compile facts and figures," returned Mrs. Dexter, with some warmth. "The chaos of the reactionary stage is n't worked out of yet. Many generations of dependence, not being allowed to stand alone, and being denied education, must be followed by many generations where the reverse course is carried out before there is any justice in forming conclusions."

The young girl smiled into the earnest face. "And as we shan't be here many generations hence, we can't prove anything, can we?"

"No, we can only make baby clothes and hope," returned Mrs. Dexter, folding up the little gown with a sigh.

Betty leaned on her elbow and began idly to gather the buttercups nearest her.

"I 've been wanting to ask you a question," she said at last. The girl had become fond of Mrs. Dexter. She got on with her more unconstrainedly than with Nathalie, and she enjoyed the sunshine of Mrs. Dexter's approval with all her motherless heart.

"And I want to answer all your questions if I can, my dear."

" Such a strange thing has just come to ma knowledge. I know a girl who has a brother she is particularly fond of. She has suddenly come to suspect that he is in love with some one; and this sister has been wretched about it, — really wretched. She cries, and grows warm and cold over it, and — and feels that the world is — almost slipping away from her. What does that mean? "

" Jealousy, of course, poor girl."

" But how absurd! Did you ever hear of such a case? "

" It is rather extreme. Your friend must be peculiarly dependent upon this brother."

" She is. She " — Betty's throat closed, and she raised herself on her knee to reach for a far-away buttercup, her back to Mrs. Dexter.

The latter picked up another piece of sewing. " It is n't at all unusual for a sister to suffer greatly when another girl becomes all the world to her favorite brother," she went on, as Betty did not continue. " Of course, it is selfish; but it is pitiful all the same. I cried for two days when my brother became engaged, and I had to use a great deal of ingenuity to dodge him and not let him suspect me. It seems very funny, as I think of it now; but then it was no laughing matter."

" And you got over it? " Betty returned to her seat at the older woman's feet.

" Indeed, I was very soon thanking him for my new sister."

"But supposing she had n't liked you?"

. "Oh, I would have made her like me," said Mrs. Dexter gayly. "Beside, it is n't half so important whether people like us as we believe it is."

"Do you think so? It is tremendously impo'tant to me."

"Then just take on a new thought about it, my dear, and realize that that is the part of the problem you have nothing to do with. Your business is to give out kindly thoughts to everybody all the time, and leave the rest."

"To everybody — all the time!" repeated Betty incredulously.

"Certainly."

"But how can one? There are right many people I don't like at all."

Mrs. Dexter smiled. "That is because you don't know them."

"Oh, it's because I do know them," rejoined the girl quickly.

"No; you only know the rubbish that has accumulated over them, and that some time they will put off. You must help them by recognizing it as rubbish and no part of them, and when they vex you, keep thinking of the Goodness and Truth that is every instant pouring into their souls and keeping them alive, — and that *of course* you love."

Betty looked at the older woman curiously.

"That's the queerest talk I ever heard in ma life."

"How do you like it?" asked Mrs. Dexter, not raising her eyes from her work.

"I reckon I'm too rubbish-y maself to act up to it," returned Betty slowly. She bit a buttercup stem for a minute in silence.

"Did you ever talk that way to Mrs. Archer?" she asked at last, with a curious look out of the tops of her eyes.

"Once or twice."

"What did she say?"

"She said," Mrs. Dexter bit off her thread while an irrepressible laugh rose to her lips, — "she said that some of the best families were talking about such things nowadays."

Betty threw back her head hilariously. "Just let souls grow fashionable, and Mrs. Archer will have one of the first," she remarked. "We were *really* speaking of an angel, were n't we? And here she comes," she went on after a pause, in a lowered voice.

"If there's so much fun going on anywhere, I should like to be in it, for I've been reading *such* a stupid book," said Mrs. Archer, who had come down the flight of steps from her favorite gallery upon hearing Betty laugh, and now joined the others under their tree. "Busy as usual, Mrs. Dexter. I'm sure it is very lucky for Betty that you have so much time on your hands. I do so much of my own sewing that taking in any for darky babies is out of the question."

"Rubbish," murmured Betty gently, meeting Mrs. Dexter's eyes with such an innocent gaze that that lady's gravity was nearly lost.

"What's that, Betty?" sharply. "Did you speak? Have I interrupted anything private?"

"No, indeed," said Mrs. Dexter. "We were just talking before you came about the importance of loving people enough."

"Oh!" Mrs. Archer pronounced the monosyllable with some disdain. "I fancy that takes care of itself."

"Christ gave the two great commandments on that subject as if he expected us to need them."

Mrs. Archer stared. "You're very religious, are n't you, Mrs. Dexter? But, do you know, I've always avoided sentimentalism."

Mrs. Dexter smiled at the abbreviated sleeve she was hemming. "Christ said we were to love, *as* he has loved us; and that means not with effusion and demonstrativeness, but with good works and helpfulness, and above all; right thought. All that requires too vigilant effort to permit of sentimentalism, does n't it?"

But Mrs. Archer's attention had wandered. "Where is Miss Nathalie?" she asked suddenly. "I thought she was here with you."

"She went out with her kodak," answered Betty, beginning to give furtive, anxious glances toward her stepmother's suspicious face.

"Where to?"

" The fort, I believe," said Mrs. Dexter.

" But they don't allow kodaks in the fort."

" Mr. Gerard was kind enough to secure a permit for her," explained Mrs. Dexter. " She promises not to forward her pictures to foreign powers ! "

Betty's heart beat fast, for her stepmother's face was growing red, and portended a dangerous frankness. To her relief, Miss Toothaker emerged upon the brick walk at the back of the house, and loudly called Mrs. Archer. That lady turned with evident impatience, but after a moment's hesitation she responded to Miss Priscilla's call and moved away.

" I think I 'm in that, Mrs. Dexter," said Betty, looking after her. " Just excuse me a minute."

She moved across the lawn and stood beside her stepmother until the short interview with Miss Toothaker was over; then she took Mrs. Archer's arm, and conducting her into the latticed walk which led to the dining-room, she opened a door in its further side and gently pushed her through.

" I must see you a minute alone," she explained. Closing the latticed door behind them, the two were in an unfrequented corner of the grounds, where weeping willows drooped their long tassels to the rich grass.

Mrs Archer stared at the determined face of her stepdaughter in surprise.

"What would you have said to Mrs. Dexter about her daughter in a minute more if Miss Toothaker had not called you?" demanded Betty.

"I don't know," angrily. "If ever there was a bold creature" —

"Don't say it. She is n't bold. She is refined like her mother, — a lady through and through. Now, Mrs. Archer, don't you see that you can't control Miss Dexter's movements *at all?* Not by *any means?* Then what would be gained by hurting her mother's feelings and making them both go away?"

Mrs. Archer laughed sarcastically. "They won't go away. You need n't fear. You could n't get Nathalie Dexter away from this place. And you would try to keep her, — blind girl that you are!"

"I 'm not blind." Betty, pale and calm, looked straight into the other's eyes as she spoke.

"Then if you 're not, you know she is going to steal your lover from you if she can."

"She cannot do that."

"You *are* blind, just as I thought!" Mrs. Archer stamped her foot on the soft turf. "Roger's infatuated behavior yesterday exposed him to me. You poor, foolish girl! I tell you, you have nearly lost him now."

"Listen. I never had him. Roger never was my lover. No girl could steal him from me."

"Then you mean you intend to hold him to his

word? Very right, too." Mrs. Archer's voice gained a satisfied ring. "That is what you meant by telling me yesterday you were sure about him."

"No. I meant what I said. I am sure about him, — sure that at last he is in love."

Mrs. Archer regarded the pale, pure face, admiringly. "Well, you are a cool hand, Betty. I would n't have believed it of you. You can keep your head steady where most people would lose theirs completely."

The girl's soft lips parted in a little smile. "I would n't hold him. You can't think that? Why, I *love* Roger."

"Then has Mr. Andreas said anything?" asked Mrs. Archer eagerly.

Betty stepped back, and lifted a repulsing hand in an involuntary gesture of displeasure. "No!" she said; and brief as the answer was, its austerity warned her companion.

The latter stood for a moment in doubt, the excited blood mantling in her face.

"You need n't put on any airs about Miss Dexter to me," she said at last. "A proud, disagreeable, unsocial girl as ever lived!"

"I don't find her so. She has come here to rest, and she evidently likes to be by herself. This is a bo'ding-house, remember. She is not our guest."

"I suppose she has gone off this afternoon to be by herself!" said Mrs. Archer, with a sneer.

" I don't know.   Perhaps not.   Roger is her friend.   We are strangers to her."

" And you will tamely give him up to her ? "

" That is something we can't talk about, for we don't know that she cares for him."

" And don't *you* care for him, you cold-blooded, queer creature ? "

The girl's sensitive lips contracted, but she felt the futility of an attempt at explanation.

" I may as well tell you plainly, Betty Archer, that you have n't the right you seem to think you have to throw away a good match. I 've never hurried you about marrying, and have given you a home without a word of objection; but that can't go on forever. You ought to see that, without making me speak of it; but you 're just as full of Southern unpracticalness as you can hold."

The girl, in her utter surprise at this onslaught, gazed large-eyed at the speaker in silence. Her long practice in repressing and concealing her own thoughts stood her in good stead now. Instead of yielding to the overwhelming grief of listening to such words in her father's home, all her powers were summoned to aid her in appearing impassive.

Mrs. Archer, concluding that this silence augured well, decided to consider her speech a Parthian shot, and to leave with flying colors ; which she accordingly did, closing the latticed door behind her with a triumphant slam.

For some minutes Betty continued to stand in

the self-same spot, and to her those minutes were hours. The dear old trees waved gently above her, and the flowering shrubs all about were the same she had seen blossom every springtime of her life; but a harsh voice had put her away from them, so that all at once she felt an alien in the familiar place. Her first thought, as it had always been in time of trouble, was Roger; and it was with a sickening sense of loneliness that the realization came over her that he, too —

She turned aside against a tree-trunk, and thankful for the solitude of the spot, broke down forlornly, crying her heart out, her soft cheek pressed against the ridges of the rough bark, and long sobs rising from the depths of her being.

It was difficult to tell which was the proper entrance to the grounds of Edgewater. The fence belonging to the dear old house did not seem to be designed to keep people out. Rather it was an invention to make gates possible, all swinging hospitably inward to welcome the happy guest. One of these gave ingress at a point which revealed Betty's present retreat; and Mr. Andreas, returning from Newport News, happened to choose this one this afternoon. His quick eye saw, and brightened at the sight, the ripple of a blue and white muslin gown, whose owner was nearly concealed behind the trees.

Miss Archer's wardrobe was not extensive, but all the same, it was astonishing with what fidelity

Mr. Andreas's mind retained the general effect of the dresses he had seen her wear.

His opportunities for conversation with her since he had been staying at Edgewater seemed to him too limited. She was always busy, either painting in some mysterious room where he had not been invited to enter, or else out bicycling with Gerard, or — and this was a very unpleasant habit of hers — she had taken her little boat before he became aware of her intention, and gone out alone on the waters of the creek.

He had seen more of Nathalie Dexter, — a girl with much more claim to beauty than Miss Archer, a girl unattached, a sensible, responsive girl, with no nonsense about her; but — somehow Mr. Andreas could n't remember the figures on Miss Dexter's gowns.

The blue and white ripple aforesaid drew him now like a magnet. Hurrying through the gate, he struck out to the left across the thick turf in its direction.

Russell's voice was deep and pleasant, as befitted his big, symmetrical person, and it now gave Betty a decided start, accompanying his noiseless approach.

"I am going to interrupt this maiden meditation," he declared; and the words were scarcely out of his mouth before it was his turn to start, his face expressing such genuine consternation that, had she seen it, she must have smiled through her tears.

He snatched his hat off. " I — I beg your pardon," he exclaimed. " I 'll go — go right away. Can I get anybody? Perhaps Roger" — He turned to leave, inspired with an idea.

" No, no! " she exclaimed thickly. " Wait a minute."

He did wait, feeling painfully awkward, the slight figure in its attitude of abandon raising something like a lump in his own throat as he stood nervously striking his trousers with his hat, wishing he had stayed at Newport News, and glad he was here close to the blue and white dress, all in the same moment.

At last he could see that she had dropped the hand that held the handkerchief, though she still leaned against the tree with her face averted from him.

" I hope nothing very bad has happened, Miss Archer," he ventured.

" No; but I don't want you to tell Roger."

He waited, and as she added nothing, he returned: " How can I, when I don't know? "

" You know that I cried."

" Oh, that! I do wish I could do something for you." Russell spoke miserably. The grieved figure pulled at his very heart-strings.

His voice comforted her somehow. He was the only one of her little coterie in whom the sight of her sorrow would not raise embarrassing questions.

"You can do something for me if you won't tell any one — not any one at all — that you saw me cry."

"I won't, indeed." A pause. "Do you want me to go away?"

"No, — not especially."

Russell smiled faintly. "If you even want it a little, I'll go."

"I'm only afraid you'll see ma face. I know I look funny."

"I won't look at you," eagerly. "Upon my honor. Let us go over there and sit on that rustic seat a little while. I feel so flattered that you will permit me, and that you don't want Roger."

"The reason isn't complimentary to you."

"I dare say not; but you needn't remind me of that."

"Let me go first, then, and when you come, you must keep looking up."

Accordingly Miss Archer moved across to the rustic seat, and when she was placed, Mr. Andreas followed, his eyes fixed obediently on the green boughs, and his arms, hat in hand, groping broadly for possible obstacles.

Betty gave an April smile at his absurd approach.

"Am I warm?" he asked, when he was within a foot of her.

"Yes, sit down; and turn yo' cold shoulder to me, remember."

"I think it is very hard," he complained, obeying.

"You need n't stay, then," she suggested.

"Oh, I'm comfortable enough," he returned hastily. "You would n't mind spreading out your dress a little, would you, so I shall know you're there? There are no tear-stains on that. Look here, Miss Archer," in a different tone, "I must learn if your weeping had anything to do with my foolish hints the other day over at the post, — about Roger and Miss Dexter, you know."

"N-o. Not exactly."

"It was that, then!" with conviction. "You have been thinking about it and making a mountain out of a mole-hill, and I could kick myself! I'll prick that bubble in a minute. I'll tell you all about it. Don Quixote Gerard will probably pink me, but a man can die but once, and I'd rather die for you than anybody, anyway. You see" —

"Don't look at me!" with hasty warning.

He turned back suddenly. "Up there at the Pulpit, one day" —

"You must n't tell me. It is n't yo' secret."

"It won't be anybody's, after I've told you." Andreas half laughed, and turned again toward her.

She whisked about in her seat. "There! I'll be the one to look away. Yo' head is on a pivot that turns too easily."

"So you admit turning my head, do you?"

"Mr. Andreas," she asked after a short, thoughtful pause, "are you engaged?"

"Oh, Miss Archer!" he returned to her averted cheek. "This is so sudden!"

She sighed. "Are you?" she repeated.

"I *wish* I were," he answered, after a significant pause.

"Oh, excuse me!" she said hastily. "I only meant — I only wanted — Mrs. Archer takes such an interest in you, I thought she — oh, really, yo' putting it *that* way makes me feel right impertinent. You will forgive me, won't you?" In her agitation she had almost turned her face to him, when she remembered and looked away.

"Yes. Here's my hand on it," he answered, with a curious inflection, and for an instant her hand lay in the clasp of his.

He sighed as she withdrew hers. "Yes, I'm hard hit," he said.

"Confess," she returned with gentle archness, "yo're glad I broke the ice, so you will dare to talk to me about her."

"No use, no use."

"Why not?" encouragingly.

"The old story. She likes another fellow better."

Betty slowly looked around, forgetfully, directly into his face. Her eyes, plaintive and reddened, stirred Andreas to a tender longing.

"That is dreadful," she said simply.

"Yes," he returned quietly, not to startle her. "I don't want you to suffer so, and that is why you must let me destroy the false idea I gave you the other day."

"Wait a minute. Let me think if I ought to let you tell me."

He waited, satisfied to sit and watch her smooth brown hair and the curve of her cheek. At last she looked up at him.

"Oh, yes!" She gave a grave smile. "My eyes! But never mind. I think I'll hear that story, please."

"Well, one day up at the Pulpit, Gerard on the rocks turned at the sound of a woman's voice, slipped on the weed, fell, and knocked his knee-cap off. Woman was Miss Dexter. She behaved like Grace Darling, — was it? Some kind of a Darling, anyway. Managed to snap the thing back somehow, got him home, and brought the doctor, who said Roger would have been lame always except for what Miss Dexter had done for him."

"Wasn't that fine of her!"

"Well, it was a very efficient introduction between the two, anyway. Unless you are tired of life, though, don't mention the affair to the heroine of it."

"Of co'se not. It must have been a very painful experience for her. Then through his convalescence she gave him her beautiful music."

"Well, — unconsciously, — yes, she did."

Betty looked off, and did not speak for so long that curiosity rent her companion as to the nature of her thoughts.

At last she turned to him again. "It is nearly tea-time, and I must go in," she said. "Mr. Andreas, will you ask me to go to walk with you some time soon?"

Russell's very ears reddened with pleasure. "Y-yes," he stammered eagerly. "W-will you go this evening? There is n't any moon, but" —

"We shan't need a moon," answered Betty, smiling.

CHAPTER XIV.

MISS ARCHER'S CONFIDANT.

MRS. ARCHER'S irritation of manner at discovering Nathalie's absence had not been lost on Mrs. Dexter. Ordinarily, she would not have regarded it, considering such an ebullition too absurd to require notice; but little straws continually blowing one way since her return from abroad had at last formed a fixed suspicion in her mind.

Nathalie, in recovering from the depressed physical state in which she had come to Edgewater, had not at the same time recovered her old elastic spirits. The spontaneous light-heartedness that these surroundings would naturally evoke in a girl was lacking. A persistent shyness of Betty Archer was one of the features that roused Mrs. Dexter's mental questionings.

With the intuition natural to a mother of an only child, she had pieced this and that together into a theory which was more likely to be right than wrong; and especially was she convinced of its correctness on this afternoon, when Nathalie returned from her kodaking expedition.

The girl's face showed her fatigue as she entered the room where her mother was, and Mrs. Dexter, who had hitherto refrained methodically from open comment, now remarked it.

"You look tired from your tramp."

"It is such a long walk around the fort." Nathalie took off her hat and sank into a chair with a frank sigh.

"Do you think you succeeded?"

"I can't be sure. The afternoon light is n't the best for some of the views I wanted."

"Well, I suppose you could go some morning?"

"It is hardly worth while to make Mr. Gerard the trouble again."

"He was with you, I suppose?"

"Yes."

"I should think he would be thankful to you for giving him something to do."

"They have enough to do ; and what a pleasant life it is!"

"Yes, here at this post it certainly is. What did you talk about?"

"Oh, kodaks," Nathalie smiled faintly, — "and music."

"I'm afraid Mr. Gerard was n't very considerate."

"Of what?"

"Of your strength."

The girl regarded her mother almost compassionately. "How little you know him!" she returned.

"Explain yourself," said the mother lightly ; but she regarded her daughter closely.

" He is the most thoughtful man I ever knew."

" Happy Betty! " remarked Mrs. Dexter.

" Well, you knew she was happy, did n't you ? "

The two continued to look at each other a few seconds in silence.

" A strange thing has come into my mind to-day, Nathalie," said Mrs. Dexter at last. " I think Mrs. Archer is a little jealous of you."

" I should n't wonder," returned the girl equably. " She is capable of any absurdity."

" It *is* absurd, is n't it ? "

" You brought me up yourself, mother."

" I know, I know," hastily. " I did n't really require reassurance so far as you are concerned."

" I should think not." The girl's tone was a little bitter. " And if you had doubted me, you could n't have doubted him."

" I don't know Mr. Gerard so well as you do. He seems to have won your confidence thoroughly."

The girl did not reply.

" Nathalie dear," Mrs. Dexter spoke gently after a moment that had been long to them both. " I think the time has come for us to go away."

" Because Mrs. Archer is jealous of me ? "

" That would be reason enough, since your health is quite recovered."

" But I have a strong reason for staying," returned the girl slowly, and the color receded from her face as she looked steadily into her mother's eyes, " a reason which swallows up Mrs. Archer's whims."

Mrs. Dexter felt dismayed at the strength of purpose in the young face.

" A reason connected with Mr. Gerard ? "

" Yes."

" My child ! What do you mean ? "

" If you knew him, you could guess."

The mother's heart fluttered.

" Why did you let me bring you here?" she exclaimed.

" I tried not to come."

" Yes, you did, dear. But you were not frank enough. How could I know ? "

" I did n't even know myself, mother. I only feared, vaguely."

They had been sitting apart; but now they clung together in a close embrace.

Nathalie's heart smote her as she felt her mother's tremulous arms. There was something wild in Mrs. Dexter's soft tone as she suddenly lifted herself erect. " But why not go at once ? "

" A week ago I should have consented gladly; but now it is too late." The voice, sounding so suddenly mature, increased the older woman's agitation.

" What can you mean ? " she exclaimed, panic-stricken. " We are not thieves ! "

Nathalie smiled again, and shook her head. " Poor little mother, you don't know him," she said. " No; I have thought it all out at last. After the tangle and the fever my thoughts have

been in so long, I see the way at last. If I should
go away now, it seems to me I should suffer all my
life. I must stay here and live it down. I must
grow well acquainted with Betty. I must give
him to her. I must see them together. When I
think of him, I must think of her too. I must be
happy in it. It is my only chance."

" But," faltered Mrs. Dexter, " how about him?
I have imagined sometimes — and thoughts are so
strong, he may feel yours, and you are a charming girl " — She stopped, breathless with painful
feeling.

" Mother, do you remember Sir Galahad? You
remember, his

> ' strength was as the strength of ten,
> Because his heart was pure.'

Those are the lines always running through my
mind. I cannot hurt him. I *would* not hurt him.
But if I leave him now, I shall mourn for him, —
I shall long for him," the steady voice suddenly
broke in a sort of sob, " I think I should die for
him."

" Oh, darling, darling ! " protested the mother.

> ' He who fights and runs away ' " —

" No ; trust me. Give me a fortnight. It is
for my life. Then if I have not made progress, I
will be honest with you and I will go."

The girl looked at her mother with eyes that
seemed to see far beyond her. She went on in a
hushed tone.

" I suppose I cannot comfort you for this. I
cannot make you believe how far rather I would
have known him and loved him than to have been
safe and calm and happy in ignorance of him."

Mrs. Dexter had regained her self-control.
"Yes, I do believe it," she answered, "but it is
an affliction that has come to us all the same.
Pray that you may not steal from Betty, even in
thought; and if I were in your place, while I
prayed to be delivered from temptation, I should
help Heaven by taking the train away from this
beguiling Eden."

"It has been anything but an Eden to me!"
exclaimed Nathalie. "The steed is stolen now,
mother. It is no use to lock the door. Let me
try what seems to me the only hope."

"God bless and help you, then, dear."

When the family met at tea, Betty's face was
flushed from her interview under the willows, and
Russell Andreas talked fast to draw the attention
of the company upon himself.

To Nathalie, grown sensitive, it seemed that perhaps Betty's preoccupation might result from the
fact of her own excursion with Gerard. It was
more than probable that Mrs. Archer had been saying waspish things. Miss Dexter was well enough
aware of her own ungracious habit toward the sweet
Southern girl, and felt in haste to do away with
the impression in that new programme which she
had laid out for herself.

But her self-command was shaken. She could not at once react from the breaking down of all reserves of the last hour, and she answered Russell almost in monosyllables when he appealed to her in the course of conversation.

" She could n't be any more grouchy if she knew what I had been telling you," he murmured to Betty, as they followed Miss Dexter up the steps of the gallery after tea.

" I think she is n't feeling well," returned Betty. " I 'm afraid Roger made you walk too far," she said, approaching Nathalie and taking a chair beside her. " You look tired."

The kindness of her tone caused Nathalie to turn gratefully toward her.

" One always walks so much farther than one realizes when tempted on by a kodak, don't you think so ?" and the responsiveness of manner thrown into the commonplace rejoinder made Betty wonder. She little suspected that Miss Dexter had thawed toward her once and for all in the sunshine of what she was striving to make an unselfish love.

" I shall have a fine panorama, though, of Fortress Monroe," Nathalie went on, " and I think I secured some very good pictures of Mr. Gerard which you will like to have. I will give you the films, too, so you can have as many printed as you like. Perhaps you will think it worth while to have one enlarged. After all, provided it is a fortunate picture, there is no likeness so correct as what one catches with the kodak. Don't you think that is true, Mr. Andreas?"

Russell did think so, quite eagerly; and the three young people talked the subject threadbare in the desire of each to respond to the cordiality of the other.

Gerard found them thus when he looked in for his evening visit. He pressed Betty's hand as he sat down beside her, for he still felt sore over that late altercation concerning the sketch of Nathalie, and thought that she might feel so too.

"Are we going to have any music?" he asked at last, turning radiant, questioning eyes toward Miss Dexter.

"No, no," interposed Betty. "You tired Miss Nathalie out this afternoon. I'm sure she does n't feel like playing. It is too much to ask."

"Playing does n't tire me," said Nathalie undecidedly. The new humility of her manner struck Miss Archer afresh.

"I don't believe you have practiced much to-day," suggested Gerard.

"I have not, indeed."

"That's right," said Andreas audaciously. "You play to Gerard, Miss Nathalie, while Miss Archer Archer takes me to walk."

Instead of laughingly resenting this slight as she would have done yesterday, Nathalie looked from one to the other in hesitating silence.

"How impertinent you are!" exclaimed Betty,

vexed with Andreas for thus clumsily carrying out her wish.

" Well, if you are going to play Sousa or Strauss, I want to stay, Miss Dexter; but you know I 'm awfully earthy. You don't want to cast pearls of melody before me, do you ? "

" Oh, take him away, Betty," said Gerard, smiling at the plaintive voice in which Russell knew so well how to make his humility effective.

" Very well, Miss Dexter," said the girl, rising, " but remember you owe me compensation for this. I decline to admit that *ma* musical ear is that material which is unsuitable for silk purses ! "

Nathalie watched them go down the steps with a thoughtful face. " What a sweet, lovely, unselfish girl Miss Archer is ! " she said deliberately. " My admiration for her is growing beyond bounds."

. " You are entirely right," replied the lieutenant, " but I did n't know you had discovered so much. To tell the truth, Betty does n't consider herself a favorite with you."

" I think I have been slow in waking up to her. She is the sort of girl who can be imposed upon. I fear she is being imposed upon now. She has not seen you all day."

" Oh, they will be back soon. Meanwhile, if you are not too tired — *Did* I let you get too tired to-day ? " Something fluttered in Nathalie's breast at his tone.

" No, not at all," she answered brusquely, as she rose. " Certainly, I will play."

And very miserable she was, sitting there at the piano, her trained fingers running crisply over the keys, while Gerard sat close at her elbow; for her mother passed through the room more than once, and Nathalie knew she could not help misreading the situation.

Meanwhile, Betty was strolling under the festooned lace of the locust-trees and reproaching her tall cavalier.

" Well, what was the use of beating about the bush?" he argued mildly. " Miss Dexter is wrapped in the spirit of her music the minute she gets into it, and Roger is up in a balloon with her. You wanted to speak to me, and — er — I wanted to have you, so here we are; and we're all happy, are n't we?" The strong curves of the speaker's mouth, the very set of his head on his shoulders, betokened his own satisfaction. Betty's hand lay lightly on his arm, for it was a clouded, soft, dark evening.

" Yes," returned Betty, after a little silence; " Roger is satisfied now, but I'm expecting every day that his satisfaction will change to anxiety."

" I've been studying you and Gerard ever since I came here," returned Andreas, " and if you think that is impertinence, I shall defend myself. People always have a right to try to guess enigmas, and it seems in this case to the interested spectator as if you two tried to be enigmatical. That last speech of yours, now! What is an unsophisticated individual, traveling in the interests of the insurance business, to understand by it?"

"We're not the least enigmatical. I came out on purpose to explain the situation to you, because I reckon you can help us." .

And Betty proceeded to tell the story of her own and Gerard's childhood and youth.

"Then you are not absolutely engaged?" said Andreas as she paused; and there was a tone in his voice that assured his companion that her narrative had not fallen upon indifferent ears.

"We always expected to be married — until — until — now."

"And why not now? I suppose you permit me to ask leading questions."

"Yes; but I wonder if you do not see why."

"Upon my soul I don't. I'm sorry to be dense."

"Well, perhaps it is rather too much to expect you to discover it before Roger does. He looks forward to our marriage still."

Andreas's face took on a startled expression there in the darkness. "Miss Archer, you aren't going to give me the task of breaking some overwhelming news to Gerard?"

"No," returned the girl quietly. "I'm not the one whose feelings change the plan."

"Then you believe that Roger" —

"Yes, I'm sure that Roger" —

"Oh, impossible! Why, there isn't anybody!"

excitedly. " I know all about his affairs. I 've been around with him over at the post. I 've heard him discuss people."

" Oh, nearer home, nearer home," sighed Betty, smiling at the impetuous tone.

" What ? — *Miss Dexter ?* Miss Archer, I shall never forgive myself. All this arises from my nonsense. It has given you days of unhappiness. It has been a deep wrong to Roger. I 'm simply no end ashamed. Do let me assure you " —

" Hush ! Wait. Your story merely threw some light on the subject. I 'm sure about this affair, Mr. Andreas, and it is nobody's, *nobody's* fault. I suppose you think it right strange that I talk to you about it," she added after a silence, " but — I 'm a very lonely girl."

Russell feared she would feel the unsteadiness of the arm on which her hand lay.

" You honor me," he answered quickly. " I thank you."

" Since you know Roger so well, you can understand how unwilling he will be to seek his own happiness. His loyalty and unselfishness will make his feeling for Miss Dexter misery to him when he wakes up to it. Another trouble is that Mrs. Archer will not want to let him off, and I 'm so helpless to influence her, or control her speech ! "

As she spoke, there came over poor Betty the remembrance of her stepmother's heartless tirade to herself during the afternoon, and a hunted sensation oppressed her.

"There is no one — no one I can appeal to," she said piteously. "Dear Mrs. Dexter is so good to me, but about this I must be silent to her. I must think for Roger, and help him to resist both Mrs. Archer and himself; and you being his best friend, you see why I turn to you."

"I was never thoroughly convinced before that my life was worth living," said Andreas, deeply moved.

"Ah! You have yo' own troubles!" returned the girl gently. "How I wish I could help you!"

Andreas was silent. To him she seemed an angel. He was longing to speak further, but felt tongue-tied. He did not doubt (because he wished so much that he might) that she loved Roger; and a new awe and timidity changed this assured man who had become a lover, beyond his own recognition.

"It is very fortunate fo' me," she went on, with evident diffidence, "that you told me what you did this afternoon. You implied that you were in love."

"God knows I am."

"You did n't know how much you did fo' me, Mr. Andreas, by confessing it. It makes it possible fo' me to mention to you a most embarrassing feature of this situation."

The breeze, odorous with the breath of the locust, cooled the girl's hot cheeks.

" This is dreadful," she went on hurriedly, " but I don't dare to have you not understand."

" Tell me all you will," said Andreas earnestly. " Your least word shall be sacred to me."

" You are so kind! Well, you have seen a good deal of Mrs. Archer. You have formed an opinion of her, perhaps."

" A worldly, ambitious woman. You pardon me? This is a time for absolute frankness, as I understand it."

" It is. You see how she values you. You represent to her all she cares fo' most. Well," — a strained pause, — " it is very hard to say it, but if you cared fo' me, and I would return your feeling, she would let poor Roger go. She has had the cruelty to declare it."

Their pace grew slower in the girl's agitated speech, and here they paused; her hand dropped from Andreas's arm, and they faced each other. " You see," she hastened on, " what will be likely to come when she knows that I have determined on giving Roger up. You have saved me untold humiliation. She would stop at nothing. She would try to win you. I should be driven to run away, or to throw myself in the water, only that you have given me a weapon. I can now tell her plainly that which will render even her helpless. I shall tell her : ' Mr. Andreas loves some one! ' "

But here vague fears of her future which she could not hint to him, suddenly pressing upon the speaker, her forced courage gave way, and her voice went with it. With a quick motion she hid her face in her hands.

Andreas shivered through all his big frame in the longing that seized him to gather her in his arms; but his love had leaped to a strength which enabled him not to touch her.

" Yes, she cannot hurt you in that way now," he answered; and his voice sounded cold to his own ears.

The girl's brief spasm of feeling passed, and she looked up at him again.

" It is an unspeakable relief to have talked this out with you," she said. " To-morrow I shall wonder how I dared; but it is done."

" And well done. No woman ever had a more obedient ally than I will be to you."

They strolled on for another half-hour, and Betty gave him the points on which she wished him to dwell in his interviews with Gerard which were pretty certain to ensue. Among these points she of course emphasized the fact that the affection between them had never been other than of a fraternal nature, — a bit of information which Russell accepted without in the least believing it, so far as she was concerned.

" You see," she remarked at last, when they were nearing home, " it will be so difficult to convince Roger that I 'm not so lonely as to need him. Ma unsupported word will not do. I want you to repeat to him that I say I'm so much attached to art that marriage would be a questionable good fo' me, anyway. He knows how many times I've put off the consideration of our wedding."

Hardly were these words spoken when the two came into the light of the main entrance to Edge-water. There they suddenly encountered Gerard himself. He paused with some disconnected phrases, and his face was white in the artificial brightness.

"You look like a sleep-walker, man," said An-dreas, forcing a jocose manner. "I suppose you are still following in spirit the erratic wanderings of Somebody-owski."

"It was — very beautiful. I hope you've been — yes, enjoyed yourselves. Good-night."

Russell and Betty looked at each other in silence for a minute after he had hurried away to catch an alleged car, whose approach was not yet audible to the ordinary ear.

Andreas was puzzled. "Why, he seemed dis-tracted! Do you think he was offended by our staying so long?" he asked.

"No," returned the girl quietly. "Did n't you see? The time has come. He has waked up. Poor Roger! Oh, Mr. Andreas," — her voice suddenly broke, and she stretched out her hand, — "you will help me?"

He took the hand, and after a second's hesitation bowed his head and kissed it. "I am yours," he answered.

CHAPTER XV.

A BICYCLE RIDE.

NATHALIE hastened to her room to find her mother after Gerard had left that evening.

"Don't distrust me, mother! Don't be anxious!" she exclaimed. "It just happened that we were left alone. It was Mr. Andreas's fault. He took Betty away."

Mrs. Dexter's thick gray hair was hanging long about her shoulders as she sat before her dressing-table preparing for bed.

"I see you playing with fire, and you ask me not to be anxious," she said sadly.

"I thought I had explained it all to you, and that you had agreed to give me two weeks."

Mother and child looked at each other. The girl's eyes were luminous from the excitement of the evening's music and talk.

"But is there no danger to him in all this?"

"Such a thought is surely needless misery," returned Nathalie. "That attachment has grown with his growth, and is a part of his very soul." She regarded her mother for half a minute in desperate silence. "This is something we can't discuss more," she said at last. "Neither can I bear, in addition to everything else, the feeling that you are disapproving of me. Either trust me and let me see if I can win peace, or let us go away to-morrow."

Mrs. Dexter's heart sank at facing the alternative.

"But if you are worse off in two weeks, what then?"

"I shall not be. I am not the first who has been forced to love against her will. I can live it down if only," — she hesitated, — "if only I can have a little time to regard them in this new light."

"But if he should be drawn to you? Forgive me, dear. I am your mother, and it seems a danger."

"He! You don't know him. He is like a knight of old. That is impossible."

"Then take your fortnight." Mrs. Dexter sighed as she turned back to her mirror.

If Betty's surmise was correct, and Gerard had awakened to a change of heart, the question to solve next was if Miss Dexter guessed it. Observation less acute than Miss Archer's would have noticed the alteration that a day had brought forth in Nathalie's manner toward herself.

"Did you ever see a cat who was planning to steal cream?" asked Mrs. Archer of her daughter at the first opportunity. "That's Miss Nathalie Dexter! She can't come around me with any of her palaver. I've cut both my eye-teeth."

"Miss Dexter strikes me as one of the most honest girls I ever met," replied Betty. "She seems to like me better lately."

"How lately? From about the time she spent the afternoon with Roger at the post, is n't it? Oh, that girl is deep. But she won't make anything. I 'm on the lookout."

Betty was painting, and her heart was full of her problem and apprehension of her stepmother's actions. But the dove had attained some of the serpent's subtlety.

"I hope you are n't going to say or do anything to spoil our pleasure just as Mr. Andreas is going to have a little more time to himself," she said innocently.

The magic name showed its checking effect on the angry woman at once. "Mr. Andreas," she repeated. "Has he anything to do with the case? I noticed you went to walk with him last evening — leaving the cat with the cream!" she finished spitefully.

"Yes; there are just four of us now, and of course, if you choose to make it disagreeable, Miss Dexter will go away"—

"And I tell you, you could n't hire her to go away."

"What is to prevent her going to the Hygeia, — especially if yo' suspicions are correct?"

For once Mrs. Archer was silenced. She had not thought of this obvious move which would give

Nathalie unrivaled opportunities for pursuing her nefarious operations secure from criticism.

" Of course, it 's much pleasanter fo' Roger and Mr. Andreas to have both of us here."

Mrs. Archer fanned herself violently, and indeed her face looked as if she needed cooling.

" Very well; but I shall watch. After your mad declaration of an intention to hand Roger over to the first rival who wants him, I naturally feel a duty in the matter. I give you fair warning, Betty, I expect you to marry this year. It will be your own fault if you don't."

Betty began to hum a popular cockney song as she bent over her work : —

> " ' If you dies an old maid,
>   You have only yourself to blame! ' "

This levity grated upon Mrs. Archer. " You are n't in a position where you have a right to play fast and loose," she went on. " As I say, I don't insist upon coercing your affections." When the speaker assumed this tone of lofty virtue, her stepdaughter was always seized with a wild desire to laugh. " If you find that Mr. Andreas is more suited to you than your childhood's comrade, I shall stand right by you, Betty, never fear."

" And the cat can have the cream, I suppose," remarked the girl, with a demure composure so provoking that Mrs. Archer looked at her with a return of exasperation.

" When you are as old as I am, you will find
that life is n't such a good joke as you think it is,"
and she flounced out of the room.

Betty wondered if she were very cowardly thus
to use Mr. Andreas as a bait instead of frankly
avowing at once that he was out of the question.
And as she wondered, a little perplexed line came
in her forehead, and moisture in her eyes blurred
the violet empire gown in which her painted girl
was æsthetically arrayed ; for Betty was not finding life a very good joke.

" May I. come in ? " asked Nathalie, suddenly
darkening the window. The artist winked away
her tears and glanced up with a cordial nod. " If
you are sure it won't annoy you to let me watch
you paint a little while. I do enjoy it so much."

" Then come ; and you will have to let me watch
you play in return."

" Very gladly." Nathalie came in and took a
chair by the painting-table. " The weeks down
here have flown away, and I have n't become nearly
well enough acquainted with you. I 'm just waking up to what I have missed. You have captured my mother's heart, as I suppose you know,
and I 'm not going to slight my privileges any
longer."

This would have been a paralyzing speech from
the cold Miss Dexter of a week ago. It was sufficiently astonishing now. Betty seemed to see the
apparition of Roger's pale and abstracted look last

evening, as he was caught off his guard in the sudden light.

"The cat and the cream." She wondered how Gerard would enjoy that simile. "Well, does n't the cream of a class rise to the top, and did n't Roger graduate nearly at the head of his?" Fantastic thoughts raced through the girl's mind before she looked up at her companion.

What honest, earnest eyes were regarding her! There was nothing feline in their expression. Had they read Roger's soul? Betty wondered. She would have been more than human if nothing of resentment and suspicion had risen in her now to be conquered. For conquered they must be. If it was a part of Nathalie's plan to win Betty Archer's friendship, it was none the less Betty's design to meet her more than halfway in every overture.

"I was a misanthrope when I came here," went on Nathalie when her companion had responded, "but Edgewater must be a specific for misanthropy, and all unworthy feelings. Whether I was looking at the humming-birds, or picking roses, or watching the magnolia buds swell, or sitting out in the pavilion, reading, I used to be conscious all the time that it was quite an undertaking to live up to Edgewater."

"I never thought of the place in the light of a sermon."

"Perhaps you were never so tired and bad as I was when I came. You know the enemy does steal a march on you when you are tired. But in this nest I have recovered my balance. Did you ever think how odd it is that such a peaceful spot should be so surrounded with the discipline of military life? I heard taps four times last evening, the air grew so very still."

Betty smiled. " Fortress Monroe, the warships, the Soldiers' Home, and Hampton. Yes, I was brought up on martial calls of one kind and another. Speaking of the military, didn't Roger hurry away rather early last evening? Mr. Andreas and I didn't realize that we stayed out so very long."

" Perhaps he left in dread of a musical indigestion," replied Nathalie. " I fear we playing-folk are more difficult to stop than we are to start. I was telling him the musical story of the Lenore Symphony as Raff gives it. I played snatches of it as well as I could, and filled in the rest with description. You know it is a very moving, exciting thing " —

" No, no, I don't. Poor Roger will have a famine when you are gone."

" He will need the rest, probably; but how appreciative he is! When I played him the love motive, and showed him how it was intertwined with the danger and pain that come afterward, he really didn't seem able to bear any more. He got up and walked about, and at last left, asking me to finish next time."

Color crept slowly up into Betty's cheeks as she nodded without lifting her eyes from her work.

"I'm not sure," went on Nathalie frankly, "but that I bored him a little, I was so carried away by the subject; but he will forgive me when he hears the Symphony performed by a good orchestra. Won't you, Mr. Gerard?" she added, smiling, for here the lieutenant came into the room.

"Yes. What is it?" he responded, and Betty looked him a scrutinizing welcome.

The brightness of his expression and the freshness of his military toilet could not cover the fatigue that showed about his eyes. Anxiety, added to sleeplessness, had left those traces.

"Did you dream of the horse that galloped by night?" asked Nathalie.

"Why don't you ask him plainly if he had the nightmare?" suggested Betty.

"I didn't dare to go to sleep at all, for fear I should dream of skeletons and an open grave waiting to engulf true love," answered Gerard. "Well, Betty, how does it go this morning? Make the most of your time, for you must go out on the wheel with me soon."

"Very well. You and Miss Nathalie go down to the pavilion and wait for me. I'll call for you when I'm ready."

"Oh, but you said I might watch you!"

"Oh, I want to watch you!" came from the two with such hasty unanimity that Betty smiled at her violet girl.

"Poor things! How scared they are!" she thought.

At this moment Russell Andreas presented himself at the open window and looked at the group.

"Well!" he ejaculated aggrievedly. "Gibson ought to sketch us in one of his conundrum groups, with the legend: 'Find the man who is out of it!' I don't want to be hypercritical, but it does seem to me, Miss Archer Archer, that typical Southern hospitality must be dying out."

"Oh, I suppose you can come in."

"I suppose I can, too — the window-sill is rather low; but I suppose I won't unless I'm sufficiently urged. Leaving guests to themselves and not hampering them with attentions is all very well; but when it comes to chilling neglect" —

"How can I work with you all bothering?" protested the artist.

"You don't call that work, do you?" asked Andreas, seating himself on the window-sill and lowering his head to obtain a view of the bolting-cloth girl.

"That's nice! I can't see a thing!" ejaculated Betty, gazing up into a face that women found good to look at.

"Then, naturally, ask me in," he suggested, smiling at her. "I should think you might see how uncomfortable I am, doubled up here like a jackknife, all for the sake of worshiping art. I

adore art. As a lady once said to me : ' Good pictures or bad pictures, — pictures I must have ! ' "

"Oh, do get out of ma light and come in ! "
smiled Betty. "But just remember I don't always
allow visitors ; so not even *yo'* assurance will always answer. This morning I happen to feel good-
natured."

"My lucky star again," remarked Andreas,
steering his long legs carefully past the painting-
table.

But Gerard, gravely persistent, continued to
urge upon Betty a flight into the open air, and at
last he carried his point.

As they were returning from their bicycle ride,
he began suggesting plans for the afternoon.

" You will come over to parade, won't you ? " he
asked.

" Oh, yes, I think so. If Miss Dexter likes to
come."

" Since when do your plans depend on her ? "

" Since quite lately. I see now that she was n't
well when she came here. But she is herself again,
and herself is charming. Yo' prophecy is fulfilled.
I see that she is a woman's woman."

" Well, she is at home here now. You need not
consult her about coming to parade. I dare say
Rusty will want to come over."

" Of course. Probably we all three shall come.
I think we make a very agreeable quartette, don't
you ? "

As she asked it, Betty stepped lightly down from her wheel, for they had reached Edgewater. She looked pretty in her trim bicycle dress, as she stood waiting for his answer to her gay question.

" Yes, I think we do," he answered, also alighting, and drawing his steel steed close beside her. " Although Rusty always shows a propensity to appropriate you whenever we four happen to be together."

" And that makes you jealous? " asked the girl, laughing a little, although his haggard face touched her deeply.

" I should hope it would," he answered with gravity.

" Nonsense ! They always separate brother and sister at every social entertainment."

" And husband and wife," he answered seriously. " I wish you would marry me soon, Betty. Don't put me off. I am very much in earnest. What possible reason is there for waiting any longer? "

" Dear Roger." The girl's little gauntleted hand stole into his. " I love you better than ever, if possible, but I 'm not going to marry you — ever."

She could see his lips grow pale. " Why not? I refuse to give you up."

" I 've thought it all out, Roger. You know I told you I was going to ; and I 've decided irrevocably."

He leaned on his wheel. "How have I lacked
to that extent?" he asked, regarding her with such
obvious wretchedness that she had need to be very
clear-sighted not to be deceived.

"I've lacked just as much· as you have. It is n't
our fault that we care for each other only as brother
and sister, is it? There is no limit to what we
would do for each other. I'm as sure of you as
you are of me. Each of us would remain single
if it would do the other any good; but it would n't.
I give you warning, I shall marry Mr. Right whenever he comes along; and I'm ready to give you
and the 'not impossible she' my blessing any day.
See how those little sisterly jealous twinges of
mine have vanished?"

His gloomy eyes met her clear ones, uncom-
forted.

"You are not rid of me so easily," he responded.
"I decline to give up my place until some one else
proves his right to it. I have had a blow, Betty!"

"I know you have, dear, *dear* Roger," she murmured, following him with misty eyes, for with his
last words he had mounted and sped off like the
wind.

She went with her two friends to parade, but
planned to arrive only in time for the ceremony, so
that Gerard could not join them until his calming
routine duties were over.

He had regained command of himself, and his
face told no tales as he came back under the trees
to greet them.

The lieutenant and Nathalie being equally determined not to walk together, Andreas soon found himself strolling across the lawn beside Miss Dexter, while the other couple preceded them.

Betty had found opportunity to tell Russell briefly the point of her morning interview with Gerard, and he felt vaguely that she expected him to begin immediately on his task of aiding and abetting her.

With a man's usual distaste for gossip, he did not relish appearing to expose his friend's private matters for discussion; but having, in addition to his desire to help Betty, an enormous axe to grind on his own account, he swallowed his fastidiousness and plunged into his subject.

" I fancy that affair will never come to anything," he remarked, with a nod of his head toward the other couple.

" I should be sorry to think so," returned Nathalie shortly.

" You are ambiguous. Sorry which way ? "

" Sorry if it should come to nothing. They seem so well suited to each other."

" I don't know. I imagine it is one of those boy-and-girl affairs which never come to anything, or if they do, it is a mistake."

Nathalie's lips took a rather cold curve, which Russell told himself humbly that he deserved, more especially if he were rushing in where angels would fear to tread.

Never mind, he had planted the seed; and Betty was pleased when he told her about it in the evening, just as he had hoped she would be.

Mrs. Archer was as good as her word. She did watch; and the things she saw gave her food for much restless thought.

The sudden intimacy which had sprung up between the two girls, who were now "Nathalie" and "Betty" to each other, was a constant source of resentment to her. She observed that the musical hours which a little while ago Miss Dexter and Gerard had often enjoyed together had now entirely ceased to be. She thought they even avoided speaking to each other; and these facts raised her suspicions to fever-heat. It stood to reason, that if they avoided public friendliness, it was because they had a more satisfactory means of exchanging amenities in private. Nothing but Betty's appalling suggestion of the Dexters' transference to the Hygeia gave her self-control; and, in fact, she did appease her wrath by an outbreak upon Miss Toothaker one day, which gave that worthy woman an overpowering surprise.

Mrs. Archer came in upon her one morning in the storeroom. "I wonder if you have any idea of the trouble you have brought upon this household!" she ejaculated in smothered tones.

"Who? *Me?*" returned Miss Priscilla, holding an egg suspended in mid-air as she looked around, dismayed at the attack.

"Hospitality ties my hands, or I would have those Dexters away from here this very day."

"The Dexters? The nicest folks that ever came into this house!" said Miss Toothaker, wondering if she were dreaming.

"Much you know the sort of people who have come into this house. You're a parcel of Yankees together. You pretending to be such a friend to Miss Betty!"

"And I wish you was half as good a friend to her!" retorted Miss Priscilla, red in the face under this furious onslaught, and half minded to throw the missile she held.

"Don't dare to speak to me that way, woman! What do you care if my child's engagement is broken by the machinations of those people you have brought here!"

"Oh! Why did n't you *say* you was talkin' about Mr. Andreas? I'll thank you not to come here ravin' about the Dexters to me."

"Mr. Andreas!" Again the name checked the angry woman. "What do you mean?"

"Why, I've got eyes, I s'pose. He's nothin' to the Dexters, nor they to him. How are they goin' to help it if he acts cracked about Miss Betty?"

"I don't think he means anything by that," rejoined Mrs. Archer, grasping after her dignity, and anxious to draw the housekeeper out.

"I guess you don't know what you do think,"

retorted Miss Priscilla. "I hope Miss Betty 'll do well. I *know* she 'll do *right*, far's she knows. My advice to you is to stand by and keep your mouth shut."

"Yes, sir, I told her to keep her mouth shut," Miss Priscilla used to repeat with relish, when, later, she described this hot and short interview. "And after that I told her I wished she'd go somewheres else, for I was gettin' out provisions for the cook. And she *went.*"

CHAPTER XVI

THIS shock to Miss Toothaker's consciousness, abstracted as it had been among the cares of her busy life, opened her eyes to see hitherto unobserved signs in her family. Most noticeable was the quiet, ·serious change that had befallen Mrs. Dexter.

It was a few days after the storeroom incident that that lady came to Miss Priscilla to announce that she and her daughter expected to spend but a week more at Edgewater.

"It seems such a pity to be goin', too," answered Miss Priscilla regretfully. "The magnolias and lilies just comin' out, so."

"But something beautiful is always just coming out here," returned Mrs. Dexter. "I fancy the right time to leave would never come."

"You ain't lookin' so bright as you was," suggested the housekeeper kindly. "I hope you have n't had bad news."

"Yes, I have, Miss Priscilla," said the gentle woman, "but perhaps it is not going to be such bad news as I at first feared."

"I do hope so, I'm sure," returned Miss Tooth-

aker, with hearty and troubled sympathy. "And
does it take you away sooner?"

"Yes, it does. Don't speak of this."

"No more 'n one o' those oysters would," returned Miss Priscilla, indicating the shining sands
outside the fence, from which the tide had retreated.
"I hope we ain't goin' to have bad news here,"
she added in the hushed tone she had been using.
"It would seem a shame to have anything break off
such a pretty match as Miss Betty's."

Her companion retreated a step; but Miss Priscilla's kind light eyes held no consciousness of
inflicting pain. "Shame would be the word,"
returned Mrs. Dexter severely. "What gave you
such an idea?"

"Oh, the stepmother's got a bee in her bonnet;
but land! Mr. Andreas is so kind o' flighty I'm
afraid it's just a sort o' second nature with him to
flirt with pretty girls. I have n't a doubt he'd
have tried it on Nathalie, if she'd have let him."

The fright Miss Toothaker had given Mrs. Dexter caused her heart to beat quickly for minutes.
Miss Priscilla remained where she finally left her,
wrapped in thought. The housekeeper had been
assailed with an idea, and she turned it over some
time in her mind before she at last remarked
aloud: —

"I don't see why not."

Junius poked his woolly head around the side of
the lattice. "I'se been watchin' yer, Miss Pris,"

he declared. "You looked like you wuz cunjerin' — standin' there talkin' to yo'self."

She sighed. "You had n't better be too sure I ain't a conjurer," she answered, moving toward the house.

"Laws, Miss Pris!" The boy's eyes rolled.

"You do your work all right, and I guess the conjurers will let you alone."

"Yas 'm, I 'm — I 'm just goin' to do the dishes now;" and immediately a clash of silver and china, accompanied by one of Junius's favorite hymns, sounded from the dining-room window.

Miss Toothaker strolled around the house to see if perchance Fortune favored her putting in her oar at the present juncture of affairs in the Archer family.

Apparently she did, for Miss Priscilla caught sight of Russell Andreas alone on the gallery, his chair tipped back, his feet on the rail, and his hands employed in folding some business papers into rubber straps.

He lowered his feet at sight of Miss Toothaker, in her gray gown and white apron, looking up at him.

"Busy?" she asked sententiously.

"I have been, but I 'm just seeing the error of my ways. It 's a great mistake to work between meals, Miss Pris. Remember that for one of your guiding rules of life."

"Will you give me five minutes, then?"

"Give you a whole day — a week — a year," he responded with enthusiasm. "Will you come up?"

"No; I want to see you alone."

"Ah! You make me thrill!" and Andreas repressed a yawn as he rose and came deliberately down the nearest flight of steps.

"You even keep your hand in with me, don't you?" remarked Miss Toothaker dryly. "I guess you're as bad a flirt as there is goin'."

"Guess again, Miss Pris. There are lots worse; and for *you* to doubt me! This is hard indeed."

"I know you pretty well, young man. Come over under the big tree. This sun's warm."

"So is this one. Fine old tree that is, but it just swarms with some little green insect, do you know. If you're going to sit on the rustic seat, you won't misunderstand me if I don't sit very close to you?"

"You keep in range o' my voice, that's all I ask;" and Miss Toothaker led the way to the honey-locust and seated herself, regardless of myriad busy aphides, while Andreas ensconced himself in the swing that hung from a large bough.

"There's a something, an indefinable tone, — just a *nuance* of expression in your voice and manner that gives me vague terrors," remarked Russell, regarding his companion with amused curiosity. "There is an absence of yearning tenderness in your face which suggests that you may be going to

cut off my preserves at tea. Tell me frankly, why
have you lured me into this lonely part of the
grounds just at nap-time, when my shrieks for help
would probably be unheard ? "

" I 'm goin' to tell you, young man. You know
I ain't any hand to beat about the bush. Just as
like 's not I 'm goin' to make you mad, but when
I think I see my duty, I do it, every time. You
know I nursed you through one fever? "   She
paused.

" Bless your heart! You did that! "

" Well,· I 'm afraid you 've got another," said
Miss Toothaker bluntly. " I 'm an old maid, and
don't know much about such things ; but I like
you, and I like Betty Archer, and I like Lieutenant
Gerard, and when I see you kind o' forgettin' yourself and perhaps bringin' trouble onto those faithful lovers, I just think to myself, who is there to
speak to you but me? "

For once Andreas was silent. He looked at his
accuser, then toward the house, then back again at
Miss Toothaker, who was evidently holding herself
up to her task with difficulty.

" I don't think for one minute that you ain't
honorable, but I do believe you don't know the
harm you may do. You 're the kind o' lookin' man
that turns girls' heads."

Andreas made a slight impatient gesture. Even
his enemies admitted that reference to his handsome person was distasteful to him.

"Now Mrs. Archer and I met up the other day like two old tabbies on a fence disputin' the right o' way. She began spittin' about the Dexters and insinuatin' her insults. I knew what she meant well enough, for I 'd noticed you. She classes you all in together as my friends, and I answered her back pretty well. I told her flat out I knew she meant you."

Andreas gave an odd smile at the grass. "What did she say to that?"

"It seemed to shut her up. She did n't know what to say; but it just set me to thinkin' that right now was when you wanted a good friend; and I am a good friend o' yours. You believe it, don't you?"

"I do indeed."

Miss Priscilla regarded him with troubled eyes. "If I could put you to bed and nurse you through this, I would n't begrudge the trouble, — not a bit," she said kindly. "But seein' I can't, don't you think, Mr. Andreas," persuasively, "you 'd better go away from here?"

"Gerard is my rival in more fields than one, it seems."

"Why, of course I want him to have his rights. You know as well as I do what his rights are." Miss Priscilla's tone was scandalized.

"Well, I thank you, Miss Pris, and I will be more careful in future." Andreas returned her look frankly and seriously. "I promise you to

avoid an approach to dishonor, and perhaps I will
go away very soon."

"And you know just how sorry I am to have
you!" exclaimed the good woman anxiously.

That afternoon Nathalie and Betty, Gerard and
Andreas, took a boat-ride together. They rowed
to a point about a mile distant, and landing, sat
under the trees in a breeze blowing fresh from
Chesapeake Bay.

Mrs. Archer saw them depart with mingled
excited feelings, uppermost in which was resentment toward Betty for slighting privileges and
opportunities which a girl of better judgment would
improve. Even that stupid Miss Toothaker had
observed the impression made upon Russell Andreas.

If Betty were sincere in the romantic idiocy of
throwing Roger over, what a godsend was this new
and even more eligible *parti ;* but fearing that the
girl was capable of clinging in her heart to Gerard
even though she gave him his liberty, Mrs. Archer
was gnawed with anxiety lest such a slippery big
fish would be deliberately permitted to get away
when perfectly willing to be caught.

"I'll make her suffer for that, if she is so enor-
mously stupid," vowed Mrs. Archer to herself,
wishing it were still *à la mode* to shut girls up and
keep them on bread and water.

Betty, unconscious of the resentful thoughts that
pursued her, was feeling more light-hearted and

happy than for weeks past. Her satisfaction in seeing Roger and Nathalie together had now become spontaneous, and she let her high spirits have their way, believing that to let Gerard see her contentment would be the best balm for his wound; indeed, convince him that his honor and self-respect had not been injured by his runaway affections.

He had not reached that relief as yet, however. The chief reason that he had come to long to confess himself to Nathalie was that he might throw himself on her compassion and beg her to go away. The sight of her face and the sound of her voice were sweet torment. He was still promising himself to conquer his love, to win Betty back, and to devote his life to making her happy.

By ill-luck Nathalie had been placed in the stern of the boat, and he, as he rowed, was face to face with her. Her white flannel suit and the reddish tendrils of hair that curled and clung up against her white cap in the wind photographed themselves on his brain.

The girl felt none of the stormy compunctions that swelled beneath his calm exterior. She wanted just this. She wished to see him and Betty together, as she meant to hold them in her mind all her life, and desired to accustom herself with more and more friendly feeling to this conception. A very sweet and serious expression was in her eyes, — one that did not at all contribute to the peace of mind of the longing man before her; and she, with her belief in him, her admiration and respect for him, did not dream that he would have been glad to avoid her, but talked to him easily, forgiving his courteous monosyllables on the score of his preoccupation, until they reached the peninsula whither they were bound.

"Going home, Nathalie and I are going to row," announced Betty, as they left the boat.

"All right," agreed Andreas. "'I would not live alway.' Would you, Gerard?"

The latter made a gesture. "So long as I die with Betty, what matter when?"

"Hear, hear!" called Andreas. "Or no. On second thoughts I take back that applause. It is excessively unmilitary for you to propose dying with Miss Archer Archer. I insist that you be murdered properly on the plains."

"You unpleasant person!" exclaimed Nathalie.

The men spread down shawls for the two girls to sit upon, and disposed themselves close by.

"Now, then, bring on some Pulpit waves," suggested Russell, regarding the softly lapping water.

"*Now* you are impolite," said Nathalie.

"We forgive him," said Gerard, half-reclining close to the hem of Betty's blue dress. "Especially we who have been there. Betty, you ought to see the Pulpit."

"Roger, that's not original. I've heard you say it befo', and I promise you the same summer I visit the moon I'll visit the Pulpit."

"You must come up again this year, old man," said Andreas. "My mother wrote me yesterday to be sure to ask you."

"Please thank her very sincerely; but I shall not be able to repeat the pleasure this summer."

"Why, do go, Roger! It did you so much good."

Gerard met Betty's earnest look. "I shall not get any leave this year."

"Want to stay where you can watch me, don't you?" she asked saucily.

"I want to stay with you, yes."

She looked down into the depths of his eloquent, unsmiling eyes. Then she poked the tip of her finger into the spot in his cheek where a dimple would be if he had had one.

"Could n't he laugh a little for the lady?" she asked wheedlingly; and Andreas began absently tearing up the grass with one hand and wondering if Roger would win after all, while Nathalie congratulated herself with a hurrying heart that this was a fine opportunity for learning the lesson she had set herself.

And Roger, infected by the mischievous sparkle in the blue eyes above him, sighed, but smiled as he was bid.

They made an early start home, for a dance was in order that evening.

The water-trip was made eventful chiefly by Nathalie's inexperience with the oars and the directions and devout comments of Russell, who had on several occasions constituted himself her instructor in the art of rowing.

Under cover of their nonsense Gerard made a serious appeal to Betty.

" No, no," she answered, with firm brightness. " I 'm happy now, and you will come to happiness too. I sleep all night like a baby. I did n't befo'. Look into ma eyes, Roger. Don't you see that I 'm telling the truth ? "

He leaned back in his seat silently, while Russell's pathetic tones rent the air.

" Miss *Dexter !* I 'm dripping ! Heaven knows I don't want to be unchivalrous, and it is painful to expose the poverty of my wardrobe ; but really, one more crab like that, and I shall have to wear my dress suit mornings."

" Cut them off and make knickerbockers of them," suggested Nathalie unfeelingly ; and Betty, whose oars here collided with the unmanageable ones behind her, lost her stroke, and laughed gayly.

" By Jove ! that girl 's a good actress, if she is n't an out and out angel," thought Andreas. He was nearly as perturbed as Gerard's self, and quite as much in need of reassurance.

CHAPTER XVII.

AT THE BALL.

THE ballroom at the Hygeia was gay to-night, and the long promenade was as popular as the glass-inclosed dancing-floor. Army and naval uniforms varied the monotony of conventional evening dress, and the women's light gowns enlivened the scene.

"What a serious beauty Nathalie has to-night," said Betty to Andreas, as he came to claim her for their first dance together. "Of co'se she's a pretty girl, but there is something so spiritual in her look in that white gown, — something different from usual. Have you observed it?"

"I noticed that she looked well. I've just been telling her so. But you are right. She is extraordinarily mum to-night."

"So is Roger," sighed Betty.

"I am not sorry to exchange her for a partner who can speak, and one who has some color in her gown as well as in her conversation. Do you know I particularly like this color?"

"So unusual, I suppose."

"Are you laughing at me?"

"Well, I fancy you've seen several pink gowns."

"Oh, but not of just your hue. It looks different from any I ever saw, really."

Miss Archer gave a little shrug.

"I thought I'd better wear pink because I felt blue."

"I knew you were acting all along," said Andreas with sudden gloom. "Did you notice Gerard as he and Miss Dexter just passed us? They look more like mutes at a funeral than people at a ball. And if you are blue, too, you ought to stop this whole business."

"Why, Mr. Andreas!" exclaimed Betty in surprise at his tone, and no more words passed between them until the dance was ended, and the couples began to hasten, chatting and laughing, out of doors.

"Do you wish to wait here for Gerard, or shall I take you to Mrs. Archer?" asked Russell stiffly.

Betty's eyes were lifted to him questioningly, and he looked down at her innocent face and girlish white neck rising from her airy pink frills.

"Why are you vexed with me?" she asked.

"Because you are making a lot of people unnecessarily uncomfortable by your mistaken unselfishness," was the severe reply. "You admit that you are blue."

"How can I help feeling sad for Roger when I see him struggling?" she asked, and her gentleness made him ashamed of his jealousy.

"Would you like to walk out a little way?" he asked briefly.

"Yes, and quickly. It will give them more time together."

"Then let me get your wrap." He moved to where Mrs. Archer was sitting, and that lady's vain heart swelled with pride that her companion chaperons should see him.

"Don't let Betty stay out too long," she said, as she smilingly handed him the silken scarf.

"One of the Andreas family of Philadelphia," she explained carelessly, when he had gone.

"When are your daughter and Mr. Gerard to be married?" asked her portly next neighbor.

"Who knows if they ever will be?" responded Mrs. Archer lightly. "They seem to think themselves boy and girl still."

Andreas placed the wrap about Betty's shoulders, and they followed the promenaders out to where the waves were booming.

"Forgive me if I seemed rough a minute ago," he said. "Surely I ought to reconsider my promise to be your ally in a crusade against your own happiness. It is wrong — why, it is fantastic to sacrifice yourself to Miss Dexter in this way! Admitting that Roger was somewhat taken with her music, you see how it has knocked him up for you to throw him over. He is sane enough now at all events, and has had a lesson. If you would let me tell him that you have confessed to me that you are unhappy" —

"And you call yourself ma friend!" exclaimed Betty.

"I don't admit a rival there, not even Roger," was the quick rejoinder.

"Then I wonder why you can't understand that I'm not unhappy for maself."

"I don't believe you think enough about your-self to know."

"Indeed I do. Don't you worry about my un-selfishness."

"Then are n't you willing to marry Roger even, if you could be made to believe that he loves you?"

A low laugh escaped the girl. "I think, Mr. Andreas, he could have made me believe it, if he had loved me."

"But you love *him*, and that makes me misera-ble!" exclaimed her companion.

"Yo're just as kind as you can be, but one of us is awfully stupid. I thought I'd explained to you that I only love Roger as a lonely girl must love the brother who is all the world to her. I'm mo' than willing he should marry some one else."

"And I'm to believe that!"

Betty laughed softly again. "I don't know. I hope so; but you seem to be unreliable. You may say something cross to me and something clumsy to Roger befo' I know it."

"I won't, I won't!" Russell's big voice trem-bled. "I can go ahead with some heart now;" but here some acquaintances of Betty stopped her

on the walk, and introductions and small talk followed.

Andreas and Gerard found a minute for a few
quiet words at the close of the evening, while the
ladies were preparing for the drive home. Russell
felt that he was about to enter upon ticklish ground
as he regarded his friend's set countenance, but
what was the risk of a few snubs to a man in his
state of mind?

"Miss Archer has been telling me an astonishing bit of news," he began, seating himself near
the lieutenant on the piazza.

"Yes?" was the not inviting response.

"She tells me that the understanding between
you has resolved itself into an agreement not to
marry."

"That is a misstatement. I have not agreed
to it."

"But you are not the man to hold a girl who
wishes to be free."

"What do you mean by speaking to me of
this?" asked Gerard, with the ultra-deliberation of
manner his chum remembered.

"Confound it, Roger, don't be grouchy. Why
should n't I speak, since Miss Archer gave me the
right? She says you are both free."

The lieutenant shook his head. "I am not
free." Then impatiently, "What do you want to
talk about it for? You can't understand."

"I understand the whole situation. Miss Archer

has been kind enough to give it to me. Her painting is everything to her. It is all she wants for
her happiness. She says it makes her feel entirely
independent for the future."

A slow smile curved the lieutenant's mustache,
and under his quizzical look Andreas smiled rather
consciously.

"You've learned the words, Rusty, but you
aren't much of an actor. You feel a trifle uncon-
vinced yourself, don't you?"

"Of course, that about her comfortable independence is all moonshine," admitted the ambassador
bluntly, although with desperate thoughts of Miss
Archer's displeasure; "but I say, Gerard," — he
looked up with sudden determination, — "don't be a
dog in the manger. Give me a show, won't you?"

Gerard changed his position, and his dreamy
eyes widened. "What?"

"I'm head over ears. I'm swamped. I'm
gone."

"What! You of the chronically 'honorable
but remote intentions'?"

"Yes; and they're deucedly remote now, but it
isn't my fault."

"Does she know it?" Gerard's pulses were
fluttering with new strivings to be free.

"Know it! *No!*"

"See here, old man, you needn't shout. Then
that is the explanation of your officiousness." Gerard fell into thought, and his companion did not

disturb him. At last he looked up. "Betty has evidently told you everything. I am going to ask you a question now that will be a strain on your honesty ; but answer it on your honor. Do you believe her decision irrevocable? Do you believe I cannot induce her to marry me? "

" I don't know *sure*," responded Russell, looking from one side to the other in a hunted way, which would have been comical to Gerard at another time. "But she *says* she isn't in love with you and does n't want to marry you. I urged her to stick to you; I did, for a fact. I believed then she really wanted you, you know."

Gerard looked away. " That would seem frank enough," he remarked. " I ask the question, Andreas," he went on after a second, " because I cannot feel as if any one would take such care of Betty as I should."

" Oh, get off the earth ! " retorted the other.

" I believe you would come next, though," and the young officer smiled ; the rigid lines of his face had slowly faded away.

" I mean to come next if a man's powers can compass it, — that is, I suppose you have no objection."

The two men looked at each other for an instant in silence as they rose ; then Gerard held out his hand, and Andreas was not slow to clasp it.

" Thank God it is you, Rusty," was the low response.

Poor Nathalie, strained and over-tired, longed
to creep to bed when the party at last reached
Edgewater, and her heart rebelled when Betty
caught her arm at the door.

"Don't go in yet," she said softly, for Mrs.
Archer had preceded them, and she feared to let
her hear. "I have something to tell you."

"But it is so late," objected Nathalie. Whatever Betty had to tell, she was sure she did not
wish to hear it.

"It won't take me long; and don't you always
want to talk over a party? Yo' mother is in yo'
room, and ma mother is in mine, and we can't have
any peace in the house. Beside, it is such a lovely
night, it is a shame to go in."

"Oh, you are going to stay out and smoke with
me! How kind!" said Andreas, seeing them
turn away from the door.

"Indeed we are not," returned Betty. "Who
ever heard of a man being admitted to an 'After
the Ball' conclave!"

"Oh, do let me," begged Russell effusively.
"I'll tell you all about my compliments, and how
the other fellows' coats were cut" —

But with a firm gesture of farewell, Betty led
her captive away.

The moon was low, and the great trees were still
beneath the star-set, velvet sky. In a remote
corner of the gallery Miss Archer found two chairs,
and ensconced her reluctant friend beside her.

"Did you enjoy it?" she asked.

"Not very much."

"Dear me!" returned Betty. "Did n't you like yo' partners?"

"Yes; the fault was wholly in myself. Sometimes I don't feel like dancing. I know this sounds ungracious; but you 're always so good to me, I know you will let me be honest. You see you would better have let me go to bed."

"No," confidentially, "because I did n't have a good time either."

"Indeed? I am sorry. I thought you were very gay."

"Oh," Betty repressed a yawn, "we girls can all smile and smile and be villains still, you know. I never have a good time if Roger does n't, and did n't you think he was out of sorts to-night?"

"I believe he was rather quiet."

"And I can tell you why. He is in a transition stage; and they are always so unpleasant, you know."

Nathalie made no comment.

"You don't seem very curious about our affairs." Betty smiled, and reaching over, squeezed her friend's hand. "But I 'm going to tell you about this little hard time I 'm having with Roger, because too many people believe we are engaged, and the sooner the truth is generally understood, the better. Now that we have arrived at years of discretion, we have discovered that neither of us has the slightest desire to marry the other; and yet, if you will believe it, that foolish boy won't agree that it is right fo' him to trust me to travel safely through life without him! Of course he will in the end ; but if you knew what Roger is, you would understand why he feels actually remorseful about the whole matter. It makes it mighty unpleasant fo' us both."

Nathalie leaned against the pillar, her heart beating almost to suffocation. Betty felt the impossibility it was to her to speak; so, looking out on the shadowy bay and feigning to repress another yawn, she continued after a little silence : —

" The worst is over, I reckon. Roger squeezed ma hand and smiled like his dear old self when he put me into the carriage to come home to-night. I felt certain that he had begun to look at the situation reasonably, and if so, Nathalie, you must congratulate me, for I shall feel as light-hearted as a bird."

" You deserve to be happy." Nathalie managed to utter the words, but in a rather breathless voice.

" Poor thing! Yo 're so sleepy," returned Betty, laughing. " I may as well let you go to bed while you can still understand what I 'm talking about."

She put her soft arms around her friend's neck and kissed her tenderly as they separated, and Nathalie hurried to her own room.

Hastening to the side of her sleeping mother,

she sat down on the edge of the bed in the dim light, and stooping over her, pressed her fresh cheek to hers.

Mrs. Dexter stirred.

"You home, Nathalie?"

"Yes, dear. You told me to wake you, and I would have had to, anyway. Can we go away to-morrow?"

The question made the mother alert at once. "Yes, indeed. You give up your experiment, then?"

"Oh, I am frightened, mother! Betty says it is all broken off."

"May we be forgiven!" ejaculated Mrs. Dexter, horrified.

"No, no, dear," the girl murmured with soft eagerness. "Betty confided in me. She does n't wish to marry him. She truly does n't."

"How can that be?"

"Yes, how can it! But it is true. I must believe her; and now I can't stay another day."

"Why — I don't see" —

"*Mother!*"

"Yes, yes; I suppose it would be hard. We will go, Nathalie."

CHAPTER XVIII.

THE Dexters' sudden departure made a stir the following day.

" It's not sportsmanlike for you to leave before I do, Miss Nathalie," said Andreas. "Just come out in the boat once more and row me about, to show that you have no hard feelings. I have still one pair of trousers that is n't shrunk quite to the knees."

"You make it very tempting," she answered. "Is n't it hard enough to leave Edgewater, anyway?"

Mother and daughter told all inquirers that they had received news which hurried them away; and only Betty Archer understood what this news was.

"I'm going to be very philosophical about this separation, Nathalie," she declared. "I feel it in ma bones that we shall meet again, and ma bones are exceptionally truthful."

"I hope your affairs will come out to your entire satisfaction," returned Nathalie, as composedly as she was able.

"You must leave some nice messages fo' Roger. "It's right strange he has n't been over this mo'ning."

"He told me last evening that his duties as officer of the day would keep him at the post," replied Nathalie. This fact had given her satisfaction and relief all through her hurried preparations. "You must give him our good-bys."

"And regrets, of co'se?" added demure Betty.

"Oh, of course."

And so, accompanied by a little concourse to the station, and laden with roses, the Dexters left Edgewater and Virginia, deeply regretted by all the company but Mrs. Archer, who moved with a lighter step and happier mien after their departure.

"It's a wonder that girl did n't go over to the post and hunt up Roger to say good-by," she remarked to Betty.

"It would have made him very happy if she had. I dread to tell him she has gone."

"Oh, you are such a dunce, Betty! It's the best thing that could happen to you to have her out of the way."

They had sat down on the piazza in cool shade after the warm walk to and from the train.

Betty braced herself for an avowal. It might as well come now as any time:

"I ought to tell you, Mrs. Archer, that I've at last told Roger ma wish that we should be brother and sister for evermore."

The older woman turned and scrutinized the girl alertly.

"Betty, don't be afraid to confide in me about

Mr. Andreas," she said tentatively. "It will be better for us both, I assure you."

"Mr. Andreas has nothing to do with the question. I wish you would believe it." The girl blushed in spite of herself, and her heart beat fast with distaste for this necessary ordeal. "If you have any regard fo' me," she added earnestly, "please try to take ma standpoint for a minute and listen to what I say. I used to believe that it would be right fo' me to marry Roger some time, but now I know it would be wrong. I did n't see it all at once. I had some pangs to bear, fo' I had been first with him so long; but in the mental struggle I have learned to understand ma own feelings, and it is of no use to argue, fo' it is clear to me as the light of day that a girl should have a sentiment fo' the man she marries totally different from any I 've ever felt fo' Roger Gerard."

Mrs. Archer eyed her shrewdly. "Yes; since knowing Mr. Andreas you have discovered all this!"

"Truly," exclaimed the distressed girl, — "truly he has nothing to do with the case."

Mrs. Archer gave a hard laugh. "I wish girls would once in a while tell the truth about these matters. Oh, well, I can apply to him, if you prefer."

"Would you be so unkind? That compels me to tell you that he has confided to me that he is in love with some one else."

The stepmother reddened. "Then he has behaved outrageously, Betty Archer! He has flirted with you till he has set every one talking. No wonder Roger relinquished you! But we will go to the poor boy together. We will tell him there is nothing in it, and he will take you back. It's ridiculous! It's wicked! You need n't think I shall sit tamely by and see you " —

But here Betty fled into the house, for the angry voice was rising, and she did not know who might be witnessing the scene.

At all events, it was over. The worst was passed. Roger was pacified, Nathalie enlightened, Mrs. Archer fully informed. The question of where Betty herself should live, and how, if her stepmother persisted in making Edgewater too uncomfortable for her, had yet to be met; and as her little paint-brush was the weapon she always thought of in possible battles with the world, she went to her painting-table now and began to work with energy, trying to forget all other thoughts in this interest.

But the storm without did not die down so quickly as she hoped it would. One victim of Mrs. Archer's indignation having escaped her, that lady looked about for another. She concluded there would be tangible satisfaction in a talk with Russell Andreas at the present juncture. Despite an undercurrent of fear of giving permanent offense to one of the best families, she could not resist her own craving to punish that exasperatingly irresponsible Free Lance.

She found him swinging in a hammock. In fact, he saw her first through the meshes of his couch, as she came with determined tread across the lawn, and he weighed the possibilities of decent escape with depressing results.

" Ye gods and little fishes ! I 'm in for it ! " he murmured. " Don't remember a thing about Philadelphia! I 've forgotten the whole outfit, from Independence Hall to the public buildings ! "

With prompt courtesy, all the same, he sprang from his couch. " Would n't you like this hammock, Mrs. Archer ? "

" I never get into a hammock," she responded, with a fierceness so disproportionate to the subject that the young man's jaw fell, and he sank upon the netting in a sitting posture and awaited developments.

Mrs. Archer took a rustic chair near him. " I have just been having the most surprising talk with my daughter Betty, Mr. Andreas."

" All right ! All right ! Come on, old lady ! " was the mental response which greeted this announcement, though outwardly Russell's countenance only composed itself, and he adopted an attitude of polite attention.

" She tells me her engagement to Roger is off."

Andreas bowed. " They have been kind enough to confide the fact to me." The cold and serious

formality into which the speaker seemed to freeze
had far from a cooling effect upon his interlocutor.

"He is your *friend*, I believe," she said, with
elaborate sarcasm.

"I believe so."

"And you believe also, no doubt, that you have
treated him well."

"Why?" asked Andreas, with exasperating
courtesy. "Don't you?"

Mrs. Archer emitted a scornful laugh. "People's standards differ. You have come here," she
began to glare at him again, "and have flirted with
his fiancée until he naturally believes that it is for
her happiness that he should give her up."

"Are n't you too excited to have full command
of yourself?" asked Russell with gentle suggestion. "Shall we not postpone this interview —
indefinitely?"

"No doubt you would like to. What are girls'
hearts to a man like you? Thanks to you, Betty
may be a struggling old maid all her life."

A darkness overspread the young man's face.
"Be kind enough not to speak of Miss Archer in
a cheapening manner."

"Indeed! I shall not ask you how I may speak
of her!"

"Yes, you will." The answer was so quick, and
the insouciant manner had changed to an attitude
so masterful, that Mrs. Archer could not retort at
once for surprise, nor could she drop her gaze from
the eyes that held her.

"You will speak of her with respect, or you will have no listener in me."

She still stared, fascinated.

"There are two people in the world to whom Miss Archer's happiness is of supreme importance. One is Roger Gerard and the other is myself. Do you suppose we are going to permit you to make her wretched, if she chooses to call her heart her own as well as her soul? From now on you will be accountable to us for every word and action concerning her."

Mrs. Archer caught her breath. "Well! Perhaps you will tell me by what right *you* interfere!" she ejaculated.

Andreas looked out to the creek frowningly, and drew his lips together in a meditative, noiseless whistle.

At last he faced her again. "Perhaps it would be better all around if I should," he answered. "My right arises from the fact that I love Miss Archer."

"As a brother, I suppose," responded the other with a sneer.

Andreas was looking off again. An irrepressible long breath rose in his throat.

"No," he answered, "not as a brother."

Mrs. Archer started and actually paled in a revulsion of feeling. What would she not give to undo the work of the past fifteen minutes! "She believes you care for some one else," she said faintly, after a stunned silence.

"I know she does. Do not undeceive her. I am capable of managing this affair, if you will have the goodness to permit me, and I shall try to take my failure decently if it comes. I am sorry to be discourteous, but the greatest favor you can do to all parties now is to efface yourself so far as circumstances will permit."

Mrs. Archer rose, too humiliated even for anger. "I attacked you under a misunderstanding," she said miserably.

"I know you did."

She waited undecidedly. It was all like a bad dream. How she would have enjoyed the position of welcoming this man graciously as a son! And here she was reduced to standing before him as a culprit, — before him, an Andreas!

"I suppose you won't shake hands with me?" she said, after a short, painful silence.

He had risen when she did.

"It would be as well to wait, perhaps," he answered, with a slight inclination of the head. "Let us see what the future brings forth."

Tingling with mortification, she turned and went back to the house.

"Betty, I feel ill," she said abruptly, entering the studio. "I've a raging headache."

The girl instantly pushed back her chair and rose with a look of concern.

Her stepmother did indeed appear to be suffering. In a minute more the girl had made her lie down, covered her lightly, and was smoothing her forehead with cool fingers.

Mrs. Archer lay with closed eyes, while Betty wondered at her passivity, for it was not thus that her stepmother usually bore physical pain.

From time to time the prostrate woman opened her eyes and looked off into space, and once she thanked Betty for her ministrations.

"She must be going to be dangerously ill," thought the girl, amazed.

"I'm afraid yo're worrying very much about Roger and me," she said timidly.

- The gentleness of her tone falling upon Mrs. Archer's harrowed feelings brought that lady nearer to shame and contrition than she had been for years. In her crushed condition it would have been a relief to confess all to the kind young girl, but she did not dare. Russell's strong face seemed still commanding her to efface herself.

"No, it isn't that. You and Roger are of age. You must settle your affairs between yourselves," she returned.

And in the alarm created by this stingless reply, Betty began casting about in her mind as to what doctor had better be sent for.

But it proved that Mrs. Archer did not require a physician. She soon rose from her bed, but with a passive and colorless demeanor astonishing to behold.

"Do you believe in sudden conversion?" asked

Betty of Andreas, as the two were on their way to
parade that afternoon. Miss Archer wished to be
the one to break the news to Gerard of Nathalie's
departure.

" Why? " returned her escort. " Has Junius got
'em again ? "

" Mr. Andreas ! "

" You need n't be horrified. Life would be a
dreary waste to Junius without his semi-annual
conversion."

" Well, it is n't Junius. It 's Mrs. Archer. I 'm
right frightened about her."

"More apt to be apoplexy than religion in her
case, is n't it ? "

" Why, Mr. Andreas ! She 'd be so shocked if
she heard you that her crimps would stand on end!
She had a regular tantrum this morning about
Roger and me, and now suddenly she seems just as
gentle as a lamb."

"Quite a relief sometimes when the wolf bor-
rows the sheep's togs, is n't it? " returned Andreas,
laughing heartily. It touched his sense of humor
irresistibly to picture the erstwhile virago amazing
Betty with her change of heart.

" Why, if she would be all the time like this,
we could have a right peaceful life," said the girl,
with such naïve wistfulness that Russell stopped
laughing and his eyes grew tender.

" I wonder if you suspect what a nice girl you
are," he said.

"The idea!" She laughed in her turn. "I don't know why it is, but you always seem to be getting a false impression of me, Mr. Andreas. I reckon if you saw me in some moods you'd change yo' mind. Roger could tell you — but he never will, that's one comfort."

They were walking instead of riding to the Fort to-day, and they moved along the quiet road in silence for a time.

"But I've been wishing," she went on shyly, "if you don't mind, that you'd tell me a little more about *the* girl, — if you really don't *mind*."

"I don't in the least," replied Russell promptly.

"I thought perhaps you might *like* to talk about her, you know."

"I do; but I didn't want to bore you."

"I *thought* perhaps that was it." Betty looked up at him with a smile, and was faintly surprised to find that he, too, was smiling. It would have seemed more fitting to find his countenance overspread with a fine melancholy.

Miss Archer's eyes were good, and she was an artist. She had observed the fact that nature had so arranged Russell Andreas's countenance that all the expressions she had so far caught were becoming to it.

Perhaps he discerned her present critical thought. At all events, he composed his features as he began : —

"She is a rather tall girl."

"That is good. Large men ought not to marry tiny girls, as they so often do, and leave the tall girls to short men."

"But she is slender and graceful, and has n't the effect of largeness. There is a sort of bright softness about her altogether, even to her voice; and her manners and movements, — well, to me they are simply perfection."

"She must be lovely," said Miss Archer thoughtfully.

"Hard not to be able to get her, eh?"

"Hard!" The girl looked up at him sympathetically. "But you have n't told me how she looks yet."

"No, I 'm afraid I can't. In the first place, I fancy she does n't look to any one else as she does to me; and, in the second, I can't describe a spirit, and that is what I see in the depths of her eyes and the expression of her lips."

"How beautifully you love her!" said Betty gently. "If only there were any other obstacle except the one you mentioned."

"A wonderful thing has happened," said Andreas, his eyes fixed on the road and his face grave enough now. "Since the night I talked to you about it I have heard that my rival is no more. Moreover, I 've good reason to believe that she was not so deeply attached to him as I thought."

"Why, Mr. Andreas!"

"But she does n't care for me. How does that alter matters?"

"But she *will* care for you. Give her a little time. Surely you cannot love her in this way for nothing!"

"Bless you for those words! But what would my next step better be? Would you tell her frankly — tell her all — at once?"

"N-no." Betty shook her head judicially. "Give her time to stop thinking about the other one."

"But I must bring myself to her notice in some way."

"Yes — you" — Russell, watching her narrowly and looking for a straw to cling to, saw her face change. "I reckon it would be better fo' you to go and stay where she is as long as you can," the girl answered slowly.

There was a ringing in Andreas's ears. She disliked the thought of his going! A blind man might discern it. It was a trifling indication, but it was something.

He crushed down his elation. "Thank you," he said briefly. "I'll see how business turns. I wonder what took the Dexters off in such a hurry?"

"They had to go." Miss Archer sighed. "What will Roger say?"

This action of the Dexters had removed the last doubt from Betty's mind as to Nathalie's attitude toward Gerard; but as yet she had not come to a peaceful hour with leisure to cogitate upon the pleasant certainty of Roger's future; and now an unexplained quietness, almost depression, fell upon her spirits, and she allowed her companion to monopolize the conversation until the Fort was reached.

It was a new Roger, or rather the old one, assured, calm, with smiling eyes, who came to greet them under the live-oaks.

The reassurance and pleasure that Betty was conscious she ought to experience in seeing him thus rehabilitated failed to swell her heart.

" Mr. Andreas thinks I 'm such a nice girl. He ought to see into ma mean soul now," she thought. " Just as soon as I find out that other people are right happy and don't need me, I begin to mope !" And with this bracing reflection she smiled upon Roger as she put her hand in his. Andreas strolled out of earshot, according to her previous instructions.

" No, she did n't come with us," she answered to the lieutenant's question. " The fact is, she has gone away."

Gerard's hand fell unconsciously on the hilt of his sword, and he looked stern in his surprise.

" Certainly I 'll give you satisfaction, if you 'll let me have the choice of weapons. I 'm partial to mahl-sticks maself."

" This is a great surprise," said Gerard, trying to recover himself. " Miss Dexter of course did not know of it last evening."

" Not until very late in the evening."

"They received some sudden news?"

"Yes, Nathalie did — from me."

Miss Archer's smiling face, trying hard for its usual demureness, was enigmatical. The band was playing loudly as it marched after the even gait of the drum-major. By the way, government should make an appropriation, if necessary, in order that the field-musicians of Fortress Monroe need not have so forlornly meagre a repertoire.

Gerard felt an added irritation in the proximity of the band just now with its well-worn chords.

"Please don't give me any conundrums, Betty," he said.

"Confess, then, that it is an important matter to you."

He looked at her dumbly.

"You will have to, some time, Roger, if things are with you as I think; and I don't want to make any blunders." The mischief had died from her sweet face, and her eyes interrogated him affectionately.

"No one can take your place. You understand that," he said at last.

"I should think not," she returned gayly. "As Mr. Andreas says, 'not if I see her first!' But," she lowered her voice, "it is that other place we are talking about."

"Then I do confess it, Betty!" They exchanged a brief hand-clasp, much to the delectation of a sixteen-year-old girl near by, who was much divided between parade and the eyes of the officer of the day, and thereafter allowed the ranks of artillery-men to present, port, or carry arms without her, while she attended to that lucky girl's delightful flirtation.

"It is fortunate fo' you that ma tongue is not tied by any confidences on her part," said Betty.

The officer shook his head humbly. "There were none to make. I am afraid she cares only for her music. Why should she think of me?"

"I could find a few reasons, if I took time to it, I fancy; but she thought, like everybody else, that you were bespoken,—until last night. When we came home from the dance I told her how things really were." Miss Archer's eyes were eloquent, as she nodded impressively.

"Well?"

"Well, it frightened Miss Muffet away."

"But why should it?" earnestly.

Betty laughed. "I don't know. Do you? Girls are n't very often afraid of military men."

"And why should she be afraid of me?" asked Gerard, much perplexed; and the question furnished his companion so much amusement that the sixteen-year-old decided that Roger must be as witty as he was handsome.

"She did n't say she was," returned the girl at last. "On the contrary, she left her good-by and her regrets just as politely as possible, and never mentioned being afraid."

"Why *do* you think it is so funny?" pleaded the lieutenant plaintively.

"Honestly, Roger, I wonder how any man manages his own love-affair unless he has some woman to help him! I 'm as sure as possible that if it were n't fo' me you would take her running off so as a discouraging sign."

"Indeed I should. And why don't you?"

"Because," Betty gave him a wise nod, "that is precisely what I should have done in her place. Suppose she believes she cares for a man who does n't care fo' her?"

"Do you think she could imagine that?" And as Roger uttered the exclamation Miss Archer saw for the first time a flash of what those eyes of his could express.

"Of course, dear. Have you forgotten your own loyalty?"

"I see. I 'm unbalanced. I have lost count of common sense as well as time of late. Betty," with sudden grateful fervor, "you trump, you sister, you angel!"

"Ahem!" coughed Andreas behind his hand. He had come up in time to hear the close of this apostrophe; and the sixteen-year-old, who had just succeeded in getting her attention back to parade, began to experience all the delicious despair induced by a three-ringed circus.

"Come back, come back!" laughed Betty, as Russell turned away. "Roger is only practicing on me."

Andreas was anxious for an opportunity to speak with his friend alone, and a little later it came. Betty recognized an acquaintance whom she wished to greet, and the two men were left to themselves.

"Well, how goes it, Rusty?" asked the lieutenant.

"Don't know. I am thinking of following Miss Dexter's example. I 've been hanging about here some time. Now I think I 'll see if out of sight proves to be out of mind."

"And supposing it does!"

"Supposing it does?" Andreas gave an exclamation. "Then you can wager your existence I will get back into sight in short order."

"Want me to keep you posted?"

Russell smiled. "Do you fancy you would find out anything? Well, you are green!"

This jeer appeared to please Gerard. He looked thoughtfully off into space. "I believe I am, Rusty; I hope I am."

"That is a modest ambition, I 'm sure," returned the other; "but I think I understand. I know you 're in the same boat with me. I never should have found it out, though, if it had n't been for Miss Archer Archer."

"She is a wonderful girl," observed Gerard, with conviction.

"Now you 're talking," returned his friend.

"This is a queer business, Rusty." The lieutenant's voice expressed perplexity, even awe. "This being captured heart and soul by another human being is a very queer business."

"I'm finding it so. With Mr. Gilbert, —

> 'The pain that is almost a pleasure I'd change
> For the pleasure that's almost pain,'

if I had the chance. But that will be as the wonderful girl decrees. Don't make the mistake of trying to help me in this, Roger. Hands off, please. You'd make a mess of it."

"I'm sure I should," agreed Gerard with much humility. "Rusty, would you mind telling me," the speaker's eyes expressed the gravest interrogation, "how it happened that you did n't fall in love with Miss Dexter?"

Andreas smiled broadly and gestured with his head toward a great live-oak beneath which Betty and her friend were talking. "There's the reason."

"But up at the Pulpit? Betty was n't there."

"I don't know. Too much Owski, perhaps; or perhaps your good angel was holding my eyes. I suspect, though, that I had taken one too many voyages up the Potomac."

"You did n't know it then, though."

"Not a bit of it. I considered myself fireproof. Oh, see here! Mrs. Archer has been bullyragging the wonderful girl on your account."

"I feared that," said Gerard, his far-away look

suddenly focusing itself on his friend's face with an alert expression.

"And after laying her low she came out under the trees and executed a war-dance around me."

"On what score?"

"On the score of making you jealous." Andreas smiled appreciatively.

"I did try to be jealous of you," said Gerard, with such seriousness that his friend laughed aloud.

The lieutenant paid no attention to his mirth. "I must settle all that. I shall have to have a talk with Mrs. Archer."

"No need of it. I have forestalled you. If you want to see a middle-aged lady of florid complexion enacting the rôle of Mary's little lamb, come over to Edgewater."

"How did you do it?"

"Oh, represented you and myself as guardians of Miss Archer Archer's peace, and then tried her own weapons. Bullied her, in fact. Took away her tomahawk, twitched her war-lock, and generally browbeat her."

"Good. But will it last?"

"I think so. I'm going to leave you on guard for a month, and then perhaps I shall come back. Miss Archer Archer knows nothing of the *modus*, and therefore is almost frightened by the metamorphosis in her stepmother. Don't tell her anything. Here she comes now, so look pleasant, and wink as much as you please."

CHAPTER XIX.

A MIGRATION.

DEAR MRS. DEXTER, — It 's only two weeks since that pleasant morning when you and Nathalie went away, but it seems *much* longer.· I have missed you *more* than I can *tell*. To make things more lonely still, Mr. Andreas left us a couple of days after you did. His departure was *sudden*, like yours, but he had *good* reasons for *going*, and I was glad to see him do his *duty*, though I 'm sure he *hated* to leave. He is a very *fine* young *man*, I think, though light in his talk.

I have some sad news that will surprise you. Miss Betty's engagement to Mr. Gerard is *broken*. They don't act as if it was sad to them, though it can't be denied they are *quieter* in their ways, Miss Betty especially ; but that is only respectful to the past, as I look at it. However they feel, it evidently has been a crushing *blow* to Mrs. Archer. She don't act like the same woman. If she should rear and tear around I would n't be surprised, but she 's so *quiet* and *peaceable*, I don't know what to make of it. Sometimes I wonder if Mr. Gerard has n't *scared* her into not saying anything ; for she *feels* it just as *sure* as this *world*. He comes over here just the same, and smiles as pleasant as ever when he says " good-evening " at three o'clock in the afternoon. There are some Southern ways that will always seem *queer* to *me*.

If I was Betty Archer, I should about lose my *reason* to lose *him*. I shall always like red stripes for his sake. He's got the nicest *ways* and *looks* ever I saw. He's the kind of man would make a woman happy, if she had to live alone with him on top of *Pike's Peak*. And yet Miss Betty paints away as calm as ever, and *laughs* with him as *hearty* as if everything was all right. He don't seem worried a mite, either. It beàts me; and it's just knocked Mrs. Archer — I was going to use slang and say *silly*, but I won't, I'll say *decent*, for she is real decent, and don't poke her nose into anything.

I haven't made up my mind yet whether I shall come North this summer. Most likely I could if I wanted to. Business will be light here.

I wish you and Nathalie could make a plan to come again. I did *enjoy* your being here.

Shall always be *pleased* to get a line from you. Don't let Nathalie practice too *much* in the *warm weather*.   Always your friend,

PRISCILLA TOOTHAKER.

This letter found the Dexters at a hotel in Boston. Mrs. Dexter read it and passed it to Nathalie in silence. Then she broke the seal of another and read it while her daughter was absorbing Miss Priscilla's underscored sentences.

" That is good advice, — not to let you work too hard this summer," said Mrs. Dexter when the girl finally looked up ; " and what do you suppose I have here? A note from Cousin Rebecca, who says that at the last minute another summer at her dear cottage is slipping through her fingers. She cannot go to Pulpit Point, and offers the cottage to us."

Nathalie's face brightened. "Let us accept it."

Mrs. Dexter looked doubtful, and though she did not speak, Nathalie read her thoughts.

" Mr. Andreas invited his friend in my hearing to come there," she explained calmly, " and Mr. Gerard refused. He said he could not get another leave this summer."

" But the associations?" suggested Mrs. Dexter gently.

Her daughter approached and kissed her. " You are too tender of me, mother dear. Are you worrying about me ? "

" I am a little."

" But I 'm not pining." Nathalie slipped down on her knees and looked smiling into her mother's eyes. "I am glad of all that has come to me, and you must not regret it either. To think of seeing the Pulpit again, and Cap'n Levi — and with *you !* We will be so happy ! "

·And Mrs. Dexter, cheered by this spontaneous

burst, hoped that the zest of life was returning to them both.

Nathalie had written once to Betty Archer since leaving Edgewater, and received a prompt reply; but she had not written again. She was through with Virginia and Virginians. She knew she could not forget the two who had entered so deeply into her life, and she felt that no other man or woman could ever so touch the quick of her affections; but she longed that the sensitiveness of her memory might be deadened by time. She would do nothing to keep it vivid.

Roger Gerard had made no sign since last she saw him. If she had vaguely hoped for a different effect of her flight, she had given no expression either to the expectation or the disappointment.

It was early in July that mother and daughter took possession of the cottage at Pulpit Point. Nathalie, ignoring the dull throbs of feeling that sights and sounds evoked, seized Mrs. Dexter's hand and drew her from window to window to exclaim over the noble views. She pointed out the Andreas cottage; she led her mother over hummock and through pitfall down to the Pulpit and made her mount its height; and she proudly exhibited Cap'n Levi.

" What ye done with Miss Toothaker? " asked the captain after the greetings had passed.

" Left her down South among the roses," replied Nathalie.

" That 's clever," remarked the old man. If he felt that life would have been quite as peaceful had Nathalie also remained among the roses, he did not let it appear. Her pleasure was disarming, even though he foresaw another piano-moving.

" Nawthin' but wild roses he-ar," he continued.

" They 're good enough for me," she responded gayly.

Nevertheless, she was struck with the bleakness and barrenness of Pulpit Point after the luxuriant vegetation of Edgewater.

The crisp, salt coolness of the air here smote her cheek, and she recalled the simile Miss Toothaker had used one morning in the pavilion.

" As much difference in this air and the Pulpit's as between a banana and a cucumber," she had said.

The moon used to rise at Edgewater behind massive boughs, through which the silvery water gleamed. Here nothing intervened between sea and rugged shore.

" This is the tonic I need," thought Nathalie. " It is my native heath. The balsam fir is better for me than the magnolia. I need bay instead of roses. I am a wiser girl than I was a year ago."

The whole of that first day she was occupied in recalling her gaze from the large boulder at the right of the house.

" Very well," she said to herself at last, with determination, " I will break that spell." Then she walked deliberately to the boulder in the sunset light, and rested her hand on its lichens.

At her feet on its further side was a strip of grass a few feet wide and the length of a man, different in color and depth from the surrounding verdure. Her heart beat in unexpected tumult.

"It is as if it were a grave," she thought; "and it is — it is a grave!"

There was a sudden rush of tears to her eyes, and she turned in the sunset glow and hurried back toward the house.

Her mother from her stand on the piazza was watching her.

"Run down to that bay bush and bring me a bunch of it, will you, dear?" she called to the girl.

Of all mind-readers, mothers are the least apt to be mistaken.

There was plenty to do to put the cottage in order, and Nathalie knew where everything was, for she and Miss Toothaker had put all away.

On the second busy day she was arranging bric-abrac in the living-room, when a familiar voice at the door cried : —

."Hello the house!"

"Already!" Nathalie turned her pleased face and greeted Russell Andreas, who seemed to fill the room as he came into it.

"How do you do, Miss Nathalie? How do you do, Mrs. Dexter?" He shook hands with them both, and the three seated themselves in a group.

"I was delighted to hear you were at the Pulpit again. You must be kind to my mother, Mrs. Dexter. She does n't get out, and I want her to know you. You will do her lots of good. It seems as if Miss Pris ought to be about here somewhere, does n't it? Do you hear from her?"

"We have had one letter," replied Mrs. Dexter, "but she speaks as if she might stay in Virginia."

"Indeed?" Andreas turned toward Nathalie. "And what is the latest from Miss Archer Archer?"

"The latest and earliest are one. We have only exchanged one little letter since we parted. I'm afraid neither of us likes to write."

Nathalie wondered how much feeling lay behind the bright attentiveness of his countenance. It had occurred to her that this young man might have had an influence in Betty Archer's love affair.

The sight of him now in his outing clothes recalled last summer too vividly. She was sorry he had come; sorry he would make her task of forgetting so much harder. Each moment she was dreading, yet longing, to hear him mention Gerard. The only reference that had been made to him since she came North was the little sentence in Betty's letter which mentioned Roger's regret at her sudden disappearance. Amiable, courteous Betty could not have said less.

"Oh, I'm disappointed in you, Miss Nathalie," said Andreas. "I was hoping you would be the

tie that binds the North to the South. Gerard
and I have for a long time relied on the philosophy
of thought transference for our communications."

"You are such a transcendental creature," remarked Nathalie.

"Don't laugh at me. Remember how sensitive
my feelings are. Then I'm afraid you can't help
me either, Mrs. Dexter. I fear you cannot give
me news of my valued friend, Mrs. Archer."

Mrs. Dexter smiled. "I fear I can't except
at second-hand. Miss Toothaker says she is — is
improving."

"Did any one think there was room for improvement?" asked Russell. "As I say, I am far from
being a complete letter-writer; but when it came
to separation from Mrs. Archer, I discovered that
indeed 'Love will find a way.' I gathered myself
together for a mighty effort, and I wrote her a
letter."

"Indeed? Did she reply?"

"Reply?" Andreas smiled consciously upon
Mrs. Dexter, then lowered his eyes and bit his lip
in coy embarrassment. "You evidently do not
comprehend the state of affairs between Mrs.
Archer and me. She did indeed reply, — beguiling
creature, — since when I have written her again."

"A remarkable case of devotion," said Nathalie.
"It would be interesting to know what you are
after."

Andreas regarded her reproachfully. "Is it

difficult to see what I was after? I have been asking Mrs. Archer to come to the Pulpit. I want to stray with her in the forest, to guide her steps down the rocky ravines; to support her delicate form among the rioting waves. I must, to be happy, — I must have Mrs. Archer here during the next moon, to sit with her, shielded from the wind, among the rocky ledges, and watch the masses of white foam break at our feet."

"And your mother so delicate!" said Nathalie accusingly.

Andreas smiled rather guiltily. "She can stand it for a fortnight. Beside, my dear ladies both," with new courage, "you have never seen Mrs. Archer on her good behavior. You remember what Miss Pris told you of her improvement? Well, I did that, all with my little hatchet. I assure you with pardonable pride that I accomplished that reform!"

"What did you do, Mr. Andreas?" asked Nathalie, with lively interest.

He gave her an impressive look. "As if I should tell any one! Why, supposing the missionary societies were to get hold of it: do you suppose I should be allowed to remain in the insurance business? Not a day! I should be packed off bag and baggage among the savages, where my humanizing powers could have scope."

Nathalie gazed at him thoughtfully. "Do you believe Betty will come?"

" Betty ? "   Mr. Andreas frowned and appeared to tax his memory. " Betty? Oh, yes! I remember now. Mrs. Archer has a stepdaughter. Yes, I think if my friend comes she will bring Miss Archer Archer. It would n't be exactly safe to leave her at home."

"Not safe for Mrs. Archer, surely," remarked Miss Dexter dryly.

When Russell had by slow and easy stages finally left mother and daughter by themselves, Mrs. Dexter spoke : —

" There, you see, Nathalie ! "

" But I don't mind," returned the girl quickly. "Mr. Andreas will absorb Betty. I shall have my practicing. It will only be for two weeks."

" Perhaps. I think this looks decidedly as if dear Betty had a new lover."

Nathalie's piano came soon, and she threw herself into her work again with abandon, and conscious of her mother's devoted espionage, she assumed a cheerfulness and interest in the small happenings of their daily life which served a double purpose ; for Mrs. Dexter became more and more reassured, and we all know that conscientiously to assume a virtue, even if one has it not, brings that virtue ever nearer.

One day Russell broke in upon her practicing, some excitement changing his ordinarily imperturbable manner.

" She is coming this morning ! " he exclaimed.

Nathalie wheeled around on the stool. "Oh, yes," she smiled at him. "Mrs. Archer."

"Yes. Won't you go to the boat with me? You know mother" —

"Certainly I will be your mother *pro tem.*; but would n't you rather have mine? It would be more appropriate, would n't it — to meet Mrs. Archer, you know?"

So Nathalie laughingly set out with the expectant young. man, who would have been very much surprised to suspect with what effort she was steeling herself for this meeting. And she again would have been all sympathy had she known the palpitation that was agitating Betty's breast out there on the steamer, already plainly visible, threading its way among the islands of Casco Bay.

The girl was half ill with the excitement of her novel journey and its goal. Her stepmother had had to use considerable persuasion to convince her that this trip was feasible and best; but ably aided by Roger, she had carried the day after the reception of a touching note from Mrs. Andreas, who called herself one of the "shut-ins" and expressed a keen longing to know her son's friends.

Mrs. Archer's walk and conversation had continued so placable that Betty never ceased to marvel and be glad; but now, with the shores of Pulpit Point indicated to her, she turned to her stepmother for a last warning, which she did not dare to neglect.

"You used to feel quite strongly about Mr. Andreas's attentions to me," she said. "I feel as if I cert'nly ought to remind you again that he is very devoted to another girl. I have an idea that the chief reason he is glad to have me come is to talk to me about her. It's natural he shouldn't like to write it."

And Mrs. Archer, on her way to be a guest beneath the roof of an Andreas, and secure in her knowledge, was doubly intrenched in good behavior, and made answer most soothing: —

"I understand quite well, my dear. Don't fear that I shall disturb you in any way."

Nathalie and Russell were ready with waving handkerchiefs as soon as the passengers' faces were distinguishable; and the length of time it took for the boat to make her landing seemed more tedious than usual.

To Nathalie's fancy there was something exotic about Betty's sweet, grave face, so far from its proper environment. The road had never looked so grim, the hill so bare. Cap'n Levi's voice had never sounded so strident; but while Miss Archer Archer evidently wondered, it was with an eager interest.

"I reckon still it's all a dream," she said, as at last Nathalie embraced her.

Andreas gave a quick, low bow and a hand-shake to his elder guest; and then Miss Dexter discovered that it was indeed Mrs. Archer she had come to meet, and she passively allowed herself to be packed into Cap'n Levi's wagon with her erstwhile foe and started off, while Russell and Betty walked slowly up the hill.

"This is so good of you," he said with satisfaction. "Now suspend all judgment of us till you get to the cottages. We're not pretty; we are grand."

"Yo're still our modest Mr. Andreas," she answered.

He stepped to the roadside and gathered a handful of the large daisies that abounded.

"Even the daisies aren't modest here," he replied, as he offered them to her. "So what can you expect?"

She tucked the blossoms in her belt and looked about her. "This is all so different. I cert'nly am in a new world."

"I hope it will be a satisfactory one."

"We think you were very, very good to ask us, — so does Roger; but I know I have a charm fo' you. I'm yo' confidante-in-chief, am I not?"

She gave him a quick smile and turn of the head.

"Yes. Oh, yes."

"I suppose you have lots to tell me."

"I have that." Andreas heaved an involuntary sigh, and then he smiled down upon her. "But I'll let you get your bearings first. We have plenty of time, — plenty of time."

CHAPTER XX

BESIDE THE BOULDER.

MRS. DEXTER and Nathalie met a number of domestic problems, which could so well be solved by Miss Toothaker's presence that that efficient person was finally summoned, and so managed her affairs that a very few days after the reception of Mrs. Dexter's telegram, she was again moving about the cottage at Pulpit Point.

"I declare for it, don't time fly?" she demanded of Nathalie. "Who'd think 't was a year since Mr. Gerard fenced that grass for me! Hasn't it come up good this year? It does seem a shame he shouldn't be here now. He's the only one lackin'."

Of course Russell Andreas was early in his welcome of the housekeeper.

"Well!" she exclaimed, as she came one morning to the kitchen window, where he had paused.

"I knew where to find my charmer," he said, removing his cap and putting in his hand to take the loose and brief shake Miss Toothaker accorded him.

"Ain't this great? I didn't much think when the Archers started off I'd be followin' 'em up so close," she remarked, smiling.

" You must excuse my not being at the dock to welcome you, Miss Pris, but Miss Archer and I were away fishing just at the time of your arrival."

" Oh, you were, were you? How 's Mrs. Archer? Broke loose yet? "

Russell grinned broadly. " I can't think what you mean by referring in such terms to the mildest-mannered lady of my acquaintance."

" I know. Mild as a moonbeam, ain't she? Well, it gets me. All I could think of when she turned around so was that place in my grandmother's primer where it told about

> ' Young Obadias,
> David, and Josias,
> All was pious.'

That woman 's got somethin' possessin' her mind; and I don't believe it 's religion. Just as sure as you 're standin' there, Mr. Gerard could tell what it is if he wanted to ; " and Miss Toothaker gave a nod and a prodigious wink which contorted the whole left side of her face.

" You think he tamed the shrew? "

" I do." Miss Priscilla stood regarding her handsome visitor, her hand on her hip. " See here, Mr. Andreas! I have n't got chick nor child, nor even folks, much of any, that belong to me. 'T ain't wonderful if I think a good deal about Nathalie and Miss Betty and you, is it? I 've thought a number o' times o' the way I talked to you under the locust-tree that day, and I 've de-

sired to speak of it. When that engagement —
melted, as you might say, — there did n't seem to be
much break about it, — so soon after you 'd gone,
I seemed to myself pretty meddlesome. What
earthly good did your goin' do ; and what call did
I have to put in my oar, anyway ? Have you forgiven me ? "

" Of course, Miss Pris. You did quite right."

" Ain't you clever ! " returned Miss Toothaker
gratefully. " When you sent down for the Archers," she went on, " I made sure Mrs. Archer would
sort o' act up — she was so down on you that spell
when she tackled me in the butt'ry ; but instead o'
r'arin', she was as pleased as Punch; and 1 must
say, Mr. Andreas, though it may sound pryin',
your sendin' for 'em *did* look pointed to me; it
did so."

" I want to know, Miss Pris ! "

" You 're laughin' at me. Well, laugh away.
But I ain't the fool I look ; and I 'm goin' to warn
you right here and now that madam has her eye
on you ! "

" Not this minute ! "

" Her mind's eye, yes. You see, what worries
me is that Miss Betty evidently ain't the marryin'
kind ; 'cause a girl that could have Mr. Gerard
and did n't " —

" Look here, Miss Pris, you will drive me to do
Gerard a bodily hurt."

Miss Toothaker waved the interruption aside.

— " she evidently don't want to *be* married. Now, I said to myself when you sent for the Archers, ' Mr. Andreas maybe don't mean anything by this invitation, or maybe he does ; ' 'cause of course I know that some time when you try to flirt your wings as usual and fly away, you 're goin' to find yourself held tight and fast, and you 'll realize you 're *caught*. Well, as I was sayin', I thought maybe you was caught now, and maybe you was n't ; but I saw Mrs. Archer calc'lated you *was*. And, Mr. Andreas, you listen to me." Miss Priscilla gestured impressively. " If nothin' comes o' this fishin', and sailin', and walkin', you 've begun on now, you 're goin' to see one o' the biggest backslides from reform that ever was known in this world. It 'll be a reg'lar *landslide*, — Mrs. Archer's will. I don't care whether it 's your fault, or whether it 's Miss Betty's, the result will be the same."

" Miss Pris, you grieve and terrify me. Perhaps you will tell me what your penetration discovered in Miss Archer's manner on the reception of my mother's invitation ? "

" Yes, I will. I think it 's only right I should. I discovered a good deal of reluctance ; yes, sir. That girl will have a good time now she 's here ; but I can tell you Mrs. Archer pulled, and Mr. Gerard shoved well, before they could get her out of Edgewater."

Andreas looked genuinely disconcerted.

"I say!" he returned. "You don't spare a fellow's vanity."

"Well, a girl who would n't have Mr. Gerard"—

"Oh"— Andreas swung away from the window, and the latter part of his ejaculation was indistinct as he strode away.

Miss Toothaker started in a listening attitude, and pursed up her lips in horror. "I *think* that was a very bad word," she murmured. After a minute she turned to the stove and ladled out some hot water into a pan in the sink, and a smile stole gradually over her face.

"He's in earnest!" she said, with a little nod.

She stooped and opened the oven door. "As if I did n't know why Betty Archer hung back about comin'!" Here she poked the loaves of cake therein with a broom straw; but the operation seemed to tickle her more than it did them, for she threw back her head in a noiseless laugh.

Several quiet days passed by, very happily to Miss Priscilla, who especially enjoyed making people comfortable whom she loved as she did the Dexters.

"It's interestin' to watch the changes that take place in young folks," she said one day to Mrs. Dexter. "Nathalie's just as different from what she was a year ago as can be."

"In what way?" asked the mother quickly.

"We-ell — it's hard tellin'. She's quieter and sweeter — oh, riper, you know."

" You like the change, then ? "

" Yes, I like it. I liked her when she was friskier, too. How her heart is all wrapped up in her music! It does seem 's if she begrudged goin' off with Mr. Andreas and Miss Betty; but Miss Betty just won't take ' No ' for an answer." Miss Toothaker nudged her companion and lowered her voice. " There 's safety in numbers, you know ; " and then she winked in a knowing manner that made Mrs. Dexter smile.

" I see ; but it is scarcely pleasant for Nathalie sometimes, although she says Mr. Andreas is always jolly and cordial. Ah, here you are, my dear," as Nathalie entered the room, flushed from a long walk. " We were just speaking of you."

" Yes," said Miss Priscilla. " I think it is an excellent thing that Miss Betty is here to keep you away from the piano so much. This is vacation."

Nathalie smiled, and proceeded to hang her cap in a curtained corner of the room. " I have told them not to dare come near me this afternoon," she announced. " They are the worst thieves of time I ever knew. I can't study, I can't read, I can't practice ; and in short, I have struck."

" It has been fine for you," returned her mother. " I am not afraid of your being too lazy."

" I 'm so hungry, Miss Priscilla! Where 's dinner ? "

" 'Most ready. Corned cod and drawn butter, and blueberry pie."

"Oh, fine! Meanwhile I'll get some ginger ale." Nathalie disappeared into the cellar and shortly returned with several small bottles, which she took to the primitive sideboard in the living-room, and emptied, hissing, into glasses.

"Here, Miss Priscilla!" she called; and the housekeeper, a clean towel over her arm, came in to join her.

"Prosit!" said Nathalie, waving her own brimming glass toward the others.

"Here's prosperity to Mr. Andreas," suggested Mrs. Dexter.

"Agreed!" replied Nathalie.

"All right," said Miss Toothaker; "but I'm goin' to drink to Mr. Gerard, all alone down there in Virginia."

"It's a touching case of loneliness," remarked Nathalie; and she drank her ale with such a relish and ate her dinner subsequently with such cheerful appetite and conversation, that Mrs. Dexter thanked God in her heart that good and wholesome times had come to them.

After dinner came the hour respected throughout the cottage element at the Pulpit as sacred to naps. Nathalie, perforce detained throughout it from her piano, took a book to a hammock, intending to read, but succeeded, as usual, only in watching the sea and its life.

She had cultivated her day-dreams away from dangerous localities. When her thoughts wandered in forbidden lines, she at once began to conjugate an irregular French verb. Miss Dexter was eminently practical — for a musician.

When sounds in the house liberated her at last, she went to the piano, and worked there till nearly teatime. Then she ran down to the Pulpit for a while.

How she enjoyed being alone! "It is a feeling that is growing on me," she thought, "and I must not allow it." But she knew that the desire to be convincingly natural and cheerful in her mother's presence was the secret of this new preference.

After tea she went again to the piano, and played until the sun was ready to fall behind the distant blue mountains.

"Come out, dear. Come out for this sight," said her mother at the window. "How Betty must be enjoying it!"

The full moon had just risen, and the setting sun's light suffused the great disk with rose color.

Nathalie stood, her arm around her mother, and watched it shining above water that shaded from purple to bronze.

"How beautiful the world is!" she said.

The two stood there in silence, looking out on the scene for minutes, until the rose tints had all faded.

At last Mrs. Dexter went into the house to write a letter, and Nathalie was again alone.

There were no trees here to cast swaying shad-

ows under the full moon. Only the great boulder
flung a long, dark curtain upon the grass. Down
among the ledges the Pulpit rose black against the
corrugated pathway of bright silver that led straight
to the horizon. Nathalie looked toward it hesitat-
ingly, but her feet stepping down from the piazza,
carried her slowly toward the boulder.

The air was soft with the mildness which, after
sunset, so strangely succeeds to the keen winds of
day in this locality. As Nathalie neared the rock
she heard Betty's laugh, and then Andreas's voice.
They were probably coming for her. With an
involuntary quick movement she sprang into the
shadow of the boulder, and sank down against the
gray moss.

She saw her friends go up to the cottage door,
and, after a minute's talk, turn away, and move
through the rough pasture toward the sea.

"Mother has probably suggested that I am down
at the Pulpit," she thought, and she remained in
her dusky nook until their figures had disappeared.
"Betty may want me, but I am certain that Mr.
Andreas will be consolable in their fruitless
search."

She smiled in satisfaction at her escape, and rose
from her hiding-place. There was a niche in the
boulder large enough for a seat, and she moved
around the end of the rock to seek it. Here she
would sit and revel in the vast outlook, and — if
necessary, conjugate a French verb!

She had her hand upon the lichens ready for a spring into the high niche, when her eyes strayed from habit toward the close-lying stretch of turf which had so often held her audience of one.

A flood of moonlight poured upon the spot. The girl's grasp tightened upon the mosses, and her other hand sought the rock for support. Had her heart held one image until it evoked visions? She was so startled that faintness almost overpowered her; for there in the flood of moonlight lay, or seemed to lie, Roger Gerard, at full length at her feet.

His outing-cap was off, his head supported on his arm, and he was sound asleep.

Nathalie, her heart beating heavily, leaned against the rock and gazed at him. It was he — it was really he; and only a minute ago she had been fearing even to let her thoughts dwell on him in this entrancing night.

She summoned her strength and her wits. What did his presence mean? He had missed Betty too much after all? He had followed her?

No, it was scarcely possible.

Then, if that were not possible, what had he come for?

Oh, the divine sweetness that poured into Nathalie's heart and brain as she gazed down into the unconscious, still face. Had he cared for her after all — her, Nathalie Dexter? Had he even at Edgewater thought of her? Had that been the reason why the loss of Betty had been cheerfully sustained?

He had secured a leave. He had come up into this out-of-the-way corner of the universe for a purpose, and, leaving his friends, had sought the spot which he had oftentimes declared held an enchantment for him.

Nathalie remembered how long she had played after tea. He had probably been listening when sleep overtook him.

Was this a fool's paradise which was enveloping her closer and closer as she realized the transcendent fact that he was really here in flesh and blood, and that after a while he would waken and speak to her? Why should she expect anything? Why should she? Nothing was proved; nothing.

Her heart beat fast as she strove with herself, exulting, yet questioning, and her eyes were fixed upon his face with an attraction under which no man could have remained unconscious. The sleeper stirred. The girl felt a sudden wild desire to fly, but she could not move.

Gerard slowly withdrew his arm from beneath his head, and his eyelids fluttered and lifted. He saw at his feet Nathalie's slight, erect form, clinging against the boulder as closely as its own mosses.

He brushed his hand across his eyes, but the white-clothed vision did not vanish. With quick bewilderment he sat up, gazing, then sprang to his feet, dumb.

"You can hardly believe it is I," she said in a low tone. " I could hardly believe it was you."

He took a step toward her. " I was dreaming, — dreaming that you were looking at me ; so it seemed all a dream. I have been trying to get to you ever since you left Edgewater. I have traveled fast. The boats are crowded. I had no sleep last night, so you forgive me ? I came right from the boat — here ! "

He was off his guard. The spontaneous acts and words of dreamland had not had time to be supplanted by the conventions of waking hours.

His manner and tone were enough. Nathalie's doubts vanished. An ineffable sweetness crept about her lips, and her bright head leaned slowly against the rock, as if swayed back beneath the passionate gaze bent upon her. The moment of tender ecstasy would be with her forever.

She could see in his face, in his attitude, that he doubted the outcome of his quest; and she did not stop to congratulate herself upon this; instead, the heavenly gladness that she could give to him flooded her soul.

"Then Mr. Andreas does not know you have come yet?" she asked after a period during which he seemed satisfied only to look at her.

"No; I shall stay at the hotel. I did not even let them know I was coming. Two guests are enough for that house."

"It is very uncomfortable at the hotel," said

Nathalie, in the same dreamy and unconventional tone they were both unconsciously using.

Betty's shrewd suggestions had been present in Gerard's mind every hour since that long-ago day under the live-oaks when she had informed him of Nathalie's sudden departure. Spoken for his comfort Gerard knew they had been, yet Betty seemed sincerely to believe them. Now they echoed in his heart again with Nathalie before him, fair enough in the moonlight to be the embodiment of the thrilling harmonies she interpreted so well.

She had not offered him her hand. Her manner was certainly out of the ordinary, but —

" I shall not care for physical discomforts, since I have attained getting here," he answered. " Especially," he added after a pause, " if you can tell me that you are glad I came."

She hesitated only an instant. " I am glad," she said.

Her hands were clasped behind her as she looked up at him. Oh, the glory of the summer night!

He came a step nearer still, and her heart fluttered for joy and vague timidity under his eyes.

" If I knew why you left Edgewater — left without speaking to me or sending me a line — if I knew that!"

He waited; but the question was too difficult. She did not answer.

" If I only knew whether the reason concerned me?" he pursued gently.

"But why do you wish to know?" she asked breathlessly.

"Because I love you so," he answered, his repressed heart thrilling through the words.

Her look made him draw her, yielding, from the rough rock, hardly believing in his own happiness.

"That was why," she answered, close to his breast. "It was because I loved you so."

An hour later, Miss Toothaker was sitting alone in the living-room of the cottage, knitting, when Nathalie entered.

"Where is mother?" she asked.

"Upstairs in her room. What's the matter? Why, see here, Nathalie Dexter, let me look at you."

The girl obediently faced about again for the housekeeper's inspection, and well might Miss Priscilla wish to catch a gleam of that radiance which shines on earth but once in a lifetime.

"I did n't know as you was so good-lookin'! But you 're kind o' queer, too, — as if you 'd been seein' things."

Nathalie's lips smiled slightly with their secret joy.

"Mr. Gerard is here."

"He is! Why did n't he come in?"

"He will be back soon. He has gone down to the hotel first."

"He ain't stoppin' at *that* one-horse tavern? I

s'pose the Andreas's cottage is full. Dear me, now! Don't you think your ma might ask him here? I 'd just as soon have him as not."

"You do like him, don't you?" said the girl, such a tenderness welling up in her voice that Miss Toothaker stared.

Nathalie returned her gaze for an instant, then turned quickly and ran upstairs.

Miss Priscilla's knitting was dropped, and she continued to stare after the girl, open-mouthed. Her mental processes were laboring. Finally she picked up her work mechanically and slowly scratched her head with a knitting-needle, while a smile of surprise and gratification stretched one side of her mouth.

"And that was probably goin' on the whole livin' time," she murmured. "I never once thought of it, not once; but, land o' liberty, who could run a house and keep track of all such doin's?"

She suddenly began knitting with excitement. "If it 's the way I think it is, won't I cook 'em a good dinner to-morrow! To think Nathalie 's the one that 's got those eyes, after all! Well, well!" Her work dropped again as she mused. At last she picked it up, lifting her shoulders and laughing to herself. "I don't know who made that match if I did n't!"

CHAPTER XXI.

BETTY ARCHER, who had known when she left Edgewater that Roger was trying to obtain a leave which circumstances rendered it difficult to obtain, was the only one of the little group not utterly surprised at the sudden advent of the lieutenant at the Pulpit, and his still more unexpected entrance into the life of the Dexter household.

"You 've been so sly about it," complained Andreas to Nathalie, as he beamed upon her and squeezed her hand the next day. "Never even told me that Roger was coming, or asked me whether or no you had better say ' Yes.' "

And Nathalie, smiling, silently turned to Betty, whose perfect and comprehending sympathy would be one of the chief joys of her life henceforward.

"I 've wanted a sister so much," the Southern girl had said, "and now I shall have one!"

Even Mrs. Archer, who ran over for a minute to offer congratulations, was as effusively gracious as if she had made the match. What wonder? Entering the Andreas home with every faculty of her being concentrated on the intention to conciliate Russell and to propitiate Mrs. Andreas, she had been treated like an honored guest, and had communed to her heart's content on her favorite subject, for her hostess quite agreed with her as to its interest.

Her closest scrutiny had so far failed to discover any mutual understanding between her step-daughter and the man who acknowledged himself the girl's lover. A hundred times a day she was tempted to give a hint that might draw out his invalid mother, and as many times she checked herself; for Russell's suggestion — which was much more a command — that she should efface herself, still rang in her ears each time she encountered his urbane but masterful glance.

It was quite true. There was no understanding between Andreas and Miss Archer beyond that of good comradeship.

"The mischief of it is, I don't want to lose her. I *can't* lose her," Russell said to the happy lieutenant, whom he dragged from the Dexter cottage to take a ramble with him around the rocky shore. He looked into Gerard's face as the latter strode along beside him, his hands in the pockets of his coat.

"Heavens!" he ejaculated. "I wonder if I'll ever look the way you do: as if you were sure of everything here and hereafter."

"I hope so," answered Roger.

"But how did you dare act so promptly?" pursued Andreas enviously. "Is it all military disci-

pline? The last time I saw you, you thought
doubtful things just as uncertain as I do."

Gerard smiled at a tall, pointed fir-tree.

"It seemed taken out of my hands."

"By George!" returned Andreas ruefully, "I
wish Miss Archer Archer would take it out of *my*
hands."

"You don't understand me. The only advice I
can give you is to sleep and dream, and wake and
go on dreaming."

"Listen to the sphinx! I can sleep and dream
all right, but when I wake, you bet I don't go on
dreaming."

"Why don't you ask her?" inquired Gerard
simply. "What are you afraid of?"

"I'm afraid of *her*, man," returned Russell,
almost shouting in his desperation. "She scares
me stiff. Why can't she be prettily conscious, and
blush and glance away, and do all those nice attractive things that other girls do? Instead, she
looks square at me with those blue eyes of hers,
and seems to be considering me as if I were something away outside of her. If she has the headache, I'm afraid I've offended her. If she is
thoughtful, I am afraid she is bored. The only
way I can get her sweet face to soften is to give
her a song and dance about an apocryphal girl up
country whom she believes I'm in love with."

Gerard laughed aloud. "That is certainly an
original way of wooing."

" Oh, it's all right for you to stand high and dry on the shore, and ridicule a man who's swimming for life. She grew to believe in that girl by misunderstanding something I said, and I get so hungry sometimes that I'll bid for a kind look from her any way I can."

The lieutenant looked at his friend's splendid proportions, and gloomy, clear-cut face, with amusement, which he contrived this time to keep to himself.

" If you expect Betty to show any preference for another woman's lover, you misunderstand the sort of girl you are dealing with," he said quietly.

" There is something in that," admitted Andreas.

Gerard picked up a tempting stone, and paused to send it skimming through the waves.

" There's lots in it — to an Archer," he returned.

Betty had more than one admirer at the Pulpit, and one of the stanchest was Cap'n Levi, upon whom her gentle and refined reposefulness had made a deep impression.

On her way home from Nathalie's on that radiant morning, when it would have been hard for a stranger to decide which of the four women talking in the Dexter cottage looked happiest, Miss Archer met the captain, who was muttering to himself as he came down the road. He stopped before the girl to express his grievance.

" Russell Andr'as has been at me to try to git my bo't," he grumbled. " He *knows* I won't lend my bo't. Jest as soon let my woman go as my bo't."

" I suppose the only safe way is never to lend it," returned the girl kindly.

" Yis, 't is. Russell knows this coast 's well 's I do ; but I ain't goin' to break over m' rule. Ef he wants to sail in my bo't and have me go 'long an' sail it, I 'm willin'. He knows that."

" Well, don't worry, Cap'n Levi. I 'll talk to him. I think a sail in yo' boat with you would be right jolly."

" Well, you jist gi' me a half-hour's notice any time, and I 'll be thar," returned the old man, his seamed face brightening.

" Have you heard the news, Cap'n Levi ? "

" No, I hain't heard no news. I seen that young soldier feller 't was here last year 'round this mornin'."

" Yes, he has come, and he and Miss Dexter are engaged to be married."

" Ye don't say so ! " The captain looked much interested. " Wall," he chuckled, " no extry charge fer sweethearts in my bo't. Let 'em come, ef they want to."

" Very well. This is my party, is n't it, Cap'n Levi ? "

" Sartin it is. Sartin," returned the old man gallantly.

"Expect us at two o'clock, then. I'll be there, if I have to come alone!"

"I'd be jest as well pleased ef ye was to come alone," returned Cap'n Levi; and delighted with his own repartee, he went, chuckling, along toward the store.

But Miss Archer did not appear at the dock alone. She had with her Nathalie, the lieutenant, and Andreas, who had swallowed his displeasure with Cap'n Levi at her command, and now submitted to the unaccustomed rôle of passenger in a sailboat.

"The old man's the fifth wheel to the coach, after all," remarked the captain when he had his load on board, and had begun to tack slowly out of the little cove which served Pulpit Point as a harbor. "Miss Dexter and Cap'n there, I wish ye much joy. There's ben lots o' sparkin' he-ar. Seems 's if the Pulpit come pretty near to heaven when it comes to the jawb o' makin' matches." The speaker turned his solitary tooth toward the young couple, who were dutifully trimming the boat by sitting on opposite sides of it.

"Say!" exclaimed Andreas. "Would n't it be great to have a wedding at the Pulpit,—I mean, have the minister actually stand in the Pulpit! You ought to be willing, Miss Dexter, to wear a waterproof instead of the usual mosquito-netting business for the sake of the romance of the thing, and be married in the very spot where you and Gerard first met!"

Russell passed his hand over his mouth, and his eyes shone wickedly. " We would scrape all the seaweed off one rock for Roger to stand on. It would n't do to have any slips on that occasion. I suppose liberty of speech has returned, Roger — eh ? "

" To a certain extent," returned Gerard, smiling at Nathalie. " I think, however, you should be the one to have the honor of being married among the barnacles, since it was your own brilliant idea."

" Won't Nathalie's wedding be pretty ! " said Betty joyously. " I love a military wedding. It is one of the nicest things about marrying an army officer. I 'm to be maid of honor, Nathalie has promised. Now mind you choose the finest lieutenant in the service fo' yo' best man, Roger. You must consider ma future."

" What are you thinking of, child ? There sits my best man." Gerard indicated Russell.

" Oh ! " ejaculated Miss Archer blankly. And then Andreas had the opportunity of seeing how the too imperturbable girl looked, colored by as violent a blush as he had ever beheld on maiden's face.

" Cap'n Levi promised to show me about sailing," she said, rising hurriedly ; and the boat at that moment meeting the first big wave outside the cove, she was promptly precipitated straight into Russell Andreas's arms.

" Do excuse me ! " she exclaimed ; and he, his usual ready nonsense all flown, replied meekly : —

"Certainly."

They sailed out to one of the islands that they knew well, and Cap'n Levi mooring his boat in a safe place, they all landed.

"I am going to hunt for fir balsam," said Nathalie, who had brought scissors and a basket for the purpose.

"Let me go with you!" exclaimed Andreas effusively. "I'd just as lief go as not."

The lovers disappeared, laughing, into the woods, and Cap'n Levi, finding a sheltered group of trees, sat down among them on a grassy bank.

"Ye kin all go, ef ye don't stay too long," he said. "I'm goin' to kind o' keep an eye on the bo't. Never did keer fer walkin' when sittin' 's jest as cheap."

Miss Archer promptly sat down on the grass near him. "I feel like staying here too," she said with decision.

Russell deliberately followed her example, and disposed himself on the other side of the captain. "It seems to be Hobson's choice for me, then," he remarked. "I never was much on wandering about alone, and soliloquizing, and carving names on the trunks of trees."

"I s'pose them two folks," the captain gestured backward with his head, "don't keer much whether they're walkin' or settin', jest so 's thar ain't anybody else around."

"Well," admitted Andreas, "I dare say they're not lonely."

" That young man 's found his commandin' officer sure," went on the captain. " I could tell him
a thing or two." He nodded knowingly. " She
looks dretful soft and biddable, — but just let him
wait." The speaker nodded again, so portentously
that Betty laughed merrily.

Cap'n Levi showed his tooth for sympathy.
" That gal knows jest what she wants and when
she wants it ; and so I can tell that soldier boy
over there."

" Well," said Miss Archer, " Mr. Gerard wishes
to find out what she wants, and to give it to her."

" Jest 's long 's he doos, things 'll go reel peaceful," returned the captain.

" And when it comes to war, you must remember
that Mr. Gerard is right in his element," suggested
Russell.

Cap'n Levi began comfortably mumbling a
blade of grass. He was having a very good time.
The trees kept the wind off, the sun was pleasant,
and since these young people preferred his society
to rambling about the island, he was bound to do
his best to entertain them.

" When 's your turn comin', Russell ? " he inquired. " Seems to me you hang fire consid'able."

" It is n't my fault, Cap'n."

" Whose, then ? Your sweetheart's ? "

" Yes." Andreas sighed. " She 's sweet enough,
but she is n't mine."

" Sho ! " said the old man contemptuously.

" Refused ye once, maybe. Some folks git the mitten so easy ! "

No woman ever had a larger bump of curiosity than had developed on this old fisherman's cranium in his narrow, monotonous life. He gazed now at Andreas, who was leaning on his elbow, and staring out to sea.

" Where 'd ye say she lived ? "

" She lives in Virginia."

" You never told me that," said Miss Archer.

" You never asked me. You have n't the Yankee enterprise."

" Down there now — eh ? " hazarded the captain.

" No, she is in Maine now." Russell smiled oddly toward Betty. " Miss Archer, this seems to be a game of twenty questions. Won't you take a hand ? "

" I think I will," said Betty gravely. " You make me feel as if I were detaining you. You have not given her up. If she is in Maine now, why are you not with her ? "

" I am."

Andreas spoke so quietly, his eyes resting on hers, that it took Betty moments to believe she had heard aright ; then the color mounted to her face, and slowly receded.

Her gaze did not drop from his, though she turned so pale, and the old captain sat there between them, his weather-beaten, nut-cracker face looking meditatively out to sea.

"You told me she loved some one else," said the girl; and Cap'n Levi smiled shrewdly.

"I 'll find out more a-listenin' than I will a-talkin'," he thought. "Women 's jest brimful o' curiosity. 'T ain't their fault."

"I firmly believed so that afternoon when I told you."

"But in the evening, when I explained " —

"I did not credit all you said. I thought you capable of any sacrifice. Yes, I believed that sweet girl was crushing her own heart."

"But at the dance — the evening at the Hygeia " —

"Yes, I believed you at last, then, and I began to dream dreams."

"Ye can't put no faith in dreams," remarked Cap'n Levi, briefly.

Miss Archer's breath was coming faster, for Andreas's eyes were eloquent, and his fine face was tense with feeling.

With an involuntary movement she suddenly came closer to Cap'n Levi, and took a fold of his faded sleeve between her fingers.

The old man, gratified at her friendliness, turned toward her.

"He 's baound to be close-mouthed, ain't he? Ye hain't found out much, I 'll bet. Russell Andr'as allers could talk the most, and say the least, of any feller that ever come to the Pulpit."

Betty laughed a little, — a laugh that was near

to tears, — and caught her lower lip with her
teeth.

" Wonder 'f them folks back in the woods thar
hev got any idee o' time ? " remarked Cap'n Levi.

" I think we had better go after them, Miss
Archer and I," returned Andreas quickly.

" Yes, that 's right, you go," said Betty, whose
expression made Russell think of some delicate
wild creature, who sees the hunter near.   Their
positions were reversed : she was the one who was
frightened now.

" I said ' we,' " he answered.

" But I think I 'll stay with Cap'n Levi."

The captain, mumbling his grass-blade, turned
to Russell, smiling triumphantly.

" Holler, can't ye ? "

" I don't want to startle them.   I wish you
would persuade Miss Archer to come with me."

" Seems skeered o' the woods, don't he ? " remarked the captain to Betty.   Then, happening to
catch sight of a water-lined rock below, he started.
" Look he-ar.   I did n't know as time was flyin'
so.   I knew the tide wuz a-runnin' out when we
come in.   We 'd better git aboard.   She draws a
good deal o' water for her size.   Git the folks,
Russell, an' I 'll go down t' the bo't an' jest keep
watch of her."

Miss Archer had charmed the old man without
doubt, but when it came to a question of his be-
loved boat, no rival had a chance.

He moved now as swiftly as he was able, and hurrying away down to the shore, disappeared behind its gray rocks.

The two he had left also rose. All was still but for the wind in the trees and the solemn murmur of the sea.

Miss Archer gave one look into Russell's speaking face, and then her eyes fell, and involuntarily she pressed both her hands to her fluttering heart.

He came near, but he did not touch her. Her pure, proud maidenhood was an appeal.

"You know it all now, Betty," he said pleadingly. "Have I not been patient? You said yourself that in time she would care for me."

A faint little smile grew about the girl's lips as she still studied the turf.

"Ever since that evening at the Hygeia," she began slowly, "I have prayed to God every night that I might not love Mr. Andreas."

"Dear heart!"

She lifted the blue eyes he loved, and her sweet lips trembled as she added still more slowly: —

"But ma prayers were not answered."

It might have been seconds, — minutes, — hours, that they had stood in that little sheltered copse, her heart beating upon his, when Cap'n Levi's strident shout from the shore pierced the Æolian music of the pines.

"I tell ye *I'm* a-goin'!"

Nathalie Dexter's voice replied: —

"But you *must* wait a minute. We haven't found them yet."

Betty started. "They want us."

"Never mind," murmured Andreas. "Let us stay here forever."

"But I shouldn't like barnacles three times a day. Are — are you going to tell them?"

"Tell them? I shall tell the very stones!" exclaimed Andreas; and so even at the moment when the lieutenant was waking the echoes in an endeavor to reach his friend, these two came out of the copse near by, hand in hand, the same light on their faces that shone upon Adam and Eve in the garden.

Instantly the other pair came to meet them, with glad comprehension. Gerard wrung the hand of his friend in silence, while his eyes gave him a solemn charge. Then he took Betty in his arms tenderly, and kissed her cheek.

Cap'n Levi's voice came desperately up the bank.

"She's a-scrapin', I tell ye."

"Ay, ay, sir," called Andreas; and the radiant quartette hurried forward and down to the shore.

"Didn't reelize the tide wuz so low," said the captain. "You 're a smart feller, Russell," he added, with biting sarcasm. "I'll send you after folks agin some time!"

"It was Miss Archer Archer's fault, Cap'n."

" Blamin' it on the woman, hey? That's an old dodge ! "

Andreas took Betty's hand to help her to the high gunwale of the rocking boat, but paused in that attitude.

" Beg pardon, Cap'n ; I called her wrong," he continued. " I meant to say, the future Mrs. Russell Forbes Andreas."

" Hey ? "

" It 's a fact, Cap'n, it 's a fact. You can't believe it, and I sympathize with you perfectly. Neither can I."

There was an ominous grating of pebbles under the keel of his precious boat, but Cap'n Levi was actually deaf to it, while Miss Archer's eyes sparkled at him, and her lips were closed demurely.

" Ye don't say so ! Then *you* wuz the gal ! "

Betty nodded.

" Wall, we 've found out who she *wuz*, anyway," said the old man with satisfaction. " And," he viewed Andreas leniently, " ye might take up with a worse feller 'n Russell, after all."

Gerard was gravely emptying the contents of his full basket on the beach.

" What are you doing ? " asked Andreas, viewing in wonder the mass of common, scentless green that fell upon the pebbles.

" Nathalie insisted on filling the basket with something at the last minute," explained the lieutenant,

" but it does n't matter now if you do know that
we forgot all about looking for fir balsam."

Cap'n Levi's tooth aided in the general laugh.

" Git aboard! git aboard!" he commanded. " I
guess neither one o' ye 'll begrech me sailin' the
bo't goin' back; and if signs an' omens caount fer
anythin', I sh'd say the very best place this party
kin head fer 's a *Pulpit!* "

www.ingramcontent.com/pod-product-compliance
Lightning Source LLC
Chambersburg PA
CBHW060527030726
47498CB00004B/1101